Close your eyes. . . .

James was a heavy sleeper, hard to rouse once he became tangled in the world of dreams.

If she kissed him, chances were good he'd never know. And oh, how she longed to kiss him.

Lowering her lips to his, she rested them there, delicately balanced, scarcely touching. . . . He didn't awaken.

Emboldened, she let her eyes softly close as she increased the pressure, turning the barely there touch into a real kiss. She savored the sensation, the feeling of skin to skin, heat to heat. He tasted like honey, or some exotic variety of fruit, lush and forbidden. She softly drew a breath, her senses swimming as the scent of him flooded through her. His essence swam inside her head, on her mouth, in her nose, down her throat, better than anything she'd ever tasted.

Suddenly he shifted. . . .

She broke the kiss and began to sit up, but before she could move away, he clamped a hand around the back of her head and crushed her lips to his.

His turn now . . .

TRACY ANNE WARREN

THE MAN PLAN

A SIGNET BOOK

SIGNET
Published by the Penguin Group
Penguin Group (USA) LLC, 375 Hudson Street,
New York, New York 10014

USA | Canada | UK | Ireland | Australia | New Zealand | India | South Africa | China
penguin.com
A Penguin Random House Company

First published by Signet, an imprint of New American Library,
a division of Penguin Group (USA) LLC

First Printing, August 2014

Copyright © Tracy Anne Warren, 2014

 REGISTERED TRADEMARK—MARCA REGISTRADA

ISBN 978-0-451-46614-3

Printed in the United States of America
10 9 8 7 6 5 4 3 2 1

For my amazin' raisin, Georgianna,
who spread light and laughter wherever she went
and who never needed sight to see the beauty in life

ACKNOWLEDGMENTS

Deepest thanks to all my wonderful fans—both old and new.

Prologue

B^{*ang.*} The church door swung back hard on its hinges, caught in an icy blast of wind that raked James Jordan's short hair and cut beneath the thick dark wool of his coat. He barely acknowledged the chill as he jogged down the stairs, strode across the concrete pathway, too deadened inside to be troubled by a little nip from the elements.

He'd been so happy just a short while ago, buoyant and brimming with anticipation. The late-December sky had been clear and sunny when he'd arrived for the ceremony, as if it too were celebrating the day. Now it was swathed in gray, broad clouds lumbering above in sullen gloom.

How could she have done it? he wondered. Madelyn, his friend, his love.

How could she have crushed him on this, the day they were supposed to have wed?

She'd suffered as she'd told him, he knew, the words passing from her lips in a strange, strangled whisper.

Sorry, she'd said, *but I can't marry you.*

She loved him, but not that way, not enough to promise herself to him for a lifetime. Her face had been ruddy and swollen from tears as she pleaded with him to understand.

But he didn't want to understand. Not now. Perhaps not ever. Nor did he want to forgive. She'd hurt him, betrayed him, shamed him in front of their guests, their families and friends.

Yet the humiliation was nothing, not compared to the chasm that had opened deep inside him. The pain of knowing he'd lost her.

He clutched a set of car keys—hastily borrowed from his best man—inside his fist. The hard-edged metal teeth bit into his hand. He squeezed harder, craving the pain.

He had to get away.

Had to be alone.

Where?

What did it matter where?

Just away. Anywhere away.

"James, wait," a soft voice called to him, satin-slippered feet rushing up from behind.

He walked onward without pause.

A slender hand reached for his shoulder, plucked at his coat sleeve. "Please, James. Please stop."

He walked on. He didn't need to look to recognize the identity of the speaker. Ivy Grayson, Madelyn's teenage sister. "Let me be, Ivy."

She kept pace with him, undaunted. "You shouldn't go, not this way. Please stop."

He did, finally, halting at the neat black iron gate to the fence that surrounded the church's rear yard. With a sigh, he turned, found her standing, slender and pretty in her bridesmaid's finery. Tiny fresh rosebuds were arranged in her fair hair, the flowers the same deep pink as her long formal gown.

"There's no reason to stay," he said in a lifeless tone. "The wedding's off."

"You shouldn't be alone," she insisted gently.

"But that's exactly what I want to be." He saw the distress in her blue eyes. "I'll be fine," he assured her. "Don't worry about me."

"But I will worry." She bit her lip. "Why don't I come with you?"

"No," he said, more harshly than he'd intended.

Her face fell at the rebuke.

A fresh gust of wind swept over them on its rush toward the west. Ivy shivered in her thin garment.

He frowned. "Why'd you come out here without a coat? You're freezing. Go back inside."

She wrapped her arms around herself, shook her head. "No, I'm okay. It's not that cold."

He made a rude noise and began unbuttoning his coat. He slipped it off, revealing the fine, hand-tailored black tuxedo he wore underneath.

His wedding clothes.

He draped the coat over her shoulders, drawing the flaps closed in front.

Ivy sighed as heat enveloped her.

His heat, his scent trapped in the sleek silk lining and soft cashmere wool. She drank it in, all of it, luxuriating in the exquisite sensations. Despite her height—she stood five feet nine in her bare feet—his coat hung on her, voluminous as a tent. The hem just barely cleared the ground.

"I can't take your coat," she protested. "You'll be cold."

"I thought you said it wasn't cold," he chided mockingly.

"No. I said not much," she hedged.

They eyed each other for a long moment, the air between them easy with the familiarity of years. For an instant the tension eased from his jaw as his natural sense of humor asserted itself. Then his eyes hardened again.

She read his pain, her heart aching. "I'm so sorry. Maybe I could talk to her—"

"No. There is no talking to her. She's made up her mind. It's done. She doesn't want me."

"I don't understand her. Any woman would be thrilled to be yours. I'd marry you in an instant," she blurted, saying the words she'd never, ever meant to say out loud. Revealing a wish she'd kept locked away inside her heart for such a very long time.

"It's nice to know someone still would after today."

Aware he thought she was joking, she lifted her chin. "I'm serious. I'll marry you. I know I'm only fifteen, too young yet for you, but if you'd wait, I wouldn't leave you at the altar. I'd make you happy. Grandma Bradford was only seventeen when she got married."

"Ivy—"

"I know you still love Malynn," she said, using the name she'd given her sister long ago, when her toddler's tongue couldn't wrap itself around the harder word "Madelyn." "I wouldn't expect you not to. But maybe as time goes on it won't hurt so much. Maybe in a couple years there'll be room in your heart for me. If you loved one sister, why couldn't you love another?"

"Shh, Ivy. Enough."

"I love you, James."

He closed his eyes for a brief moment before meeting her gaze. "I love you too, sweetheart. We've always been the best of friends, haven't we?"

She nodded, a spark of hope flaring to life inside her.

"And we'll continue to be friends, good friends, no matter what. But, Ivy, as flattered as I am by your proposal, it wouldn't be right. There're a lot of years between us, too many years. Besides, what would you want with an old man like me when there're so many young guys just waiting for a chance to be with a beautiful girl like you?"

"But I don't want any of them. I want you. And you're not old," she protested.

"I'm thirty-one. When I was fifteen, thirty-one sounded as close to ancient as you could get without actually being dead. Come on; admit it. You know I'm right."

She shook her head. "I don't see you that way. I see you as you, as James. Your age doesn't matter to me."

"But it matters to others; you know it does. Your parents, your family, your friends—what would they think?"

She knew exactly what they would think, and they wouldn't approve, no matter how much they liked James. And they did like him, even adored him. Her parents had all but adopted him years ago, when a then-teenage Madelyn had dragged him over from the house next door.

Maybe he was old enough to have known her since she was a baby. But she didn't care. She loved him.

He gave her a sympathetic smile. "I know you won't believe me, but six months or a year from now, you'll look back on this and wonder what you could have been thinking. You'll have met some great guy at school. You'll be worrying about which college to attend and what dress to wear to the prom. I'll be the last thing on your mind."

A lock of her hair came free of its carefully styled knot and blew across her face. He reached out to tuck it behind her ear. She caught his hand, pressed his palm to her cheek and closed her eyes. "You're always on my mind," she murmured earnestly.

When she opened her eyes again, he met her look and sighed. "Ivy, you seem to have forgotten that until a few minutes ago, I was going to marry your sister. I love Madelyn and I wanted her for my wife. Getting over her is going to be one of the hardest things I've ever had to do. But I'm going to try my damnedest and so are you. You're going to get on with your life and get over this . . . this crush you have on me."

He pulled his hand away.

A tear slipped down her cheek. "You're going, then?"

"Yes, I'm going."

"When will I see you again?"

He tucked his hands in his suit pockets, hunched his shoulders. "I don't know. A while. I have some business in Europe I've been neglecting because of the wedding. I may see to that."

"Be careful."

"I'm rarely anything else; you know that."

"You'll need your coat." She slipped it from around her shoulders and held it out to him. "Mine's inside the church."

He shrugged into his coat. "You'd better run on. Someone's probably looking for you by now."

But she stood her ground, her eyes serious and intent. "She's a fool, you know, to have let you go," she stated, her words those of an adult.

He paused, then pressed a kiss to her forehead. "You're a sweet girl. Don't ever let that change."

He turned and unlatched the gate.

She watched him walk away, the skin on her forehead and cheek hot and tingling where he'd touched her. She wished he'd kissed her on the lips, but it was too soon for that.

James was right about a great many things, she knew.

She was too young for him.

Her family would disapprove.

And less than an hour ago, he'd been pledged to marry her sister.

But not anymore.

Before, Ivy had been willing to let him go. For Madelyn's sake. For his sake. Because she'd known he loved her sister, and above all else, she wanted him to be happy.

But now he was free. Now he could be hers. And he was wrong about her feelings; they would never change.

She loved him.

She always had.

She always would.

And someday, she promised herself, he was going to feel the same.

CHAPTER ONE

Present Day

"James. How are you, sweetheart?"

James heard the clear, rounded tones of Laura Grayson's voice over the speakerphone on his desk. He never minded receiving a call or a visit from her, despite his ill-fated engagement to her eldest daughter, Madelyn, more than five years before.

Lord knows Laura and Philip Grayson had been better parents to him over the years than his own—who, at last report, were sunning themselves somewhere on the coast of southern France. No doubt they were spending more money in a week than most people earned in a year. His mother in particular had no idea there was such a thing as a budget.

"I'm fine, Laura," he said, signing his name to a thick set of documents. "And you? All's well, I trust?"

He tossed down his pen and handed the paperwork to his executive assistant. She hurried away.

"Quite well," Laura answered. "Is that work I hear you doing? I hope I'm not calling at a bad time."

"Not at all." He lifted the receiver to make their conversation private. "Just finishing up."

"Well, we're all too busy these days. I'm due to zip out of here any moment myself—evening rehearsal for the Caldicott wedding. Then there's the Jay affair on Friday. I have so much on my to-do list, it's a wonder I can keep my head on straight now that spring has sprung."

"Glad to hear your business is booming."

"The wedding consultation business is always booming, even though the divorce rate's high. But I didn't call just to chitchat. I have a favor to ask; Philip and I both do." Her voice lowered. "It's about Ivy."

"What about Ivy? Problem at school?"

"You might call it that. She's decided to drop out."

He straightened in his chair. "What?"

"Yes. Despite all our efforts to convince her otherwise, she's dead set on withdrawing from college and moving to the city to be an artist. She's always been such an easygoing, levelheaded girl. I don't know where this defiant streak has suddenly come from."

"Would you like me to talk to her, then? Get her to reconsider? She only has one more year before she graduates, doesn't she?"

Laura sighed. "Yes, and if I truly thought your talking to her would do any good, I'd have her on the phone right now. But she's like a piece of granite, as fixed on this as I've ever seen her fixed on anything. Besides, it's already too late. She's officially withdrawn. The college has given her spot away for next year."

"I'm sure something could be arranged," he said.

In addition to the many charitable organizations he contributed to each year, he made sizable donations to a number of colleges and universities. If enough money was at stake, he felt certain Vassar would be more than pleased to make an exception for Ivy. No matter how impossible such a request might seem on the surface.

"No. It's useless," Laura said. "She won't go back. And to be completely honest, her father and I have no real objection to her pursuing her painting, if that's what she really wants. What we do object to is her living arrangements.

"James," Laura went on in horrified tones, "she's planning to move into some horrible artist's garret in *Bushwick*. I'm sure it has cockroaches and rats and God knows what else. I can't bear to think of my darling girl living in some dingy, run-down old hovel."

He frowned. "Well, it's not the best part of Brooklyn, but from what I've heard, it's undergoing a rapid transformation. Maybe it's not as bad as you think."

"No, it's worse. She's going to be sharing the hovel with three men."

"What!"

"Yes, some friend of hers from college—an actor who's moving to the city this year and two friends of his. One's a musician, and I can't remember what the other one does. Dancing, I think. Anyway, she simply cannot be allowed to do this." Laura audibly slowed to catch her breath. "That's where the favor comes in. James, are there any available apartments in your building? Anyone who might consider subletting one?"

He frowned. "Doubtful. People tend to stay put once they move into my building."

"Ivy's father and I will pay whatever it costs if you could just find something, anything. We'd both feel so much better knowing she was near a person we trust. Someone to watch over her and make sure she doesn't come to any harm. I know she'd be safe with you around." She paused. "We considered Madelyn and Zack, but since they bought the house on Long Island last year . . . Well, it would be such an imposition, what with the twins and all. And I don't think Ivy would ever agree to it."

He tensed at mention of Madelyn, a reflex he couldn't seem to shake even after all this time. "But you think Ivy would be willing to move into my building?" he ventured. "You don't think she'll feel she's not suffering enough for her art on the Upper West Side?"

"She should be grateful not to suffer at all. Her father and I will make her see reason, at least on this. Now, tell me you think there's hope and that you'll help us."

"Of course I'll help, if I can. Let me look into things and I'll call you tomorrow. Okay?"

"Thank you, dear. We love you, you know."

"I love you too," he responded, and hung up the phone.

So Ivy was turning stubborn, was she? Displaying that famous streak of Grayson obstinacy at last.

Ivy. Lord, he hadn't seen her for . . . well, nearly two years now, he realized. Except for holidays, she'd been away at college while he'd been busy making deals and dollars in the world of international finance.

Fortunately, he thrived on the business, savoring the risk, relishing the challenge of juggling vast sums and gambling on ventures that often had as much chance of going bust as they did boom. And he'd done well for himself, and for the family, as the head of Jordan Enterprises. Since his father had handed over the company reins with a stiff handshake and a grateful sigh nearly twelve years ago, James had more than tripled their holdings.

Lately, though, he'd begun to wonder if that's all there was to his life—work and profit. He had so much, and he was thankful for it. He tried never to take his life of privilege for granted. Yet sometimes when he awakened in the darkest black of night, an emptiness would sweep through him. A void none of the luxuries he possessed could ever fill.

A home. A family of his own. Children.

If he'd married Madelyn, they'd have those things now. . . .

But no, he refused to dwell on her. He was over Madelyn. She was in his past. He needed to focus on his future. As he knew all too well, she'd built a life for herself, found a happiness separate from him.

If only he could find a way to do the same.

The intercom buzzed. He pressed a button. "Yes?"

"Mr. Jordan, Ms. Manning is here to see you. Shall I send her in?"

Parker.

"Of course. Show her right through. Then why don't you go on home, Tory?" he said to his assistant. "It's getting late. You can finish up that report tomorrow."

"Thanks. Andrew's got soccer practice tonight, and Bill's taking Cara to ballet. If I leave now, we can have a quick bite together before we have to run."

"Go be with your family. I'll see you tomorrow."

"Good night."

Moments later, the door to his office opened as Parker Manning let herself in. She made a dramatic entrance in a minidress that hugged each and every one of her lean, feminine curves. The color, a bold slash of red, accented her sleek dark hair and olive complexion. A pair of three-inch red heels, a narrow yellow wrap, and a trendy purse shaped like a lemon slice completed the ensemble.

He and Parker had been lovers now for the better part of a year. They'd met at a play, introduced by mutual acquaintances who shared an appreciation for live theater. Divorced with no children, Parker lived off a trust fund from a wealthy grandmother and dabbled in whatever amused her at any given moment.

Right now, it was real estate.

He rose from his chair and went to greet her, taking her into his arms for a warm kiss on the mouth. "I didn't expect you tonight."

"I decided to surprise you. I'm celebrating." She

showed him a set of well-straightened teeth. "I sold my white elephant today."

He raised a brow. "The loft in Tribeca?"

"The very one. I'd about given up hope of ever un-loading the thing, but the ideal buyer came along. A computer entrepreneur from California who didn't bat an eyelash at the price. Just asked me where he could sign. I've been in heaven all day. With the commission I'll be receiving, I decided I deserved a well-earned treat. New outfit, new hair, a complete facial and mas-sage. I feel positively yummy. I thought you could take me out to dinner and make the evening perfect."

He held back a sigh. He'd been looking forward to a quiet evening at home, a good book and a full night's sleep. But she'd be disappointed if he said no. He feigned a smile. "Of course we'll go out. And congratulations. I know how hard you worked selling that property."

"I did, didn't I?" she agreed as if the notion amazed even her. "You haven't mentioned my new look." She held her arms out at her sides and turned a slow circle. "What do you think?"

He perused her from head to toe, ending by meeting the expectant look in her wide brown eyes. "Stunning as always. But then you know you don't need a make-over to look gorgeous. You always are."

She smiled at the compliment.

He closed the distance between them and slid a hand down the taut flesh of one arm. "Perhaps we should forget dinner, go to my place, and celebrate in bed."

"Aren't you the naughty one?" She laughed and gave him a playful tap on the shoulder. "But save the thought. We'll skip dessert and enjoy each other later instead." She moved away, heels silent on the Aubusson rugs spread over the dark, wide-plank walnut flooring. She stopped in front of a wet bar concealed behind a clever faux niche and pushed the panel to open it. "Drink?" she asked him.

"No, thanks." He moved in the opposite direction, stopping before the floor-to-ceiling span of glass that formed the outside wall. Beyond it lay an unimpeded view of the city. Twilight was upon them, lights beginning to wink on in the buildings opposite, creating all sorts of interesting patterns and designs.

"I don't know how you can stand being so close like that," she remarked. "Gives me the willies wondering if I'll fall out."

His lips curved but without humor. He lifted a hand, rapped his knuckles on the thick glass. "Safe enough, I think."

"Anything wrong? You seem pensive." Ice clinked in her crystal glass as she took a swallow of vodka and tonic.

"A little tired, nothing more. Long, busy day."

"Then a good dinner is exactly what you need. We should go."

"Anywhere in particular you had in mind?"

He stifled a groan when she named a trendy, hideously expensive restaurant that was always booked solid months in advance. If he twisted an arm or two and greased the right palms, he might be able to find them a table for the last seating.

"All right. Let me make some calls."

*   *   *

A grunt, followed by a curse, drew Ivy's attention away from the kitchen linens she was unpacking. She watched as her friend Neil Jones muscled a huge packing box through the doorway of her new apartment.

"I think this is the last of them," he huffed. He struggled a few more feet, then let the box slide to the floor. "I lost Josh somewhere behind me," he panted, beads of sweat dotting his tanned forehead, dampening his short, sun-streaked brown hair.

She set her hands on her hips. "I wish you guys would have let me help."

"You helped. You lugged up your clothes and a few of the lighter boxes. Believe me, cupcake, you wouldn't have been able to manage these last few."

She wasn't entirely sure about that—she was pretty strong for a woman—but male pride could be a delicate thing, so she didn't argue. It's why she hadn't hired professional movers. Neil and his friend Josh had offered to help her move, and she hadn't wanted to offend by refusing. Neil in particular took affront at paying anyone a thousand dollars for a few hours' work.

"How come you've got so much stuff?"

"It's from my mother," she said. "She wants me to be comfortable."

He snorted. "I don't see how you could you be anything but comfortable in a swanky place like this."

He was right. A twinge of embarrassment went through her as she surveyed the space. The ocean of plush cream wall-to-wall carpeting, the gleaming cherry woodwork and cabinetry, the crown molding coated with fresh glossy white paint, and the wide windows with their elegant view of Central Park. In addition to the living room, the apartment boasted a spacious bedroom, full kitchen, fireplace, one and a half baths, and a bonus room she planned to use as her art studio.

Perhaps she should have stuck to her principles and refused to give in to her parents' wishes. She'd been all set to share Neil, Josh, and Fred's modest apartment in Bushwick. She might have grown up in wealth, but she wasn't a pantywaist or a snob.

Then her folks had to go and tempt her.

Oh, not with the obvious lures—a luxury apartment in Manhattan, the chance to paint full-time and not worry about finding a job, the free rent. No, they'd reeled her in with a far more insidious temptation. Though to be fair, she knew they had no idea that's what they were doing. They'd persuaded her with the most compelling enticement of all—the chance to live only seven floors down from James Jordan, the man she'd loved as long as she could remember.

At least she thought she still loved him.

She'd scarcely seen him these past few years, his long-ago breakup with her sister having driven an awkward wedge between him and her family. Still, they'd traded presents and postcards and phone calls during that time. And he'd never really been more than a glimpse away, his handsome, patrician features smiling dependably out at her from the photograph of him she kept on her nightstand.

James.

Her nerves hummed at the thought of him.

What would it be like, seeing him again?

How would she feel?

How would he feel?

Would she want him with the same intensity? The same desperate yearning that had consumed her for nearly the whole of her life? Or would time and distance and newfound maturity have altered her perceptions, her emotions?

Would she meet him again and be chagrined to discover her devotion was nothing more than an illusion? A faded crush? Or would she see him and experience once more the old breathless thrill? Know, as she always had, that he was the one for her?

Moving to New York was her chance to find out. Her opportunity to explore her emotions and to act upon them if she found her feelings unchanged.

"What in the hell've you been doing, man?"

Neil's question ended her reverie. Josh Moran was shouldering his way through the front doorway, the muscles in his arms bulging from the weighty carton he carried. Tall and stocky, his auburn hair trailed in a neat ponytail halfway down his back. "Where's this go, Ivy?"

She rushed over to check the top. *Books* was scrawled in black felt-tip marker across the cardboard. But what kind of books? she wondered. After three years of college, she'd collected a lot of them, from cheap paperbacks to fine-art first editions.

"Living room!" she decided.

As he headed in that direction, Neil followed close behind.

"So, where'd you disappear to, man?"

His burden unloaded, Josh dropped down onto the L-shaped navy blue sofa that dominated the space. "I didn't disappear anywhere."

"Then where've you been?" Neil persisted.

"I was thirsty. I stopped at the water fountain for a drink and missed the elevator."

"It took you ten minutes to get a drink of water? You've been smoking again, haven't you?"

Josh bristled. "No, I haven't been smoking. I've got this damned patch on, haven't I?" He yanked up the short sleeve of his shirt, flashed it at Neil. "You're not supposed to smoke if you're wearing the patch."

"What's that mint scent, then? Smells like breath spray."

"It's not breath spray," Josh said in a hard voice. "Must be the Tic Tac you smell. The one you shoved up your butt alongside the stick you've already got in there."

"Hey, guys," Ivy said, stepping between the squabbling pair. "Take it easy. It's been a long day and you're both tired."

"If you've been smoking again—," Neil warned, shaking a finger.

Josh bared his teeth. "You'll what?"

"Please, enough. I'm sure Josh only took a few extra minutes to catch his second wind. And, Neil, you probably smell the mouthwash I used last time I was in the bathroom. Don't fight, guys, hmm?"

Neil retreated a step, stuck his hands into his jeans pockets, and ducked his head. "Sorry, Ivy."

"Yeah, sorry," Josh said. "*Not* smoking is making my fuse kind of short today."

She waved aside the apologies, already accepted. "You guys must be hungry. I know I am. There's a market a block over. How about I run over and bring back sandwich fixings?"

"Sounds great, but we can't stay." Neil checked his watch. "The rental truck has to be back by seven, and the Prince of Pop here has a late gig at the club tonight. Don't mean to leave you in the lurch, cupcake, but we have to bounce. Will you be okay?"

Deflated but determined not to show it, Ivy pasted on a wide smile. "Of course I'll be okay. The building couldn't be more secure, the neighborhood's great, and God knows I've got plenty to keep me busy." She gestured toward the mass of packing boxes.

"You're right about that, but it's not what I mean. Will you be okay *alone*?"

She smiled, touched. "Yes, I'll be fine. I have been by myself before, you know."

"Yeah, but being alone and living alone are two different things. I'll call you tomorrow, see how your first night went."

"I'll be waiting by the phone," she promised with a grin. "Now, you two get going before I make you late." She gave Neil a fierce hug, then Josh, who'd risen from the sofa to join them. "Thank you, thank you, both of you."

"I'm still pissed you aren't moving in with us," Josh grumbled. "Don't be a stranger. Drop by the club some night. I'll make sure you get a front-row seat."

"And we'll have lunch," Neil offered. "I'll tell you all about the latest cattle call my manager sent me on. Little Shop of Horrorsville."

She laughed.

The moment they were gone, a thick hush descended on the apartment. She'd never lived alone before. It was scary. . . . No, it was exciting. She would make it an adventure, she decided.

Forcing herself not to mope, she marched into the kitchen and keyed open a music app on her tablet. Humming along to a tune, she dug into a box and got to work.

"Good evening, sir." The doorman held open the front door, looking resplendent in his black uniform. His steel gray hair and crisp British accent lent him even greater distinction.

"Good evening, Barton," James said. "I hope you had a pleasant day."

"Yes, very pleasant. Thank you for asking, sir."

"Did Miss Grayson get moved in?"

Barton smiled. "Indeed, yes, she did. Some friends of hers helped with her belongings. She seems a delightful young woman, a very welcome addition to the building."

James nodded. "Ivy's a special girl."

Once inside the elevator, James punched the button for the fifteenth floor instead of inserting his passkey and going directly to his penthouse. Since he owned the building and had made the arrangements for Ivy's move, he knew exactly which apartment was hers.

It will be nice to see her again, he mused.

Two years ago Christmas, that's how long it had been since he'd stood in the same room with Ivy. He'd accepted her parents' long-standing invitation that year because her sister Madelyn, and Zack Douglas— the man she'd jilted him for and then married—had been absent from the family festivities. They'd been visiting Douglas's sister for the holidays or some such.

Ivy had been there with a date, a thoroughly smitten college boy whose brown eyes had followed her every move, who'd wanted only to please her. Just as James had predicted, she'd outgrown her childish adoration of him, her anguished lovesick proposal to him all those years ago nothing but a faint memory.

The elevator came to a halt with a soft *ding,* and he stepped out. He walked briskly down the well-lit hallway. The walls were a crisp, light blue, the carpet a tidy gray. Her apartment was all the way down on the left— a cozy end unit.

Reggae music throbbed like an aching tooth, reaching his ears long before he neared her door, which was propped wide with a packing box. More boxes were stacked inside, piles of them ranged in every direction.

He peered inside, rapped his knuckles on the door. "Ivy?"

No answer.

He moved inside, called again. "Ivy, are you here?"

He stopped and set his briefcase on the floor beside the living room sofa.

But there was no sign of her, only the beating rhythm that grew louder the farther into the apartment he went. He followed the noise, walking down a hallway and past a guest bath to the bedroom. He stopped in the doorway, his eyes widening at the sight that greeted him.

Snugged into a pair of tight plaid cotton shorts, a woman stood bent over a huge cardboard clothing wardrobe. The entire top half of her body was concealed beneath masses of hanger-hung clothes as she quite obviously searched for something on the bottom of the box.

Friend of Ivy's?

A grin of pure male appreciation spread across his lips.

What a pair of legs. He whistled silently.

They were smooth and golden with a supple length that went up—all the way up. And her rear end, it was trim but softly curved, lush.

He tucked his suddenly itchy palms into his pockets and reminded himself to act like a gentleman. Still, gentleman or not, it didn't mean he couldn't enjoy the show.

He watched as her backside did a provocative dance, wiggling up and down, side to side, as she strained to reach whatever it was that eluded her.

He was trying to decide on the politest way to announce himself when she overbalanced, her legs and feet splaying wide.

A small screech echoed from inside the cardboard depths.

He rushed forward and grabbed her hips to keep her from toppling all the way in.

She screeched again, louder this time, then jerked and stiffened. Her bottom arched backward, pressing for a long, electrified moment smack-dab against his fly. He sucked in his breath as if he'd been seared by a live brand.

Fighting the urge to press even closer, he hauled her up and out of the wardrobe.

Dresses, shirts, and skirts exploded across the floor as her head popped free.

He let her go and stepped back.

"Who's there?" She spun around, shoving aside the long blond hair covering her face.

"It's okay," he shouted over the music. "I'm just here to see—" And then he noticed her eyes, familiar and blue. "*Ivy?*"

She froze. "*James?*"

He didn't respond.

"Where'd you come from?" she asked. "You scared the living bejesus out of me."

He could say the same, but for different reasons, still trying to wrap his head around the fact that the mystery woman—whose spectacular ass had just been pressed against his crotch—was Ivy.

Little Ivy, whom he'd known since she was a baby.

He scowled. "Yeah, well, you shaved a good year off my life too. What in the hell did you think you were doing, standing on your head in that box?"

"Unpacking," she said simply.

Suddenly her expression changed, delight illuminating her face. "James! You're here." She raced forward and threw her arms around him in a fierce hug.

Hesitantly, he put his arms around her and squeezed back.

After a moment, he gently pulled away.

He moved across the room. "You suppose you could turn that noise down?"

"What?" she called, giving her head a little shake.

"The music." He motioned with a hand. "Turn. It. Down."

She nodded in sudden understanding and moved to click off her sound system.

A refreshing wave of silence swept through the room.

"Don't you like reggae music?" she asked.

He shook his head. "Not this far north of the Caribbean. Sounds a lot better on a beach with a tall rum punch in hand. Helps numb the misery."

She grinned and met his eyes, blue against blue. "Your loss. Bob Marley and me—" She crossed a pair of fingers. "We're tight, if ya know what I mean, *mahn*," she said in a bad Jamaican accent.

He laughed.

"But hey," she said, reverting to her normal voice, "what are you doing here? I thought you were out of town on business."

"My meetings wrapped up early, so I flew back a day ahead," he said. "And what do I find when I stop by to welcome you to your new place? Your door standing wide open, inviting anyone to stroll right on in. You ought to know better. What if I'd been a thief or a lunatic?"

This time she was the one who laughed. "Please. This is the last place I'd be in danger. The security here is as good as Fort Knox."

"Actually, it's better. It ought to be since my company is the one who financed the design of the army's latest security-system upgrade. But you aren't supposed to know anything about that, and I never mentioned it."

She stared for a moment. "Of course not. I have no memory of anything you just said."

He grinned.

"As for my leaving the door open," she went on, "I needed to air things out. I painted the spare room, the one I'm going to use for my studio. It still smells of latex, even though I used the low-VOC kind." She wrinkled her nose. "I opened a couple windows and the front door to get a cross breeze."

"Airing paint fumes out of an artist's studio? I'd think an artist would love the smell of paint."

"The smell of oil paint for canvas, definitely, but not wall paint," she defended. "Linseed oil's like a fine wine; you never get tired of the bouquet. Latex is just stinky plastic. Plus, it's healthier to air things out."

James crossed his arms over his chest. "Well, whatever the reason, I want you to promise me that you won't leave your door open again when you're alone. Safe building or no safe building."

She planted her fists on her hips. "And if I don't?"

"I'll tell your mother, of course," he replied in a serious tone.

She made a face and stuck her tongue out at him.

For the first time since he'd walked into the room, he relaxed, recognizing his old Ivy.

Only she wasn't, not anymore.

Looking at her now, it was impossible to ignore the physical differences from the last time he'd seen her. There was a newfound maturity in her heart-shaped face with its high cheekbones and angular chin, all her familiar youthful softness winnowed away into clean, refined lines. Her mouth was a full, womanly pink that beckoned with sweetness and something more, something mysterious. And in her deep-set blue eyes, a wisdom and determination he'd never glimpsed before.

Then there was her body.

A woman's body, curved in all the right places despite the reedy length that lingered from childhood.

Six feet two himself, he liked tall women. They didn't intimidate him the way he knew they could other men. Still, he wasn't used to standing next to a woman who could turn her head and nearly look him in the eye. Particularly not when the female in question was his little friend Ivy Grayson.

Disturbing, that's what it was. Not just her height but the whole dynamic package.

Disturbing and sobering and unwanted.

I bounced her on my knee, for God's sake.

He'd played peekaboo and got-your-nose with her when she was a gurgling toddler. The thought of her sitting on his knee now . . .

He cleared his throat and glanced around at the stack of packing boxes. "Looks like you have your work cut out for you."

"You got that right." She shot him a hopeful look. "Wanna help?"

Her question caught him off guard. Professionals always did his packing and unpacking; he'd never had the need or inclination to bother with such mundane domestic chores. A quick phone call and he could have someone over here to help Ivy, but somehow he didn't think she would care for the idea.

He had work to do tonight. Then again, he always had work to do, and Ivy looked so hopeful. Maybe helping her for a couple of hours wouldn't be so bad.

"Sure," he said. "If I'm allowed to have dinner first. Have you eaten?"

She shook her head. "I keep meaning to take a break and run out to get something, but I just keep working instead."

"Then let me treat you to dinner. How about Per Se? I know them there, and they can usually squeeze me in even on a crowded night."

She bent to pick up a few of the clothes scattered across the carpet, then crossed to hang them up in the walk-in closet. "That sounds wonderful, but would you mind terribly if I asked for a rain check? I've been on the run since five this morning and I'm pooped." She plucked at her shorts and T-shirt. "Plus, I'd have to shower and change and fix my hair. I'd rather stay casual tonight. You understand, don't you?"

He did understand, actually. There were many times

he wished for just such an evening and the chance to stay casual.

"Okay," he agreed. "Why don't we order in something, then? How about Chinese or Italian? I know good places for both and they deliver."

She tossed him a smile. "Now you're talking. You call in our order; then I'll point you toward a box to unpack while we wait for the food to arrive."

James groaned in mock agony before pulling out his cell phone to dial.

After finishing off the last of her Szechuan beef in spicy ginger sauce, Ivy leaned back in her chair, replete and content.

She looked across the small table she and James had cleared earlier of packing paraphernalia and watched him finish his meal. His elegant fingers maneuvered the chopsticks with easy grace, his masculine jaw and the beautiful lines of his strong throat something her artist's eye couldn't help but admire.

Warmth settled low and spread through her belly, thighs, and in between—physical reactions that had nothing to do with the spiciness of her meal. Just watching him made her want. His simplest movements were dynamic, compelling, appealing.

When she'd first seen him—after she'd gotten over the initial shock—part of her had hoped the old feelings would be gone. The sensible side of her had wished she wouldn't experience the rush of love for him that had consumed so many years of her life. That they would be friends and only friends.

But nothing had changed, at least not for her.

From the moment she'd touched him, she'd known—all the emotions, all the love, surging back like a turbulent sea rushing to shore. As she'd hugged him, pressing her body to his, she'd breathed him in, savoring the clean, male scent of his skin so uniquely his own.

And she'd clung, wanting never to let go again.

But he'd pulled away, reestablishing boundaries.

She skimmed her eyes over his urbane, classic beauty. His thick, close-cut golden hair and his brows that were two pale slashes across his patrician forehead. His nose that was straight and sized to suit his handsome face, while his masculine lips retained just enough softness to invite a woman's kiss.

She wondered what he'd do if she leaned across the table and planted one on him. A big, hot, wet smooch that would rock them both all the way to their toes.

Knowing James, he would probably pat her on the head and tell her to find a nice boy her own age, exactly as he had all those years ago.

Only she didn't want a boy her age, she wanted a man.

She wanted James.

And by God, I'm going to have him, no matter what it takes.

She'd have to take it slowly though, she realized. She'd have to work hard in order to make him see her in a new light—a mature, desirable light.

Could she do it?

Of course I can, she assured herself.

No dream was impossible if you wanted it badly enough. Isn't that what had given her the courage to pursue a career as a painter despite the astronomical odds against success? Wasn't that what had brought her to New York City to strike out on her own, even though chances were good she'd fall flat on her face?

Still, if she wasn't daunted by the riskiness of her career choice, then why should she be daunted about the likelihood of winning James? All she needed was a plan of action and some good insider information.

But who was close enough to him to give her the inside skinny about his private life and habits—and any current girlfriend competition, of course?

In the next second, she knew exactly who.

She did a happy little dance inside at the thought.

Outwardly, she sipped her lukewarm China tea and smiled at James.

Suspecting nothing, he smiled back.

CHAPTER TWO

Ivy spent the next four days unpacking and arranging her belongings in her new apartment just the way she liked them. Only when she was satisfied with how everything looked, and only when she knew James would be busy at work, did she use the passkey he'd given her that first night and take the elevator to his top-floor penthouse. After all, on this particular occasion, it wasn't James she was going to see.

She exited into a small, tastefully decorated foyer done in warm, inviting shades of green and blue. An elegant Persian rug lay atop an intricate parquet wood floor, the plush wool comfortably soft beneath her shoes as she moved toward the door. A large window to her right brought in a cheery dose of sunlight. The fine eighteenth-century rosewood table positioned before it added beauty and visual éclat. The effect was further enhanced by the tall porcelain vase centered on its top, a lavish arrangement of fresh flowers spilling forth in a burst of color and fragrance.

Drawing a deep breath, she took a moment to savor the sweet scents of peony and lily of the valley before pressing her finger against the discreet brass door ringer.

A moment later, she heard muffled footsteps, then a no-nonsense voice coming through the intercom. "Yes? Who's there?"

"It's me. Ivy." She smiled, aware she was being observed through the peephole.

"Ivy who?"

"Ivy Grayson. Don't you remember me, Estella?"

After a brief silence, the door was pulled wide to reveal the ample figure of James's housekeeper. Teeth gleaming pure white against her coffee-hued complexion, Estella Johnson raised an eyebrow. "Miss Ivy, is that you?"

Ivy grinned and cocked a jeans-clad hip. "In the flesh."

"Well, dear Lord, child, I didn't recognize you," Estella declared, her melodic Mississippi accent still intact despite the many years she'd lived in the North. "Why, you've grown tall as an oak tree and twice as thin," she clucked. "I can see God's been busy raising you."

The two women stood a moment, inspecting the changes time had wrought.

Estella was short and wide with lively brown eyes and a chin that didn't tolerate sass of any kind; Ivy thought she looked wonderful. A critical eye might have noted the extra lines on the older woman's fore-head, the additional gray hairs threaded among the dark, but to Ivy she looked just the same.

"Well," the housekeeper demanded, "we just gonna stand here staring at each other, or are you goin' to give me a good old hug?"

When she spread her arms wide, Ivy walked straight into them.

"Come in. Come in," Estella said. "I was just folding up some laundry when I heard you at the door. Thought you were some infernal deliveryman come up here without security letting me know first. That boy they hired new down at the desk has you to thank. I was priming myself to deliver him a sermon, but seems he's doing his job all right after all."

Ivy followed Estella inside, where the interior of the penthouse was every bit as beautifully appointed as the entrance. Across more polished wood floors and antique rugs they made their way through the main hall and past James's large study and the dining room on the right, then turned left into an expansive living room. A series of wide windows gave a spectacular view of the city.

Hugging the distant wall, a graceful stairway curved up to a balcony. Ivy knew the entire second story held James's master bedroom suite. To the right on the first floor lay a glass-enclosed conservatory, and through a set of lovely French doors, a full-sized pool and sauna. On the opposite side, there was a well-stocked library, four guest rooms with connecting baths, a laundry, a butler's pantry, and a state-of-the-art kitchen.

It was to this last room that Estella escorted Ivy.

"Sit down." Estella motioned her toward a chair. "You want something to drink?" The housekeeper bustled over to the stainless-steel, commercial-sized refrigerator that hummed in near silence against one wall. "He's got nearly everything you could want, including fresh-made iced tea."

"Iced tea sounds lovely."

Estella reached in for the pitcher, then went to retrieve a pair of glasses, filling them with ice. "So, when are you moving in? Mr. James said you've decided to take a place in the building."

"I already did—moved in last week. . . ."

"Last week? Why, that man never breathed a word."

"He's probably been busy."

Estella snorted. "He's always busy, too busy if you ask me. He needs to slow down. Course, you can't tell him that. Won't listen to a word a body has to say." She brought the glasses of iced tea to the table. "What's this I hear about you dropping out of school?"

"Obviously, he told you about that."

"He mentions things here and there. So, spill it."

"What's there to spill?" Ivy shrugged, taking a sip of her tea. "I want to paint, not study about other people doing it. Working here in the city will be the best classroom I could have."

She decided not to mention her ultimate fear, that had she stayed in school, she might have given in to the subtle pressure of her peers and her parents to take the easy route. Attend graduate school, study for her master's, earn a PhD in art history or museum curation.

How simple it would have been to delay her art career, stay in school, let time pass. And wake up one morning to find the years gone by and herself trapped inside the comfortable prison of academia.

She wanted to create her own art, put brush to canvas in the real world, not do so from inside the safe, sterile confines of an elite ivory tower. Whether she succeeded or failed here in the city, she told herself, at least she'd have the satisfaction of knowing she'd tried.

Estella shook a reproving finger. "Painting's fine and all, but you should have stayed and finished up your education. Bet your parents were none too happy."

Ivy rubbed a line of condensation off the glass. "They've come around."

"Hmm, I'm sure they did once you didn't give 'em any choice. I heard about that too."

"I never realized what a big mouth James has."

"It's not big. *I'm* just nosy." She chuckled. "You want somethin' to eat with that?" She motioned toward Ivy's glass.

"Oh no, thanks, I'm fine. Actually, I came up here to take a swim. James gave me a key so I could use the pool, but I thought I'd better ring the bell the first time instead of scaring you to death."

"Appreciate that, child. You always did have a step as light as a cat. I remember how you used to slip in here like some quiet little ghost when the rest of your folks were out visiting in the main room. I'd look up and there you'd be."

Ivy smiled, remembering. "I must have been a dreadful pest."

"Why no, honey. You was always fine company and a good helper too. I'll tell you true. I've had paid party help come in that couldn't slice a cucumber as nice as you or arrange the trays prettier either. You always was a natural that way. Sure you don't want to take up catering instead of painting?"

"I'm sure." Ivy spun her glass in a slow circle. "Does James entertain a lot?"

"Oh, he has a mess of people over on occasion. Mostly business folks in for drinks and such. He usually asks me to do up canapés for those. Hires caterers for the rest, if they're all to stay to supper. And don't think I feel slighted lettin' others cook, 'cause I don't. No sense getting your back up if all it means is less work and bein' able to go home at the regular time. A woman's got her own family to look after too, you know."

"How is your family, Estella?"

"Why, they're wonderful. Blessed each and every one of them. My husband, Joe, has four more years and he can put in for retirement. Course, he may decide to stay on longer. Says he'd go crazy sitting around watching them talk shows all day." She laughed. "As if he ever would. There's just us and our youngest, Joleeta, at home these days, only one of my babies still in the nest. She'll be finishing high school this next year. Mr. James said to tell her so long as she keeps her grades up, she's to pick out any school she likes, any one in the country—private ones too—and he'll foot the bill."

Estella lifted the corner of her printed blouse and dabbed an eye. "He's done the same for my other three young ones, paid for whatever the scholarships wouldn't cover. The boys are both at the University of Michigan. Darnell's studying engineering and Clevert, well, he's still trying to decide, but that's okay; he's only a sophomore. Then there's Julia. Graduated top of her class from Tulane. She starts at Harvard Law this fall. She's going to be a lawyer."

"That's where my sister Brie went. Tell Julia to give her a call to talk about the particulars."

Estella's eyes lit with pleasure. "I may just do that. Yeah, Mr. James, he's a good man. Just wish he could find somebody special for himself. I keep telling him he needs a good woman and a bushel of babies to put a smile on his face. He tells me he's happy just the way he is and to mind my own business. But, of course, I know better," she added with a wink.

Realizing Estella had just given her the perfect conversational segue, Ivy strove to make her next question sound as casual as possible. "So, is he seeing anyone these days?"

"Hmmph." The housekeeper stood, reached for the empty glasses. "You done, honey?"

Ivy nodded.

Estella crossed to the dishwasher, lowered the door. "Yeah, he's seeing someone. If you ask me, she thinks a bit too much of herself, but I suppose she's all right. Pretty, dark hair, dark eyes, lots of cleavage. You know how men can be, always being led around by their"— she paused, adjusting her vocabulary—"eyes."

"Eyes, huh?" Ivy smirked.

"Hmm-hmm," she hummed in a sweet singsong. "Eyes, child."

"What's her name?"

Dishes loaded, Estella closed the dishwasher door and turned, arms folded at her thick waist. "Parker Manning. Sells real estate, though from what I hear she gets most of her money from a nice fat trust fund. I can tell she wouldn't mind having more, seeing how taken she is with all of Mr. James's fine things every time she comes to visit. Appears she'd like to dig her nails in more permanent-like, if you ask me."

Alarmed, Ivy straightened. "You mean marriage?"

"Mmm-hmm—she'd like it, anyway. Been divorced once, and she's working hard to earn herself a new ring."

"How long have they been together?"

"Oh, on about a year now, if I'm not mistaken."

That long? Ivy thought, her spirits lowering at the news. "What about James? How serious is he about her?"

"Couldn't say. Men are nothing but a mixed-up puzzle at the best of times." Estella narrowed her shrewd black gaze. "How come you're so all-fired interested in Mr. James's love life anyhow, Miss Ivy?"

Ivy blinked and glanced away. "Just curious. I'm living close by now and I . . . I care about James—always have. He's my friend."

"Sure, he's your friend. You thinking you want to be something more than just his friend? Seems I recall you always was especially partial to him."

Ivy lifted her chin, arched her back, and slipped on what she thought of as her "mature look." "And what if I am? I'm twenty now, you know."

Estella's lips twitched but she didn't laugh. "That old, huh?"

"Twenty-one come March."

"He's a might-bit older than you, honey, even if you are almost twenty-one."

"What does that matter? Age doesn't count where feelings are concerned." Ivy caught Estella's look. "At least it shouldn't count. You think I'm wrong?"

Estella rubbed a finger over one cheek. "No. I think you're young and in love. And don't you never tell your mama this, but I think you might be just the thing he needs."

Relieved, Ivy beamed. "I think so too. I only want to make him happy."

"And yourself too, I expect?"

Ivy laughed. "It would be a nice fringe benefit."

Estella joined in, chuckling. "Well, you have your work cut out for you, lamb. How you plannin' to get started?"

Ivy pulled off her shirt to reveal the skimpy red bikini top that barely covered her firm young breasts. She struck a sultry pose. "I thought I might take advantage of the pool. What time is he expected home?"

James found Ivy in his pool, cutting knife-clean lines through the clear blue water. He set his briefcase on a lounge chair and turned to watch her swim.

He'd passed Estella at the front door. "Ivy's here," she'd chirped as she bade him good night, a mysterious gleam in her eyes. He'd wondered at the look and the cheery tune she was humming under her breath. She'd worked for him for more than a dozen years and still there were times when the woman was a total enigma. He'd shaken his head as she closed the door behind her.

He walked across the earth-tone Italian tiles to the pool.

At the far end, Ivy made a neat flip and began to retrace her path. She slowed as she drew closer, gliding up to the edge, her skin beaded with water.

"Hi," she said.

He gazed down. "Hi back. Having fun?"

"Yeah." She blew at a pair of water droplets dangling from her lashes, flashed him a welcoming smile. "The water's great, perfect for doing laps. Swimming here will probably ruin me for any other pool, especially public ones. How will I ever force myself to swim in one again?"

"If you're really worried, I think there's a Y over on West Sixty-third you can join."

"No, thanks." She laughed. "I'll take the risk of being hopelessly spoiled." She pushed off, glided into a shallow float, soundlessly treading water. "Why don't you come in?" she invited.

He held his arms out at his sides, displaying his hand-tailored navy pinstripe suit, white cambric shirt, and matching tie. "I'm not dressed for swimming."

"You've got trunks upstairs. Go put them on."

"Can't." He shook his head. "I need to shower and change for dinner. I have a date tonight."

A barely perceptible frown passed over Ivy's pale brows. "A quick swim, then," she coaxed. "It'll relax you after a long day."

He was tempted, the clear, translucent pool beckoning like a siren. Or perhaps it was the girl in the pool who beckoned. He liked being with Ivy. He'd known her so long he had nothing to hide, no expectations to meet, no one he had to be except himself. She was as sweet as they came. With her, he never had to wonder which she enjoyed more—being with him or his money.

His thoughts turned to Parker and their date tonight. She had the whole evening arranged. Dinner at a prominent restaurant where they would see and be seen by all the right people. Next the opera—*Tosca*, if he wasn't mistaken—followed by coffee and dessert at some stylish nightspot. Lastly, sex at her well-appointed brownstone. She'd called that afternoon to remind him about their plans and to let him know how much she was looking forward to the evening, especially the end of it when she'd have him all to herself in her bed.

In that regard, he had no complaints. Parker was a skilled lover. Inventive, indulgent, willing to try something new just for the experience. She'd even taught him a trick or two in their time together. Yet as satisfying as the sex was, he never mistook what he shared with her for love. He knew what love was. Knew how it hurt when you lost it. He never wanted to hurt like that again.

"Well? How about it?" Ivy called from the pool. "Are you coming in?"

He glanced at his watch. "It's past six thirty already and I'm running late. Let me take a rain check and we'll do it another day."

"I'll hold you to that. Hey, before you go, would you grab me a towel? I forgot to bring one in."

"Aren't you going to swim some more?"

"Not since you reminded me of the time. I promised myself I'd put in a few hours painting tonight."

"Okay. I'll be right back."

The trip to the guest bathroom was a quick one, just down the hall. Grabbing a large peach-colored bath towel off the shelf, he strode back. His steps slowed though when he reentered the room, eyes transfixed as he watched Ivy lever herself up out of the pool. Raining like a falls, water sluiced over her translucent skin, slid down her naked limbs, soaked into the two tiny swatches of red cloth that barely constituted a bathing suit.

With her back turned, he had a full, unobstructed view of her graceful back, her lovely rear end, and long, thoroughbred legs. His breath caught as she hooked a pair of fingers into the lower half of her suit and gave the spandex a short tug. Even properly positioned, the suit left most of her rounded bottom exposed.

Saliva dried in his mouth as she faced forward, then bent, tossing her long wet hair over one shoulder. Swelling in their microscopic cups, her breasts all but popped out of the teeny-tiny, sin red bikini top. His eyes nearly popped out too when she reached up a pair of hands and squeezed the excess water from her hair, her ripe breasts jiggling. His fingers tightened against the towel he'd forgotten he held, gripping the soft cloth as though it were a lifeline. Teeth clenched, he forced his eyes away.

God damn, he swore to himself, *what in the hell is wrong with me?*

That was *Ivy,* for Christ's sake.

Ivy, his friend.

His little sister.

And there he stood, ogling her like a construction worker watching a stripper straddle a nightclub pole.

Fighting temptation and losing, he flashed another glance over her from under his lashes—pert breasts, flat stomach, lean thighs—and felt his body react in ways it had no business reacting. She was barely more than a kid. So why didn't she look like a kid? A twenty-year-old girl shouldn't be so sexy, so desirable. At least not to a man his age.

Sex on the brain.

That's what it must be, he assured himself. Parker's comments from earlier had put ideas into his head. Sex on the brain, that's what it was. Anything else was inconceivable. Anything else was obscene.

He blanked his expression as Ivy strolled toward him, his fist clutching the cotton towel as if he were trying to strangle it. He wished now he'd dropped the damned thing on one of the chairs and headed upstairs to his room. He could have made up some excuse for his rudeness later. She would have believed him.

But it was too late now. She was on her way, breathtaking as an Amazon goddess as she walked along the side of the pool.

When did she become so stunning?

He swallowed, his throat tight.

She reached for the towel. "Something wrong?"

"No," he lied, his words sounding strange to his ears. "What would be wrong?"

She rubbed the towel along one damp arm, the fabric drinking in the tiny beads of moisture. His eyes followed against their will.

"Thanks for the towel," she said.

He nodded abruptly, a muscle twitching in his jaw.

She stooped over and dried her legs, one at a time. Her wet hair swung forward, drops of water splashing onto his shoes. She straightened up. "Oops, sorry. I've gotten water on you. Here. Let me—" She reached out a hand.

"No." He stepped back as if she might burn him. "Leave it. It's fine."

"But—"

"I'm late. I told you I'm late. Let yourself out, okay?"

"Sure."

"Good night, then." Trying not to look like he was fleeing, he turned and headed for the door.

"Good night," she called.

He didn't listen, didn't want to listen. He just wanted to get away. He took the steps to his bedroom two at a time and slammed his bedroom door behind him.

Downstairs, Ivy hugged the towel to herself and smiled.

Much later that night, after dinner and drinks, Puccini and coffee, James escorted Parker to her door. He paused on the threshold.

She turned. "What is it? Aren't you coming in?" She slid her arms around his neck, feathered her fingers into his hair. "I've been looking forward to you coming in all day," she purred, rubbing her body against his in a suggestive slide. She tugged his head down for a kiss.

He kissed her forehead instead. "Forgive me, Parker, but not tonight."

"Why not? I thought we had plans."

Yes, they had. And earlier in the day he'd intended to take full advantage of those plans and spend the night in her bed. But for some inexplicable reason, he no longer wanted to, not tonight, not with her. Tomorrow this odd mood of his would pass, he told himself. By morning he'd be back to his normal self. Right now he just wanted to go home.

He touched a pair of fingers to his temple and fell back upon the oldest excuse in the book.

"I'm sorry, darling, but I have a headache."

Ivy added a dollop of quinacridone red to a blob of cadmium yellow, mashed the paints together with a palette knife, and watched a warm, lustrous orange blossom before her eyes. Deciding it was too intense, she added a speck of blue to gray out the tone. Purists might have chosen black instead, but Ivy preferred the result she could achieve using the color's complement—in this case blue with orange. She mixed the paint well, added a tiny hint more blue, mixed again. Finally satisfied, she reached for her brush and dipped in.

Nice, she mused, as she spread the paint across the

bare white stretch of canvas. A sunset come to life. She worked on, slowing to feather in an edge before switching to a smaller brush.

Despite an open window, the room stank of paint and linseed oil, overlaid with the pungent bite of turpentine. Oblivious, Ivy chose a fine-tipped sable brush, wiped the worst drips on a soiled rag long ago turned gray and greasy from a saturation of turpentine and smudged paint. Tossing the rag aside, she gave her brush a final cleaning on the tail of the oversized shirt she wore, the once-white garment stiffened by smears of dried paint in a rainbow of hues.

She worked briefly with the orange, then swished her brush clean in the turpentine jar. Wiped again on rag and shirt, then coated the bristles anew, this time in vivid pink. Humming to a tune blasting from a pair of lightweight speakers, she labored, minutes slipping by.

At half past noon, she plunked her brush in the jar and stretched her arms over her head to ease the slight ache that had settled in her lower back. Up since dawn, she'd put in a full day already. It was time for a break—and lunch, her empty belly reminded her.

She stood for another bit, studying her painting and the progress she'd made. If she kept on track, she should be able to finish the piece in another week or two—three at the outside. Added to the four completed paintings she'd brought with her from home, she'd need only another ten to fifteen to make up her portfolio. Once that was accomplished, she could start making rounds at the galleries. And if—fingers crossed—someone actually liked her work and offered her a show, she'd have to get busy painting twice that many more.

Cleaning her oily, paint-streaked hands as best she could, she removed her big painting shirt and hung it from a corner of her easel. She needed a hot bath and a meal.

Then she needed to see James.

Despite the progress she felt she'd made that evening by the pool, she hadn't seen him in more than a week. The first five days she could excuse, since Estella had told her he'd flown to Germany on business. But he'd been back in town almost that same number of days and she'd seen him only once, in the lobby, just long enough to exchange quick hellos and good-byes.

She was beginning to wonder if he was avoiding her. Maybe she'd come on a little too strong in her come-hither bikini. But she'd had to find a way to make him take notice. Perhaps a new strategy was in line.

If he wouldn't come to her, she thought as she headed for the shower, she'd have to go to him.

CHAPTER THREE

"Hi. Is James in?" Ivy asked.

James's executive assistant, Tory Harris, looked up from the report she'd been reading, her eyes cool. "Mr. Jordan," she said pointedly, "is occupied at present. May I help you?"

Ivy bounced up, then down, on her tennis shoe–clad feet, a huge canvas carryall slung over one shoulder. "No, thanks. If he's tied up, I'll wait." She paused, then smiled. "You don't remember me, do you? Though I don't really expect you to, considering how long it's been since I was here, and then only a time or two at that. I'm sure I've changed quite a bit. You haven't. You're every bit as pretty as ever."

The executive assistant lost some of her arctic demeanor. "I'm sorry. . . . I don't remember you."

"Ivy Grayson." She gestured toward herself. "It's Tory, right?"

"Yes." Tory frowned in thought. "Ivy Grayson?" Her features began to clear. "Not Madelyn Grayson's little sister?"

"The very same."

Tory's face lit up with a smile. "Why, my gosh, I do remember you. You were just a skinny kid last time I saw you. Boy, have you grown. Wow."

"Thanks. I think."

"You look great!" Tory nodded her head toward a set of tall polished double doors that led into James's office. "In case you're wondering, he really is on a conference call. He shouldn't be much longer. In the meantime, tell me what's new with you."

Ivy perched on the edge of Tory's desk as they chatted, offering Tory one of the homemade chocolate chip cookies she'd brought with her.

That's how James found them ten minutes later, laughing and chatting, cookie crumbs littering a small napkin placed in the center of Tory's desk. "Ivy, I didn't know you were here."

She shifted her hip and smiled at him. "Oh, I'm just stopping by. If you're horribly busy, I can leave."

He frowned, looked down at the file folder in his hand as if he'd forgotten it was there. "I am busy, yes. But not so busy I can't spare a few minutes. No calls, Tory," he ordered, handing her the file.

He escorted Ivy into his office.

"Is something wrong?" He motioned her toward a comfortable side chair, then took a seat himself.

"No, nothing's wrong. I just felt like a visit."

"A visit?"

"Exactly. Thought I'd stop in to say hello and bring you a treat." She reached into her shoulder bag.

"A treat?" he repeated warily.

"The baking bug bit me this afternoon—chocolate chip cookies. I had so many by the time I finished, I decided I should give some of them to you rather than eat them all myself. Tory and I split a couple while I was waiting. Hope you don't mind." She grinned impishly at him.

His eyes widened in amazement. "You came fifty blocks to bring me cookies?"

"Is it that far?"

"Why didn't you just leave them for me at the penthouse?"

She shrugged. "I didn't know when you'd be home, and I thought you might enjoy an afternoon snack. Here." She passed him a well-burped Tupperware container. He took it without a word.

"Besides," she continued, "it gave me a good excuse to leave the apartment. I painted all morning; then I started baking. An outdoor excursion seemed perfect. Aren't you going to have one?" She pointed to the unopened container. "Or are you afraid to try my cooking?"

James pried off the plastic lid, the scent of freshly baked goods drifting up. Ever polite, he offered her one first. She refused. He chose a cookie and bit in. His eyes closed in an instant of bliss.

Pleased, Ivy watched him polish off the first cookie, then dive in for two more. "These are fantastic," he declared between bites.

She waved off his remark, glowing inside at the compliment. "They're pretty simple to make."

"Simple or not, they're great. I can't remember the last time I had chocolate chip cookies."

She imagined that when he ate dessert, it was usually something elaborate and complex, the inspiration of some classically trained chef striving to outdo his competition. She was glad he was so thoroughly enjoying her plebian offering.

"You said you were painting," he asked. "How is it going?"

"Not bad. I'm making steady progress, although it never seems fast enough. When I'm out and about here in the city and something snags my attention, I make time to do a sketch, which of course sets me back on my canvas time. It'll all come together though, I'm sure," she declared with more confidence than she actually felt.

He nodded. "Give yourself time." He palmed one more cookie, then closed the box. "I'll have to drop by to see your work."

"Anytime. Why don't you stop over tonight?"

"Tonight?" He froze, looking abruptly uneasy once again. "Oh, I can't tonight."

She did her best not to look crestfallen, forcing a smile. "I understand, short notice and all. Another date?"

"No. Business dinner."

Relieved, she tried again. "Tomorrow, then?"

"Friday night? You must have plans of your own."

"Not this Friday. Look, come over and I'll make dinner. Something else simple like hamburgers or spaghetti. Even I can't ruin those."

James hesitated, shifting in his chair.

The past few minutes with her had been so natural. Easy. Familiar. The Ivy of old looking like a kid again, dressed in jeans and a baggy T-shirt.

He had been neglecting her, he realized, avoiding her because of the other evening by the pool. She didn't even know she'd done anything to unsettle him. Why should she be punished because he had issues? Besides, he was over that now. The whole event—like the other one that first day in her apartment—firmly in the past.

And she'd brought him cookies. No one, to his recollection, had ever brought him cookies.

"All right," he said. "I'll be there. But right now I have another meeting"—he broke off, glanced at his watch—"that I'm already late for. What do you say to seven thirty on Friday?"

"I'll have dinner waiting."

"Great." He picked up the Tupperware, held it out to her.

She refused it. "No. Those are for you."

"The cookies are delicious, pumpkin," he said, using his old nickname for her. "Thanks for a nice surprise."

"My pleasure."

At 7:25 Friday evening, Ivy flung aside another outfit, the seven earlier ones she'd rejected heaped on her bed. *Make up your mind,* she thought, her stomach jittery as a handful of Mexican jumping beans. It wasn't even a date, she reminded herself, not an official date anyway, since James had no clue that's what it really was.

Oh jeez, what should she wear? Cutoffs and a T-shirt were too casual—she didn't want him thinking of her as a fourteen-year-old kid. And all the dresses she'd tried on were way too formal, like the green silk cocktail dress she'd just decided against. If he saw her in something like that, he'd probably make a sprint for the elevator.

She glanced again at her bedside clock: 7:27.

Decide, decide, she chanted to herself.

If she didn't, James would arrive and she'd be left standing in her underwear. She grinned at the idea, imagining his expression if she opened the door wearing nothing but lacy pink panties and a bra. *Ah, well,* she mused. She'd have to save that one for later.

She was rifling through her wardrobe for the fifteenth time, when the doorbell rang.

She jumped, then cursed as she stubbed her toe against the closet door.

Why, of all nights, did he have to be so prompt?

Ignoring her throbbing toe, she flew into action, grabbing what came most easily and most comfortably to hand—a pair of slim-fitting white chinos and a short-sleeved blouse dyed the color of newly mown grass. She yanked on the clothes, then, careful of her toe, thrust her feet into chunky sandals. Running a quick brush through her long hair, she raced from the bedroom as the doorbell rang for a second time.

Hand to her chest, she willed her heart to stop pounding. Inhaling deeply, she opened the door.

Breath rushed from her lungs at the sight of him. Gorgeous—it was the only word that did him justice. He was dressed in crisp camel trousers and a white Cuban-style shirt with intricate white stitching on the single breast pocket and front placket. His short hair gleamed, rich and golden as a roman coin. The firm, clean line of his jaw smooth shaven, smelling faintly of soap, a temptation that called out for her touch.

She curled her fingers into a loose fist instead and greeted him with an easy smile. "Right on time," she chimed.

"You okay? You seem winded."

"Just running late. Come in. Come in." She held the door wide.

He strolled in, looked around. "You've definitely been busy since I was here last. I seem to remember lots and lots of boxes."

"Gone, each and every one of them, thank the Lord."

They moved into the living room. She waited while his eyes roved over the space, taking in the wall she'd daringly painted sunshine yellow and the huge, framed fine-arts posters from exhibits of Gauguin and van Gogh that she'd arranged on the walls.

"The place has your touch," he commented.

"Loads of garish color and bric-a-brac, you mean?" she teased.

"No, lots of atmosphere and style. The space suits you. Everything looks great, Ivy. Really great."

She let his compliment wash over her, pleased.

He held out a box wrapped in pretty pink checkered

paper. "Here. For you. A belated housewarming gift. Or should I say apartment-warming gift?"

Ivy accepted the present with a smile and took a seat on the sofa. She gave the box a gentle, experimental shake. "Not much rattle. A vase maybe?"

He stood over her. "Not even close. Try again."

It was a game they played whenever he brought her a gift. Per the rules, she had three guesses.

She sniffed at the box. "No scent. Hmm, not chocolate or perfume." She shook the package again, then raised her eyes to his.

They offered her no clues; he had a killer poker face when he wanted.

"You may have me stumped," she admitted.

"I double-boxed it to give you a real challenge." He crossed his arms over his chest and waited.

"Book ends?"

"Nope. One guess left."

She stroked her palm over the polished surface of the paper. "Hmm, something for the apartment maybe? From Germany since you were there only a few days ago. A cuckoo clock? No, too noisy. Mosel wineglasses?" She shook her head. "No, too touristy." She worried a fingernail between her front teeth as she considered. "Candlesticks. Aha, it's candlesticks!"

His expression remained neutral. "Is that your final guess?"

She hesitated. "Yes."

"*Nanh*," he mimicked, making a sound like a game show buzzer. "Wrong again. You lose."

"Damn it. I thought I had it with that last one."

"Why would I get you candlesticks? You've already got half a dozen pairs."

" 'Cause I like them."

"You like a great many things. Maybe next time." He slipped his hands into his pants pockets. "Well, open it up. We haven't got all night."

"You know I have to take my time. These things can't be rushed." She was notoriously slow at unwrapping presents despite the fact that it drove everyone she knew crazy, including James.

"You have two minutes," he warned, "or I'll tear the paper off for you."

She hugged the gift protectively. "Don't you dare."

James tapped his toe while she made a production of removing the wrapping, both sets of it. Eventually she revealed the gift.

"Blu-rays." She examined the titles. "Old Cary Grant movies."

"I know they're nothing extraordinary, but—"

"No, they're wonderful. I love them," she said with a grin.

He returned her smile. "You don't have any of them already, do you? I know you've always enjoyed his movies, so—"

She put the DVDs aside and leaped up from the couch. "I have a couple I'm always trying not to erase on my DVR, that's all. Now I can quit worrying. These are so cool. I couldn't have asked for a better, more thoughtful gift. Thank you." She reached out and hugged him.

He quietly accepted her embrace before giving her a quick, avuncular pat on the back and inserting a reasonable distance between them again. Not exactly the response she was looking for. She sighed to herself. Then again, he'd never been standoffish about her hugging him before.

Am I unsettling him?

Hmm, maybe she was making progress, after all.

"So where are these paintings I came to see?" he asked abruptly. "In your studio?" Without waiting for her response, he strode down the hall.

She smiled to herself, her spirits lighter as she trailed after him.

"Ignore the one on the easel," she warned as she walked into her studio. "It's only half finished, not much more than blocked in. I should have thrown a sheet over it before you arrived."

Hands on his hips, he studied the piece, a cityscape depicting a street vendor and a line of customers—a range of people from ordinary businessmen to a fully costumed mime having a smoke. "I don't see why," he said. "Looks like it's coming along well to me."

"Most people have trouble visualizing what a piece will look like before it's completed. Like showing someone a skeleton and expecting them to see Robert Pattinson."

"Good thing, then, that I'm not most people."

She smiled. "Yeah."

"Even half finished," he went on, "there's no question it's going to be terrific. As the rest already are." He gestured to the other paintings on the walls.

She held her clasped hands beneath her chin. "You really think so?"

He nodded. "When I heard you'd quit school to paint full-time, I had my doubts. I thought you should have stayed in school, stuck it out for another year."

The inner glow she'd been feeling began to fade. "Is that why you came here tonight? To convince me to give up and go back?"

He shook his head. "I wanted to see your paintings. You always were a competent artist, Ivy. I knew you had talent, but I didn't know if you had more. And it takes more. Art's a rough field, fine arts one of the roughest. As you know, I invest in a wide variety of endeavors, art included, so I'm not a complete novice in the field. I've seen a lot of highly talented artists toil away in obscurity."

"And poverty," she added, crossing her arms defensively over her breasts.

"Yes," he agreed. "And poverty. But looking at what you've accomplished here, what you are accomplishing here, I think you have that extra something special. You've come a long way with your art. If you can do this at twenty, I can't wait to see what you'll be creating a decade from now and beyond. Your paintings are beautiful. Don't ever let anyone tell you otherwise."

Shock warred with delight as his words sank in. Of course she shouldn't care what he thought, shouldn't let his opinion—good or bad—affect her self-esteem, her determination and belief in her own talent. Yet she couldn't contain the prideful flush of joy that washed through her at his approval.

She wanted to toss her arms around his shoulders, wanted to pull his head down to hers and plant a long, exuberant kiss on his lips. But before she could do either, James moved away.

"I have a number of good contacts," he continued. "Why don't I make a couple calls, put a few words in the right ears? Even with the limited number of finished pieces you have, I think you could sell—"

"No."

He raised an eyebrow at her clipped refusal.

"It's lovely of you to offer," she hurried to explain, "but I wouldn't feel right having you help me."

"Why not? Part of success is luck, and if I can help you get lucky by putting you in touch with the right people, then why turn it down?"

"Because I'd never know," she said in a soft, clear voice.

He frowned, crossed his arms. "Know what?"

"Whether I succeeded on my own or simply because of you. Assuming one of your art contacts did offer me a showing, I'd always wonder why. Does the gallery owner really like my paintings? Or is he just doing a favor for a friend? You're a wealthy, powerful man, James, and wealthy, powerful men wield a great deal of influence even in the narrow confines of the art world."

He waved away her words. "My influence might get you into a gallery, yes, but it won't sell your paintings. Succeed or fail, it'll be on your own."

It was her turn to raise an eyebrow. "Are you sure? You've said it yourself—the right whispers in the right ears can make all the difference."

"What I'm offering isn't a cheat," he shot back, "only a leg up, one you deserve. I meant it about your art. It's wonderful. Believe me, any success you achieve will be honestly earned."

"And knowing you think so is enough for me." She laid a hand on his shoulder. "Please, James, don't imagine I'm ungrateful. I know you're only trying to make things easier for me and I thank you. But sometimes I think things are already a little too easy for me. I need to do this on my own—"

He opened his mouth.

She cut him off before he could speak. "*All* on my own. Promise you won't interfere."

"I think you're letting foolish pride stand in the way of a good opportunity. But fine. If you don't want my help, I won't give it. With this stubborn streak, I'm surprised you didn't move into that rat-infested dive in Bushwick like you'd planned, so you could starve like a proper little artist."

She cocked her head, surprised. "What do you know about that?"

It took him a moment to respond. "Your mother mentioned something or other about it. You know she calls me from time to time."

"What else did she happen to mention?"

She could almost see the wheels spinning in his head before his face cleared of expression. "Nothing of any significance."

For a moment she considered pursuing the topic, then decided there was little purpose. Her mother had told him her original plans. So what? Surely there couldn't be anything more to it than that. What else could there be? She decided it best to change the entire subject.

He obviously decided the same thing. "So when's dinner?"

"Anytime." She smiled. "I just have to toss the salad and put the spaghetti noodles on to boil and we'll be ready to eat."

"Lead on, then, Macduff. I'm starved."

The end credits of *To Catch a Thief* rolled across the television screen, the elegant, unforgettable faces of Grace Kelly and Cary Grant consigned to memory once more. With a quick touch to the remote, Ivy stopped the movie.

From her spot on the large L-shaped sofa, she leaned up on a single elbow and looked over to ask James if he had the energy to watch another film. Seeing him was all the answer she needed.

He was asleep.

Hair ruffled, limbs loosened in a relaxed sprawl across the plush sofa cushions and flowered throw pillows, he was breathing slowly and rhythmically, which indicated a deep sleep. His skin radiated warmth, bathed in a buttery glow of lamplight. His eyelashes lay straight against cheeks grown rough with stubble, pale as wheat chaff after a harvest cutting.

Ivy silently climbed to her sock-covered feet and edged closer.

Jet lag, she mused.

Even with the convenience and privacy of his own

jet aircraft, transatlantic travel took its toll. Hours shuffled back and forth as casually as playing cards while he winged from one time zone to another, then back again. And knowing James, he hadn't been easy on himself since his return home, running on too little sleep and too much caffeine. A good meal, pleasant conversation, and simple entertainment had done their work, lulling him into the slumber his body so obviously needed.

He shifted, his shirt bowing open at the neck, giving her a peek at the mat of golden curls covering his chest. Did that hair feel as silky as it looked? Was it as soft as the hair on his head?

Without pausing to think, she dropped to her knees next to him and stretched out a single finger. Close, closer she moved until a solitary curl wound around the tip.

Her lips parted on a rapt sigh.

Soft yet wiry, the hair clung with a tensile strength. Heat rose from his skin, luring her nearer. How easy it would be to rest her palm on that broad plain of flesh, to thread her fingers into the short curls and stroke the skin beneath. How simple to touch her lips to the spot. How much better to touch them to his mouth, parted invitingly in sleep.

She flushed at the thought, desire making her pulse points throb. She curled her hand into a fist against her chest.

Do I dare?

She studied him, time slowing to the texture of winter molasses.

He was a heavy sleeper, hard to rouse once he became tangled in the world of dreams. Everyone in the family knew it. Hadn't they all laughed on countless occasions, recounting tales of the summer he'd vacationed with them in Maine? How her father had finally resorted one morning to using a foghorn to blast James awake.

If she kissed him, chances were good he'd never know. And oh, how she longed to kiss him.

But what if he woke to find her there . . . ? Hmm, what if he did?

Half-hoped-for imaginings swirled in her brain, and she couldn't resist her mind's urgings. Lowering her lips to his, she rested them there, delicately balanced, scarcely touching. Firm, smooth, the shape of his mouth matched hers exactly, as if it had been designed for that express purpose.

He didn't awaken.

Emboldened, she let her eyes softly close as she increased the pressure, turning the barely there touch into a real kiss. She savored the sensation, the feeling of skin to skin, heat to heat. He tasted like honey, or some exotic variety of fruit, lush and forbidden. She softly drew a breath, her senses swimming as the scent of him flooded through her. His essence swam inside her head, on her mouth, in her nose, down her throat, better than anything she'd ever tasted.

Suddenly he shifted, his head rolling against the pillow. A groan soughed from deep in his throat.

She broke the kiss and began to sit up, but before she could move away, he clamped a hand around the back of her head and crushed her lips to his.

She squeaked as he took possession of her mouth. His turn now, he kissed her the way a man would, hungry and demanding, feeding upon her with a kind of dark intensity that permitted no resistance, expected only surrender.

Heat washed through her like a roaring blast furnace. Blood raged like a river through her veins, clouding her brain, shredding every inch of her control. She whimpered and gave herself to him completely. Let him ravage her mouth, drink in her unknowing cries, tangle his tongue with hers in a slick, velvety duel. Draped over him, she shuddered, lost in a sea of bliss.

Abruptly, he broke their kiss, his chest rising and falling in a sharp inhale, exhale. His hand fell away, body growing slack, eyes tightly closed.

Stunned, Ivy slumped onto her haunches.

Is he asleep? Had he been asleep the entire time? Impossible, and yet there he lay, slumbering on as if the entire episode had never occurred. She might doubt it herself except for the evidence, her lips bruised and swollen, well kissed. She touched a pair of trembling fingers to them.

Shell-shocked, she stumbled to her feet and nearly tripped over the coffee table. Body aching with unanswered desire, she wondered who it was he'd imagined he was kissing. Dear Lord, if he'd truly been asleep, it could have been any woman. Appalled by the possibilities, she turned and fled to her bedroom.

James woke groggy and disoriented, the light from a single lamp shining in his face. He squinted against the glare and sat up, taking a moment to realize where he was.

On Ivy's couch. In Ivy's apartment.

He blinked and scrubbed a hand over his face. *Whew,* he'd really dropped off. The last thing he remembered was watching Cary Grant kiss Grace Kelly while fireworks exploded behind them. Then he'd been, as the saying went, out for the count.

Ivy wasn't there, and except for the dim lamplight, the apartment was dark. Obviously, she'd gone to bed. He couldn't blame her for not waiting up.

What time was it anyway? he wondered.

A quick check of his watch showed him it was late— or really early, depending upon your way of thinking.

It was 3:42 a.m. Way past time to go home.

He raised a hand to cover a yawn.

It wasn't like him to be so rude, falling asleep on his hostess's sofa in the middle of the evening's entertainment.

But Ivy wouldn't hold it against him. That was the great thing about her. She was a comfortable person to be around, family in a way his own family had never been. If he'd had the bad manners to fall asleep on his mother's sofa, he was sure she would have given him a hard rap on the head.

And how about that dream?

It sure had been a doozy, so vivid and clear it had almost seemed real. He remembered the woman, her sweet scent, her vibrant touch. The way she'd bent across him, her lovely, gentle mouth pressed to his with delicate pressure. She'd made him yearn, carnal need raging to life inside him, her whispering kisses not nearly enough to satisfy. In the dream, he remembered reaching up, pulling her closer to take more. And he had, exploring the silken depths of her mouth with eager thoroughness. She'd kissed him back, giving herself to him utterly.

The sound and taste and touch of her had burrowed into his soul.

Ivy, he realized suddenly.

The woman had been Ivy.

Ivy?

Alarmed, he glanced down the darkened hallway that led to her bedroom as if she could hear his shameful thoughts. He shook his head, mortified.

He scraped a hand through his hair. *Jesus, what's wrong with me lately?*

As if it wasn't bad enough that he was noticing the way she filled out a blouse and a pair of jeans these days, now he was having erotic dreams about her.

What was next?

Nothing, he assured himself harshly. *Nothing is next.*

He had to get out of here.

He sprang to his feet, and that's when he noticed it. The single golden hair stuck to his shirt. Ordinarily he wouldn't have thought twice about it since his hair was blond. But as he plucked the strand off his clothing, he noticed the length.

It was long.

Ivy long.

CHAPTER FOUR

Her cell phone rang, jolting Ivy from a sound sleep. She fumbled for it on her nightstand. " 'Lo."

"Oops. Did I wake you up?"

Ivy slumped against the sheets as she recognized her sister Madelyn's voice on the other end of the line. She let her eyes slide shut again. "Umm. What time is it?"

"Eight fifteen. Sorry, but it's been so long since I've slept past six that I've forgotten what it feels like. If the twins aren't up by sunrise, there's something wrong."

Slowly waking up, Ivy scooched herself up against her pillow. "And how are my little nieces?"

"Little terrors, you mean. They made a mess of breakfast this morning. I turn my back for a second and there's Cream of Wheat and mashed banana everywhere—all over them, all over the walls. I gave Zack bath duty while I stayed to clean up the kitchen. He's got them splashing in the tub right now."

Ivy couldn't keep from chuckling.

"Hey, watch it," Madelyn warned. "Just wait until you have a couple of your own. We'll see who's laughing then."

Ivy just laughed harder.

Madelyn loudly cleared her throat. "If you can contain yourself long enough to listen, I called to ask if you'd like to have lunch at Daniel on Tuesday. They had a last-minute cancelation, and I managed to snag a reservation. As Weston-Drake's newest creative director, I figure I'm entitled to a special meal every now and again."

Ivy sat up. "You got the job?"

Satisfaction rang in Madelyn's voice. "I got the job. My promotion starts effective immediately, and the best part is they're going to let me telecommute two days a week so I can be here at home with the girls."

"That's fantastic, Malynn. Congratulations."

"Zack's really happy for me, even if it is killing him that he lost our bet. You know the one we made years ago about who'd step up to the big chair first?"

Ivy did know. Madelyn and Zack had been business rivals working for the same advertising firm when they'd fallen in love. Despite their undeniably successful marriage, their competitive streaks remained firmly intact, even with each other.

"So what'd you win?"

"A bottle of hideously expensive French champagne," Madelyn crowed. "Since I switched firms, seems the grass turned greener on my side first. It won't be long before Fielding and Simmons moves

Zack up too. Although he's making noises lately about quitting to become a house husband."

Ivy snorted, imagining her robust brother-in-law pushing a vacuum cleaner, washing dishes, and chasing after a pair of energetic toddlers full-time. "That'll be the day."

"Oh, I don't know. He adores our babies, so much sometimes it surprises me. Says he wants to have another. I told him fine so long as he agrees to be the pregnant one this time."

"But you're considering it," Ivy said, hearing the wistful tone in her sister's voice.

"Yeah, I'm considering it."

Ivy smiled at Madelyn's obvious contentment.

From the background she heard a flurry of high-pitched childish squeals, followed by the noisy thunder of tiny running feet and the stomp of bigger adult ones.

Madelyn laughed. "The troops have returned all scrubbed and polished. Apparently, they're being chased by a terrifying monster." A loud, playful masculine growl came clearly through the phone.

More screams erupted, then a series of helpless giggles and cries of "No, Daddy, no tickle."

Ivy grinned at the hilarity.

She and Madelyn firmed up the time for their lunch date, then discussed the progress Ivy was making on her painting. The talk wound around until it landed on their mother's annual Fourth of July party, now less than a month away. Every year for as long as Ivy could remember, Laura Grayson had hosted a lavish party at the family home in Connecticut. This year would be no exception.

"What are you bringing?" Madelyn inquired. "And please don't say brownies, since it's the only decent from-scratch dessert I can make."

"I'm not bringing brownies, so you're in the clear." Ivy paused, twisting a piece of her long hair around one finger. "Actually, about that . . . I might not be able to make it this year."

A long moment of surprised silence followed. "What do you mean, not make it?"

No one missed Fourth of July at their parents' house, certainly not family members. It was an understood rule.

Ivy stifled a sigh, sorry she'd brought it up. But, she reminded herself, if she couldn't tell Madelyn, she'd never be able to tell their mother. "I have other plans . . . friends, you know, here in the city. They're throwing a big party and want me to come."

It wasn't a lie. Well, not exactly. Neil and Josh were throwing a big party and they had invited her. But the person she was actually hoping to spend the holiday with was James. Of course she couldn't tell Madelyn that. Her sister might be understanding about most things, but she doubted Madelyn would approve of her pursuing the man who'd once been Madelyn's fiancé, even if Madelyn had ended up jilting him.

"So," her sister wanted to know, "have you told Mom yet?"

"Not yet. Working up the nerve."

A hearty laugh sounded over the line. "Good luck. You'll have to let me know how it goes. She still brings up the Fourth that I *deserted* the family for Daytona Beach."

"That's 'cause you went down there with Derek Childs. She never approved of Derek Childs."

"With good reason, I later found out. He was a two-timing creep, but that's beside the point. The point is you and this party. What's up? Some new man in your life? One who might just happen to also be attending this party, hmm?"

Damn, does Madelyn have radar or something?

Carefully modulating her tone, she worked on lying without actually lying. "No new man." *Just the same old one I've always wanted*, she thought, fingers crossed. "And no one at the party besides me, some of my college buddies, and their neighbors."

"You sure?"

"Totally sure. It's just a party, Malynn. You remember parties, right?"

"Yeah, I seem to recall a few despite the senility setting in, ha-ha. I also remember how easy it is to get into trouble at them."

Ivy stifled a sigh. "I'll be fine. I'm very responsible."

"I know. It's not you I worry about. Sometimes I think you were born an adult. It's all the other people who'll be there. And just for the record, if Mom asks, I know nothing about this subject, okay?"

Ivy laughed. "Coward."

"Damned straight—Hannah, take that out of your mouth," she broke off to tell one of her daughters. "Look, I'd better go. Zack's about to send up an SOS flare. See you soon."

"Yeah, couple of days."

Smiling, Ivy pushed the end-call button and set

down the phone. She flopped back against the pillows, listened with half an ear to the drone of street traffic and the gentle tick-tock of her bedside alarm clock.

Then she remembered James.

Was he still out in the other room, sleeping on her couch?

Heady warmth rushed through her at the notion.

Rolling out of bed, she pulled on a lavender terry-cloth robe. Feeling unaccountably shy, she opened her bedroom door and moved on silent feet down the hall.

But she needn't have bothered with the stealth. The room was empty.

Fighting the disappointment, she leaned over to switch off the lamp that was still burning. She noticed the scattered throw pillows, honing in on the one with the faint dent where he'd lain his head. She reached out, lifted the pillow to her nose, and inhaled.

The scent of him filled her.

James.

Senses adrift, her eyelids drifted downward as she remembered their kiss.

James forked up a final bite of breakfast—soft-boiled eggs on toast with a side of Niman Ranch bacon—while he perused a sobering article on the nation's economy in the Sunday *Times*. He snorted softly when he moved on to an op-ed piece about a recent political scandal and was rolling his eyes at another bit of nonsense when the doorbell rang.

Who could that be? he thought, frowning as he swallowed the last of his now-lukewarm coffee. Setting his cup back into its saucer, the china making a faint clink, he rose to find out.

He discovered Ivy on the threshold, fresh and sporty looking in a powder blue T-shirt, hip-hugging black spandex shorts, and a pair of clean white tennis shoes. She'd gathered her long hair into a neat ponytail, darker and damp on the ends from a recent shower. Some sort of skates—he couldn't tell what kind—hung looped by their strings over one shoulder.

She looked delicious and adorable, like a dish of fresh peaches and cream just waiting to be enjoyed. He shifted uncomfortably at the thought, the dream he'd had last night slamming into his mind. The velvety softness of her lips, the delectable flavor of her tongue tangling passionately against his. Her scent. Even now he could smell the feminine heat of her as if she were wrapped in his arms instead of standing innocently on the other side of the doorway.

He just wished the damn dream hadn't been so intense, hadn't felt so real.

Incredibly real.

He wondered again about the hair he'd found. That long length of gleaming gold he'd plucked off his chest after he'd awakened.

How had it gotten there?

Off the couch, of course. It was her couch, so it wasn't all that extraordinary. And yet . . .

And yet what?

Stop being ridiculous, he told himself.

It was a dream. A disturbing, bewitching, thoroughly unwanted dream, and if he was smart, he'd forget all about it.

Mentally, he gave himself a good, hard shake.

Snap out of it.

Having dreams about Ivy, *erotic dreams* . . . Well, it was just plain wrong. He didn't even understand why he was having them. He didn't lust after girls her age— at least not since he'd been her age.

He liked women.

Mature, adult women who knew the score and didn't waste time playing games. Whatever this weird phase was that he was going through, well, it had to stop.

It will stop, he counseled himself, *right here, right now.*

Feeling like a letch and half wishing he hadn't opened the door in the first place, he made himself hold it wider. "Hi there."

"Hi," she chimed. "Hope I'm not interrupting."

"Not at all. I was just finishing breakfast."

She trailed him through the penthouse into the light-filled dining alcove attached to the kitchen.

"Coffee?" he asked, covering his uncharacteristic discomfort in her presence with politeness.

"No, thanks. I've already had enough caffeine this morning to fuel a small power plant."

"I think I'll have some more," he murmured, knowing he needed the distraction. Picking up his empty cup, he carried it across to the sleek metal coffeemaker that rested on the counter.

She set her skates on the floor near the dining table, then slid into a chair. She peered out the broad windows at the blue swath of summer sky above.

"What a great day," she declared. "Much too nice to stay cooped up inside, don't you think?"

She noticed the dish of fresh raspberries he hadn't quite finished, dipped a pair of fingers in and fished one out. He tried but couldn't prevent himself from watching as she popped the berry between her pink lips and chewed.

Sweet Jesus.

He turned away as she went diving for another berry, worked hard at not burning himself on the coffeepot.

"Anyway, you're probably wondering why I'm here," she said.

Lord, he hoped it wasn't to swim. He didn't think he could take any more of *that* today.

He cleared his throat. "The thought had crossed my mind."

"I've come to take you Rollerblading."

His eyes widened in genuine surprise. "Pardon me?"

"Rollerblading. It's great fun. Have you ever been?"

He leaned back against the counter and sipped his steaming beverage. "No, and I don't plan to start."

"Why not?" she demanded. "You're athletic."

"Not that athletic."

She made a dismissive sound. "You ski. You ice-skate."

"Yeah, in Aspen, where it's cold and there's plenty of snow to cushion any falls. Spending the afternoon leaving pieces of my bare skin on the pavement lacks a certain appeal."

"If you can skate, you can Rollerblade. You won't fall. . . . Well, not once you get your balance. We'll get you pads and a helmet, rig you out in full protective gear. You'll do great. I'll teach you everything you need to know." She paused, pursed her lips in a brief pout at the implacable expression on his face. "Oh, come on. You won't know if you like it unless you try it."

"I won't know if I hate it either," he quipped, taking a careful sip of coffee.

She lifted a pair of beseeching eyes, cast him a look he'd never been able to withstand, not since she'd first turned it on him at age two. "Please. I don't want to go to the park alone."

"Call one of your friends."

"*You* are my friend. Besides, I still don't know too many people here in the city. And Neil and Josh are busy today."

A twinge of guilt nagged at him. She did have a point. She was new to the city, was probably lonely and bored, longing for the company of someone familiar.

If he was having certain inappropriate thoughts about her lately, that was his problem. A problem he could and would control, he assured himself. It didn't seem fair to punish her for something that wasn't her fault—even if it would be in his best interest to shoo her out the door and return to the safety of his newspaper.

"How about a game of tennis instead?" he suggested on a hopeful note. "I'll take you to my club."

She made a face. "I'm all jazzed up to skate. And you will be too once you give it a try."

He made one last attempt to escape. "I don't have any skates."

She waved a hand. "No problem. We'll rent you a pair." She leaned forward, showered him with an irresistible smile. "Please, James, come with me. If you don't enjoy yourself, I'll never ask again."

And how on earth was he to defend against that?

She got him rigged up, laced up, and ready to skate before he issued his first protest.

"Where's *your* helmet?" he grumbled, shooting a meaningful look toward her bare head.

"I've done this dozens of times. I don't need one."

"Of course you need one. Your head'll crack open as easily as mine if you hit blacktop."

She gave him a superior look, gliding on her Rollerblades in an easy circle in front of where he sat on a park bench. "Ah, but you see, I won't be hitting the pavement."

"Accidents happen. Someone might bump you from behind, knock you over. This place is crawling with people."

"Central Park's always crowded, especially on the weekends. Why do you think they close the streets to cars on Saturdays and Sundays?"

"To irritate motorists?"

"Ha-ha. Very funny. Come on. Let's get moving."

"Uh-uh. Not until you cover up that pretty little head of yours." He crossed his arms over his chest and leaned back. "If *I* have to wear a helmet, *you* have to wear a helmet."

Ivy thrust out her lower lip. "I don't like 'em. They're hot and they ruin my hair."

"Hey, I'll be happy to return all this stuff and go home. There's a very fine bottle of Bordeaux in my wine room just waiting to have its cork popped."

She knew him well enough to realize he'd make good on his threat if she didn't give in. He might be fair and reasonable most of the time, but when James turned stubborn, he could be as immovable as a ten-ton granite boulder.

She tossed up her hands. "Fine. I'll wear a helmet."

"Pads too. You don't want to scrape up those delicate elbows and knees."

"Don't push your luck, buddy," she warned before turning to skate over to the rental booth.

She returned shortly, helmet fastened with a strap beneath her chin. "Satisfied?"

He nodded, an amused gleam in his eyes.

"Okay, then," she declared. "Enough stalling."

"Who's stalling?"

"You are. Now, up and at 'em. Remember what I told you: Find your center, then gently push off. Think ice-skating without the ice. And don't forget to use your heel brake."

"Yes, Teach, I remember. Stand back and give a man some room."

She did as he asked, hovering anxiously as a mother hen watching a fledgling chick leave the nest for the first time.

But she needn't have worried. James found his balance after an initial bobble and a quick grab at the park bench for support. Steadying himself, he rolled easily toward her before coming to a perfect stop.

Looking pleasantly surprised and more than a little pleased with himself, he shot her a grin. "Hey, this isn't as hard as I thought it'd be."

She grinned back. "I knew you'd be a natural."

He rolled a few more feet, circled slowly, stopped again, then spread his arms wide. "This just might be okay."

A trio of kids picked that second to come whizzing by on skateboards, whooping and hollering at the top of their teenage lungs. One of them raced toward her and James, veering off at the last second to try a fancy leap over the bench.

The velocity and abruptness of his move was enough to overset them all. The kid went flying, board winging out from under him before he crashed on the grass beyond.

She swiveled, legs splaying, arms pinwheeling as she fought to retain her balance. By some miracle, she stayed upright, but James wasn't so lucky. Out of the corner of her eye, she caught sight of him as he flipped up, clear off his skates, then came back down with a hard thud onto the pavement.

Her throat squeezed tight. She skated forward. "Oh God. Oh, James. Are you okay? Are you hurt?"

She knelt down next to him where he lay on his back. Without thinking, she reached out and began running her hands over his shoulders and chest and arms as she blindly searched for injuries.

He groaned, his eyes closed.

"Can you hear me? Can you talk? Say something, James."

"*Ow.*" His eyes popped open. "*Ow, ow.*" He winced before gently grabbing her hands to stop them.

"Are you all right?" she asked, a big dose of guilt washing over her.

What if he was hurt?

What if he was seriously injured?

She'd never forgive herself, especially since she'd practically twisted his arm, making him try something he hadn't wanted to try in the first place.

She'd just wanted to spend the day with him. She'd just wanted him to have some fun. As far as she could see, he didn't have nearly enough fun. Now she'd probably never get him to try anything new again.

He groaned. "Stupid punk kids."

She looked around for the boys, but they were long gone. "They're not supposed to be skateboarding here. Where's the skate patrol when you need them?"

"Probably on a doughnut break like the rest of the city's finest."

If he could joke, she thought, he couldn't be too seriously injured. Then again . . .

"Lie still," she told him. "I'll get help."

"No." He released her hands, levered himself onto his padded elbows. "I think I'm all right." After a long moment, he sat all the way up, rolled his shoulders, his neck, tested his arms and legs. "No permanent harm done, I guess, though I'll probably be stiff as an arthritic old man come morning."

"I'm sorry. I never dreamed something like this

would happen. If you want to pack it in and go home, I'll understand."

"Pack it in? Hell no. I'm not going to let some stupid kids chase me off. I came to learn to Rollerblade, and by God, I'm going to learn to Rollerblade."

She stared at him for a long, surprised moment, and knew again exactly why she loved him. Only through sheer force of will did she stop herself from throwing her arms around him and giving him a big smacking kiss.

But she couldn't afford to scare him off.

If only she knew whether her plan was working or not. He still treated her like his little sister most of the time, and today's fiasco wasn't helping matters any. Still, every once in a while she thought she caught a glimpse of something else in his eyes, something more.

A shiver ran down her spine at the possibility.

"Here, let me help you up."

She reached down and slipped an arm around his back, placing her chest at his eye level. She shivered again as she glanced down, noticing where his gaze had landed. On her breasts, following their movement, the gentle rise and fall of them with her every breath beneath her shirt.

She imagined him leaning closer, pillowing his head against her willing flesh. Imagined stroking her hand over his cheek, his forehead as she leaned down to kiss away all his hurts and oh, so much more.

Abruptly, he stiffened and pulled away. "I'm fine. Let go, Ivy."

Stung, she sat back as he turned away.

She managed to compose herself by the time they were both on their feet again, a sunny smile she didn't feel pinned to her lips.

This making him love me thing is going to take time, she reminded herself.

But she'd waited her whole life so far. She could wait a little bit longer.

She would wait forever if that's what it took.

"Ready to try it again?" she inquired.

He smacked a smudge of dirt off the butt of his shorts, then turned her way. "Ready as I'll ever be, assuming the coast is clear this time."

She looked around. "Seems to be. Now, push off like you did before. . . ."

James eased into a hot bath, tendrils of steam rising from the water's surface. He sighed as his aching muscles began to relax. He let his eyes slide closed as he rested his neck against the rim of his wide, white marble tub, wiggling his toes to stretch the muscles of his calves.

He smiled, thinking about the day. Despite his current aches and pains—and a less than stellar beginning to the experience—he had to admit he'd had fun.

Ivy was right. Once you got the hang of it, Rollerblading was sick.

Listen to him, he thought—*sick*.

He sounded like some college kid, which he conceded with a grimace as another sore muscle complained, he clearly was not.

Not at thirty-five.

Still, he was a long way from a rocking chair. He was physically fit, a man in the prime of his life, and today he'd had fun acting half his age. Speeding along on a pair of in-line skates, wind skimming over his skin, trees flashing by overhead, pavement racing past below . . . well, it was an exhilarating, invigorating, carefree experience.

Good thing he'd let Ivy talk him into trying it.

Maybe he should invest in a pair of skates so he wouldn't have to rent them next time.

He considered it, then wondered which companies manufactured in-line skates. What sort of profit potential was there in the product? What kind of investment opportunities? He decided he'd have to make a note to look into it when he got into the office. Perhaps Ivy'd inadvertently led him down a lucrative new avenue.

He smiled again, thinking about the pizza and beer they'd had after their skating adventure. And the mammoth banana split they'd shared after the meal. Ice cream, hot fudge, and whipped cream mounded so high they'd barely been able to see each other across the table.

She'd giggled as she'd plunged in, eyes flashing in mischievous delight as she ate her first bite. A shiny, sticky glaze of chocolate had remained on her pretty lips. He'd watched in a kind of agony and ecstasy as she'd licked them clean.

How easy it would have been to lean over and clean those lips for her with a kiss. He remembered how he'd sat there thinking that very thing before plunging his

spoon into the dessert, settling for vanilla and chocolate ice cream instead.

He shifted beneath the water, uncomfortably aware
of his semiaroused state. Much more of this kind of
thinking and he'd be rock hard. He groaned and forced
himself to relax.

He'd have to stop seeing her. Put a halt to these impromptu visits. He'd have to encourage her to widen
her horizons and cultivate some new friends, women
her own age.

And men.

He supposed she'd want to see men.

Date men.

Sleep with men.

Christ.

He sat up in the tub, his good mood taking a sudden
nosedive. He didn't dwell on the reason for his abruptly
irritable humor as he reached for the soap.

He'd just finished scrubbing his body, his hair, and
rinsing himself clean, when the phone rang. He thought
about ignoring it, letting the voice mail pick up, when
he changed his mind.

With dripping fingers, he reached out, hit the button
for the bathroom wall phone. "Hello."

"Hi, it's me. I wanted to check in and see how you're
doing."

Ivy.

He sank deeper into the tub, struck by the rhythm of
her voice.

Had it always been so honeyed? So rich and throaty
like warm buttered rum?

"James? Are you there?"

"Yeah, I'm here. What's up?"

Wrong question, he thought, stifling a moan as his erection returned.

"I know it's late, but I was concerned, because of your fall. How are you doing? Are you terribly bruised?"

He had some doozies, dappled like patches of wild blueberries all over his hips and backside, but he wasn't about to discuss them with her.

"I'm fine. Taking a bath."

"Oh?" Her answer came out on a tone of curious interest.

"I mean, I took a bath. I just got out. Just got dressed for bed."

Shit, that didn't sound any better than the other.

"I thought the heat, you know," he said, "soaking in hot water would help."

This conversation just gets worse and worse. I really need to quit talking.

She paused before continuing. "It should help. I hope you're not too stiff in the morning."

I'm pretty stiff right now.

He scrubbed a hand over his face and closed his eyes, wondering how he'd gotten himself into this situation. "So, umm, thanks for checking on me, Ivy," he said, hoping to put a quick end to their conversation. "I had a nice time today."

"Did you? Oh, I'm so glad. I wasn't sure."

"Yeah, it was fun. Well, it's getting late—"

"I know, but I wanted to ask—"

"Ask me what?"

"About Wednesday. What are you doing Wednesday evening? There's an art show, a traveling retrospective of Miró. I know you like his work and so do I, and I thought . . . well, I thought we could go together."

"Oh, well, I don't know. . . . Wednesday, middle of the week. It's not such a good day."

"Friday, then? The show's here until the end of the month. It would be a shame to miss it."

He hesitated, knowing he should refuse. That's all he needed to do, spend more time with Ivy. Hadn't he just gotten through telling himself not half an hour ago that he was going to put some distance between them?

But she had such a hopeful note in her voice. She'd be hurt if he brushed her off, and he couldn't very well cut her out of his life entirely. They'd known each other forever. She wouldn't understand if he pulled away. This little problem of his—he glanced between his legs and amended—this big problem of his, well, it would go away soon enough.

He thought of Parker, realizing he couldn't use her as an excuse. She was visiting her mother in San Francisco. She'd left yesterday for a two-week holiday. Besides, it wasn't as if going to an art show with Ivy was a date. It wasn't, any more than today had been a date. Just two friends getting together to have a couple of laughs.

Still, he should tell Ivy no.

"All right," he said. "Friday sounds good. What time?"

"Six, then we'll grab some dinner after. Can't wait.

Well, I'll let you go. Get a good night's sleep and hope you don't have to count any sheep."

It was an old thing they used to say to each other when she was a child.

Well, she wasn't a child any longer. He was finally beginning to realize that fact.

"Good night, Ivy. See you Friday."

He disconnected, wondering what he'd just done.

Gingerly, he stepped out of the bath, dried himself, and put on a robe. Then he went in search of a nightcap. He didn't usually drink before bed, but tonight he decided he'd make an exception.

CHAPTER FIVE

He didn't quite know how it happened, but Friday at the art exhibit turned into Saturday at the movies and Sunday at a street fair in Little Italy.

He'd told Ivy that Monday was out—he had work to finish.

Monday evening arrived. Tired and hungry after a long day that had included a protracted videoconference with a company in Japan, he'd eyed the mountain of reports he still needed to review and heaved a resigned sigh.

Tory had gone home a few minutes earlier and he was alone in the office. The whir of a vacuum cleaner hummed in the distance. He was about to call down to a nearby deli and order dinner—a sandwich and coffee—to be sent up, when Ivy appeared.

She'd strolled in with a smile on her face, a large Balducci's shopping bag swinging on her arm. Before he'd known it, she was spreading a red-and-white-checked cloth over the thick Aubusson rug on his floor and arranging a delectable array of foodstuffs upon it.

He was a sucker for Balducci's and she knew it. Especially their Greek salad with imported feta and kalamata olives and their freshly sliced Prosciutto, which she'd brought, along with several other mouthwatering items. Refusing her became impossible once she pulled out dessert, a tender Italian cream cake soaked in rum and loaded with nuts.

He'd tossed down his pen and surrendered to temptation, settling onto the floor of his office for the first picnic he'd ever had there.

Remembering it now, he looked across at the spot and smiled.

Every time he told himself he needed to put some space between him and Ivy, make their most recent outing their last, she would suggest something new, and he'd find himself agreeing to go along.

Nearly two weeks had passed since their skating expedition. Two interesting, exciting, enjoyable weeks, the ramifications of which he refused to dwell upon.

She was his friend.

Just his friend.

If they happened to enjoy each other's company, well, there was no harm in that. If he happened to like the way she looked and smelled and moved and laughed, it just proved he was a healthy male. Only a blind, gay eunuch would fail to find Ivy attractive, and even then it was questionable.

But her appeal came from more than her good looks,

he realized. There was something special about her. Her sweet, giving nature. Her unique, buoyant personality. A vibrancy so strong she illuminated a room the moment she entered it, as though she were the sun, spreading light and warmth wherever she walked.

He felt good when he was around her. Young, in a way he hadn't felt in a very long time.

Barely aware, he began to whistle a tune under his breath while he perused the latest stock figures on his computer. After only a couple of minutes, his thoughts drifted back to Ivy.

They were going to a Yankees game tonight, but weren't sitting in his box, which he kept primarily for business reasons.

Ivy wanted to sit down close to the field, saying it was the only way to truly experience the game. James wasn't so sure he agreed, given the comfortable, air-conditioned seats in his box and the private chef who would be there to cook an array of fine dining options. But Ivy was so enthusiastic about being in the "heart of the action" that he couldn't bring himself to disappoint her. He'd never sat in the regular seats before. Who knew? Maybe it would be fun.

He smiled at the thought, then returned to work.

Not long after, his intercom buzzed. "Mr. Jordan, Ms. Manning is on line two."

Parker.

A little twinge of guilt went through him, her unexpected call making him realize that he'd barely thought of her in days.

He picked up the receiver. "Parker, hi. How are you doing? You aren't back in town yet, are you?"

She wasn't due to return from her vacation for another three days.

"No, still here at Mother's," she said. "I'm looking at the Golden Gate Bridge even as we speak."

"So how is San Francisco this time of year?"

"Muggy and full of tediously impossible hills, but the sailing's wonderful. We took the yacht out yesterday, sunbathed and sipped cold daiquiris on the foredeck. Purely divine. I wish you could have been with us, but I know you have to work. Busy making millions, hmm?"

"Something like that. So what's up? Why'd you decide to call?"

She paused. He could almost see her perfectly painted lips form into a well-studied pout. "Do I need a reason to call? I miss you. Have you missed me?"

Had he missed her? Actually, he'd been spending so much time with Ivy, he'd hardly had the chance.

"Of course," he lied, more guilt rising. "Of course I've missed you."

"As well you should. When I get back on Saturday, I won't waste a minute before I rush over to see you. I want you all to myself, preferably naked," she added on a sexy purr.

"Hmm, there's a thought."

He frowned. He was supposed to see Ivy Saturday night.

"Doesn't your plane get in late?" he said. "You'll

probably be worn-out from the trip and the time change, won't you?"

"Not so much that I can't stop by." She paused. "Why? Is there a problem?"

"No, no problem. It's just I wasn't expecting you Saturday night. I made other arrangements."

"What kind of arrangements?" Her tone turned chilly.

"Just an evening out with an old friend," he hedged.

At least he wasn't lying this time. Ivy *was* an old friend, and he couldn't—wouldn't—disappoint her by canceling. She'd gone to a lot of trouble to get concert tickets—Justin Timberlake at Madison Square Garden. She loved Justin Timberlake. He had to admit he liked the guy's music too.

"And just what gender is this *friend*?" Parker asked in arched suspicion. "I wasn't going to mention this— I'd decided it was unworthy of either one of us—but now I'm beginning to think differently. Taffy Hughes gave me a call a couple days ago."

"Did she? How is dear old Taff?" he asked with a sarcastic edge.

Taffeta Stevenson Hughes was a catty socialite who thrived on spreading rumor and innuendo when she wasn't otherwise occupied battling the signs of aging with her bimonthly visits to the plastic surgeon and hair colorist.

"Full of disturbing news—that's how she is," Parker grated. "She says she saw you. *With a blonde.* She says Daphne Price saw you too, coming out of Zabar's last Saturday afternoon. *Laughing*," she added, as if laughter were a crime. "Who is she, James? Who's this girl you're seeing behind my back?"

"Calm down, Parker. It's not what you think."

"Really? Then what the hell is it?"

He rubbed the bridge of his nose, held back a weary sigh. Why couldn't people just mind their own damned business and stay out of his?

"Look, she's a friend—," he began.

"The one you made *arrangements* with on Saturday night, I suppose?"

"Yes, and you have nothing to worry about. There's nothing between us, nothing romantic, that is. She's an old family friend. I've known her forever."

"Then why have I never heard of this *old family friend*?"

"Because she's been in college. Jesus, Parker, she's twenty years old. Do you really think I'd be involved with a twenty-year-old girl?"

When she said nothing, he knew he had her attention.

"I've known Ivy since she was in diapers. I used to cart her around on my shoulders for piggyback rides and take her to the zoo and the amusement park on summer vacations. I've been . . ."

Yes, what had he been doing exactly? And why did he suddenly feel like a philandering dog when his and Ivy's relationship was strictly platonic?

He swallowed, abruptly uncomfortable. "I've been showing her around town. She's new to the city and she's still finding her way. There's nothing between us, Parker. Nothing at all."

His mood abruptly deflated, he picked up a pen and started doodling on the corner of a notepad.

"Well," she said slowly, "I didn't realize. I'm sorry if I misjudged, but you should have told me you'd be spending time with this . . . child."

"I didn't realize I would be until after you'd left. I apologize for the misunderstanding." He flung his pen aside and ripped the piece of paper he'd been drawing on off the pad. Squeezing it into a ball inside his fist, he tossed the wad toward the waste can.

He missed.

It pinged off the wall and rolled to a stop a couple of feet away.

"Shall I come by Sunday, then? Take you to brunch at the Plaza?" he asked.

Brunch at the Plaza was a favorite of Parker's.

Her voice warmed considerably at the invitation. "That would be lovely. I'll be ready by ten. Maybe afterward we could take in a matinee. I understand the latest revival of Cats is excellent."

By sheer force of will, he kept from groaning. Seeing Cats once in a lifetime was enough for him. If he lived to be 105, he'd never understand the appeal. Cats floating to heaven on a big tire while they sang—how ridiculous.

"I'll see if I can get us seats," he said.

"Wonderful. I'm so glad I called. I wouldn't have wanted this . . . trouble to come between us."

"No."

"Oh, and don't forget, we've got dinner and drinks at the Belfords' on Friday. Fourth of July, you know."

"Right." He crumpled another slip of paper, tossed it the way of the first.

The Belfords were society people. Conservative, tasteful, refined. The sort his parents liked. The sort with whom he'd rubbed elbows for as long as he could remember.

Upright, uptight, and boring.

"I'll be by to pick you up," he said.

"All right. Be good, dear. Kisses."

He wished her a safe trip, then hung up the phone.

He buried himself in work for the rest of the afternoon, and for once, he refused to think of Ivy.

James was brooding and Ivy didn't know why.

She dug her hand into her popcorn box and ate a few kernels. Although he denied it, he'd been quiet and preoccupied ever since they'd left for the stadium.

The crack of ball against bat sounded, the Yankees' batter racing for first. He made it easily, giving them two runners on base. It was only the second inning, early yet, so she wasn't worried by the fact that they were down by two.

She and James had lucked into some pretty decent seats, a pair not far from the dugout. She knew James would have preferred to watch the game from the comfort of his club-level luxury suite, but she held firm in her conviction that they'd have a much better time right where they were. Their present location might lack some of the nicer amenities, such as personal concierge service and a private restroom, but it made up for it in spades with the raw natural energy

and excitement of being in the crowd, close to the players and the action.

She nudged the popcorn box toward James. He
grunted, took a handful, then chewed without a word.

There was a lull in the action, so she knew his lack of
response wasn't because his attention was riveted to
the game. In fact, he barely seemed to have been watching it at all.

She sighed. "James, you're moody. What's wrong?
And don't tell me nothing."

He gave her a sharp look, then turned his eyes back
to the field. For a moment she thought he was going to
refuse to answer.

"I have a lot on my mind, that's all," he said. "Don't
worry about it."

"Maybe I could help. Why don't you try me?"

He shot her another look, an odd glint in his brilliant
blue eyes. "I don't think so," he said, his words ringing
with sarcasm.

She hid her hurt at his rebuff by watching the game,
barely aware of the action even when the Yankees scored
another run.

A cheer went up from the crowd.

She ate a few more pieces of popcorn, the kernels
sticking in her throat. She washed them down with a
long pull from her bottle of spring water as the second
inning moved on to the third.

"If you didn't want to come to the game," she murmured, "you should have said so."

He turned his head. "Of course I wanted to come to
the game. I'm here, aren't I?"

"Yes, and apparently having a miserable time. Is it because I insisted we sit here in the stands? We can go up to your box if you hate this so much."

"It's not the seating, although my legs might disagree." His knees were jammed up against the seat in front of him. "It has nothing to do with the game."

She watched the players prepare for the next pitch. "Then what? Have I done something wrong? Tell me and maybe I can fix it."

He expelled a breath and angled his body toward her. "You haven't done anything wrong, okay? It's me. Just me."

"Well, all right. But I don't like to see you unhappy." On impulse, she slipped her hand into his, threading her fingers between his much larger ones. She gave a gentle squeeze, relishing the warmth, the strength of his hand entwined with her own. "I'm always here for you, you know. I always will be, 'cause we're friends, right?"

His expression softened, some of the hard lines easing from his face. "Yeah, that's right, pumpkin. We're friends." He gave her a too-bright smile, then extracted his hand from hers as if her touch made him uncomfortable.

Her heart sank.

"Hey, you want a hot dog?" he asked in a poorly disguised attempt to change the subject. He dug into his pocket for his wallet as the hot dog vendor slowly made his way up the rows, the tangy scent of steamed, preservative-laden meat drifting in the air.

"No," she said, "and neither do you. You never

know what's in those things—hair and rat poop. Plus, I've read they give you butt cancer."

He gave her a wry look. "Well, thanks for officially ruining hot dogs for the rest of my life. I'll never be able to visit the steam cart up the street from my office again."

"You don't visit the steam cart now."

He shot her a sideways glance, his lips twitching.

Her lips twitched back.

"Here." She leaned down and dug into the large carryall she'd set at her feet. "I brought us some nice, healthy trail mix."

He made a face.

"There're dried apricots and pineapple in it, just the way you like." She waggled a clear plastic bag full of mix at him.

Resigned, he tucked his wallet away. "Yeah, okay, hand it over."

She passed him a bag and got one for herself.

"Good?" she inquired a minute later.

"Hmm, good," he agreed, chewing a roasted almond and a plump apricot.

On the field, the Yankees' coach sent in a fresh pitcher to stave off what was quickly turning into a new round of Orioles' hits. She cheered with everyone else on the Yankees' side when the next batter got sent back to the bench empty-handed after three strikes.

"They're performing Shakespeare in the Park Sunday afternoon," she said. *"Twelfth Night.* It's such a great play. What do you say we take a big lawn blanket and go?"

He kept his eyes on the game. "Sounds wonderful, but I can't."

"Why not? Don't tell me you have to be in the office. Even you don't work on Sunday, at least not much."

"No, it isn't work." He cleared his throat. "Actually, I have a date."

"Oh." The words hit her like a slap in the face, her spirits plummeting to her sneakers. "I didn't realize. Who is she?" she murmured, even though she already knew the answer.

"Just someone I've been seeing for a while. She's been out of town for the last couple weeks. She's flying back Saturday and we're getting together Sunday, which means I'll have to pass on the play."

The hurt inside her expanded at his casual explanation. She'd been so sure her plan was working, optimist that she was. She'd thought she was making progress, that by spending so much time with him, she was gradually getting him to see her in a different light. But apparently, he'd just been passing time with his little friend—his little *sister*, she thought derisively—until his girlfriend returned from her vacation.

Still, it wasn't as if she hadn't known she had competition, known her quest would be far from easy. Unless she wanted to withdraw from the field, she'd simply have to swallow her anguish and find other ways to make him want her, to make him love her.

She wondered what he'd do if she stood up right now and snuggled into his lap. Wondered how he'd react if she locked her arms around his neck and kissed him senseless.

Would he kiss her back or push her away? Her pulse thumped at the daring notion.

But she couldn't take the risk, could she?

No, not yet.

Not here.

The time, she feared, still wasn't right.

"Well, that's fine," she lied in a breezy tone. "It'll give me time to do some extra painting." She worried a fingernail over a seam in her jeans. "What about the Fourth of July? You all booked up then too?"

A peculiar, guilty look swept over his features, his eyebrows drawing together. "Aren't you going home for your mother's annual get-together?"

She shook her head. "Not this year. I decided to stay and see what the city has to offer. I assume from your expression you're already busy that night," she finished, anger and frustration adding a crisp tartness to her words.

"Parker and I are promised for a dinner party. Ivy, I'm sorry. I didn't know—"

She waved a hand. "Doesn't matter. Actually, it frees me up to go to another party."

His frown deepened. "What party?"

"Didn't I tell you? Josh, Neil, and Fred are throwing a big Fourth of July bash at their apartment. They've been after me for weeks to come, but I wanted to keep my options open. Seems I can say yes now."

"Those being the guys you were once planning to move in with?"

She crossed her arms. "As a matter of fact, they are. I see my mother's kept you well informed."

"Well informed enough to know they live in a sketchy part of town."

"There haven't been any problems at the apartment. One of their neighbors is a cop, and he's invited to the party too. In fact, I think most of the building's invited. I'll be fine."

"It sounds like trouble waiting to happen. I think you should stay home."

"Oh, so I'm supposed to sit home, am I? While you run off and enjoy yourself at some party with"— she broke off, circling a pair of fingers in the air— "whatshername? Palmer?"

"Parker."

"Right." She shook her head. "I don't think so. I'm a big girl now, grown up enough to go to parties without getting permission. Three years at college taught me all I need to know about that particular scene. I don't think Josh and Neil will be throwing any surprises my way."

He sat silent and simmering, a hint of color rising beneath his tan.

They didn't say a word to each other for the rest of the game or later during the drive home.

He finally broke his silence when they reached her apartment door. "What time should I come by to pick you up tomorrow night?"

Six thirty, she thought. *Six thirty, so we'll have time for a quick dinner before the concert.*

But instead of those simple, nonconfrontational words, some devil prompted her to say something else. "You still want to go to the concert, then? I thought maybe you'd decided to pick Parson up at the airport instead and spend the evening entertaining her."

His jaw tightened, his blue eyes turning hard. "I wasn't, but it can always be arranged."

She knew she should back down, knew she should do whatever it took to end their fight, to smooth over the angry words and nasty silences. But her feelings were hurt, and damned if she was going to let him treat her like some spoiled child who didn't enjoy sharing her toys.

She squared her shoulders and looked him in the eye. "If that's what you'd rather, it won't put me out. Fred can use your ticket. He's been salivating over the concert ever since he heard I was going. He's a nice guy. You'd like Fred."

For a moment James looked ready to explode. Then it passed, a chill sweeping into his eyes. "I sincerely doubt that, but it doesn't matter. If you don't want to go to the concert with me, that's fine. Good night, Ivy."

He turned and strode down the hall toward the elevator.

When he was gone, she closed the door and leaned back against it, tears already sliding down her cheeks.

God above, what have I done?

She'd let hurt and resentment drive him away. She'd let pride get in the way where it never had before. Now she was the one who was sorry.

Tomorrow night he'd be with Parker Manning instead of her. Tomorrow night he'd be in another woman's arms, and she would have no one to blame but herself.

CHAPTER SIX

Ivy set down her paintbrush and stepped back from the canvas to inspect her work.

It looked good, she decided. Not perfect, but good.

Best of all, it was nearly finished. Another painting to add to her steadily growing stack of completed canvases.

Over the past week she'd thrown herself into her art with a vengeance, fueled in great measure by the need to forget her misery over her fight with James. In all the years she'd known him, they'd never fought, not once. But she supposed there had to be a first time for everything.

She sighed and began to clean up, screwing tops back onto paint tubes, washing her brushes, covering her mixing palette with a damp cloth to keep the unused blobs of paints from turning hard. A glance at her Kit-Cat wall clock, with his cute back-and-forth eyes and swinging tail, showed it was nearly five in the afternoon. Time to grab a quick shower and slip into her party clothes.

Today was the Fourth of July, and no matter how low she felt, she wasn't missing Neil and Josh's party. Certainly not after making such a point of telling James that's where she'd be.

She had her doubts about the evening, but perhaps while she was there she'd manage to have a bit of fun—eating and drinking, chatting and watching the fireworks explode into colorful starbursts in the night sky. Perhaps she would also manage to forget James for a little while. Forget how horribly she'd botched their last outing and how desperately she'd missed him since.

As the week had passed, she'd thought about calling him a dozen times a day, but something always held her back. At first she'd hoped he would change his mind about the concert and come knocking on her door. But as the hours went by and it became increasingly clear he wasn't going to show up, she'd phoned Fred to ask if he'd like the tickets.

Without James, she no longer wanted to go to the concert.

But Fred wasn't home, so Neil and Josh agreed to take the tickets off her hands, offering massive thanks and pledges of eternal gratitude for the unexpected bounty.

After that, the days had slipped by with the speed of a sloth climbing a tree. One day became two. Two melted into three, and so forth until she realized the whole week was nearly over.

This morning she'd decided she would wait until the weekend to contact James. If he didn't drop over or call by Sunday, she'd pop up to his penthouse and put an end to their rift.

She may have lost the battle, she reminded herself, but she was a long way from losing the war.

Forty-five minutes later, attired in a powder blue sundress bedecked with cheery yellow daisies—a dress that made her look a lot perkier than she felt—Ivy set off for Bushwick.

The party was in full swing by the time she arrived. She took off her sunglasses and tucked them into her purse as she squeezed down the already-crowded corridor toward her friends' apartment.

Inside, she paused for a moment to get her bearings, searched for a familiar face. Loud salsa music throbbed like a heartbeat, the floorboards vibrating beneath her sandals. The air smelled of warm bodies, nachos, and Dos Equis.

This year's party theme—A Fourth of July Fiesta.

Neil found her before she found him, pulling her up into a rib-crushing embrace that made her giggle. "Cupcake, you came," he declared, giving her a quick, smacking kiss on the lips. "I was starting to wonder if you'd had a last-minute change of plans."

She shook her head. "Got caught on the train. It was a madhouse."

"Well, now that you're here, you can relax. Grab a beer out of the cooler and settle in. Josh is outside grilling fajitas. Your choice of chicken, beef, or Tex-Mex vegetarian." He grinned and gestured toward the open

window that led to a box-sized fire escape they'd eu-
phemistically dubbed "the patio."

"Sides and dessert are across the hall in Lu's place,"
he continued, referring to their neighbor, Lulu Lancaster.

A leggy bombshell with artfully dyed blond hair,
Lulu was a dancer like Fred, though not exactly like
Fred since she did chorus work instead of ballet. Ivy
had met her only a couple of times in passing, but she
seemed nice, with her Queens accent and no-nonsense
attitude.

Neil picked up a trio of empties off a nearby coffee
table. "Trying to keep things at a dull roar," he explained. "Go mingle. Go enjoy. I'll catch up with you as
soon as I can."

She gave him a wide smile, watched him thread his
way through several boisterous groups of partygoers
before he disappeared into the apartment's tiny kitchen.

She looked around for another friendly face; her
throat tightened as she realized she didn't know a soul.
She'd worked hard over the years to overcome her natural shyness. Still, at moments like this, it crept back
over her, urging her to find the closest convenient corner and disappear into it.

Then she remembered Josh.

Of course. She'd go perch in the window, watch him
cook, and hang out with him for a while.

She was about to head that way when a hand tapped
her shoulder. She turned and looked into a pair of soulful brown eyes. "Fred."

"I thought it was you. There're only so many tall,

gorgeous blondes, even in the Big Apple. Especially in this apartment." He gave her a quick hug. "And remember, it's Frederick these days. Frederick Picarovsky. I have a professional image to maintain, you know."

She lifted an amused eyebrow. She didn't know him all that well but had heard enough stories to know he'd been a struggling ballet dancer and part-time waiter up until three months ago. Then he'd gotten an audition with one of the premier ballet companies in the city, and to his astonished elation, received an invitation to join.

That's when he'd started reinventing himself.

Everybody knew the greats were from Russia or France, he argued.

Baryshnikov.

Nijinsky.

Now, those were names with staying power, with resilience.

What hope did plain Fred Pike from even plainer Newark, Ohio, have to go down in the annals of dance history?

And so, Frederick Picarovsky was born. A mysterious rising star whose heritage could be traced all the way back to Peter the Great, or so said the rumors he'd put out.

She smothered a smile. "Oops, I forgot. Frederick's just such a mouthful."

"Mouthful or not, it's starting to get me noticed. *World Ballet* did an article last week. I got two paragraphs."

"That's wonderful, Fred—erick, I mean."

"Thanks. The company's tough, but I love it." He

glanced down at Ivy's empty hands. "So why aren't you eating, drinking? It's a party, you know. Even I'm breaking my diet for the occasion. Here, let me go get you a beer."

Before she could say a word, he was halfway across the room. It didn't take him long to return, two ice-cold bottles in hand.

He gave one to her, then tapped his bottle to hers in salute. He took a long drink. "Ahh. Now we need some food. What d'you say we load up one big plate and slip off to a quiet spot where we can share?"

He grinned, the movement softening the long lines of his face. He had a devilish gleam in his dark eyes and a sensuality in his long, lean dancer's body. If she hadn't already given her heart to James, there was every chance she might have found Fred irresistibly attractive.

She smiled back. "I think it would be better if we each got our own plate and found a nice, noisy spot in the center of the action."

He flattened a hand on his chest. "Ouch. You've stabbed me straight through."

"You'll recover as soon as the next pretty girl goes by. Besides, I'm already seeing someone."

At least, she would be as soon as she could smooth things over with him.

"Oh, slashed again," he said, pantomiming the act. "So where is the lucky bastard? Is he here?"

"No. He couldn't make it." Her spirits deflated a bit at the thought.

Fred eyed her a little too shrewdly. "Doesn't sound

like he appreciates you properly. If you change your mind about him, remember me. Ballet dancers have incredible stamina and amazing flexibility. I'd love to show you sometime."

She gasped at his outrageous statement, then laughed, wondering if he might really have a trace of Russian blue in his blood, after all. He was certainly a charming enough rogue, naughty and unpredictable—a little like her brother-in-law, Zack.

Before she could respond, Neil showed up. "Hey, enough hitting on Ivy. If her cheeks get any redder, we'll be able to use her as a firework. Go on, now. Shoo."

Fred grinned again, then winked at her. "Later, sugar."

She giggled, realizing her cheeks really were hot enough to ignite.

Neil took hold of her elbow, steered her toward the open window and the fire escape beyond. "What d'you think about fajitas?" he asked conversationally. "Personally, I always prefer the beef."

"Umm, try this. It's delicious." Parker held out an hors d'oeuvre skewered on a toothpick.

After a quick visual check, James dutifully opened his mouth to receive the delicacy.

"Good?" she asked.

He chewed. Lobster with a hint of chervil, if he wasn't mistaken. He swallowed before replying. "Very good."

She beamed and selected another hors d'oeuvre for herself.

Polite chitchat drifted on the air. Soft murmurs that rose and fell, punctuated by an occasional laugh or the clink and tap of silver on china. Background music—airy harmonies by Mozart and Bach—floated past.

Original works of art graced the walls, and various modern sculptures were arranged at precise angles around the room. Striking as the Belfords' collection was, James suspected the items had been purchased with more of an eye toward investment potential than a genuine love of the works themselves.

He treated himself to another lobster canapé as he noticed a particularly hideous clump of twisted black metal squatting in a nearby corner. The artwork—and he used that term loosely—reminded him of an exploded toilet that had lost its lid. He leaned his head to one side to view it from another direction.

Trendy? Perhaps.

Appealing? Definitely not.

He smothered a smile. If Ivy were here, they'd both be laughing.

His humor fell away.

The silence from Ivy's direction had been deafening.

He'd expected her to call or come up to his penthouse long before now.

She hadn't.

He'd expected her to say she missed him, wanted to forget their foolish spat and be friends again.

She hadn't.

Then again, neither had he.

He'd thought about calling her, but he'd kept putting it off. After all, she was the one who'd gotten angry and backed out; she should be the one to mend fences.

But she hadn't, and before he knew it, the week had passed.

Maybe the distance between them was for the best, though; they each had their own life to live.

Still, he wondered what she was doing right now, and more, who she was doing it with. Had she really gone to the concert with that guy like she'd threatened?

His fists tightened at his sides.

"I see you're admiring the Krapfsmear. New artist. Up-and-comer, don't you agree?"

Krapfsmear? James turned to his host, Paul Belford, and struggled for something neutral to say.

Parker stepped into the breach. "It's very bold. The texture speaks on such a powerfully visceral level. And the color . . . How to describe it? So apocalyptic yet so penetrating. Once you've witnessed a piece like this, you'll never be untouched again."

James blinked. Was she kidding? From her expression, he feared she wasn't.

"My thoughts precisely." Belford nodded his balding head and took a sip of vodka from his crystal highball glass. "Portia St. George over at Gallery DuPres turned me on to the artist. Said only a special buyer could appreciate the subtle charm of the work. The lush anger contained in such an elegant, compact form."

"Oh, she's right," Parker agreed. "It's incredible."

Belford looked James in the eye. "J.J.? We haven't heard from you. What do you think?"

For one, that he detested being called J.J. That was his father's name for him, a diminutive he'd always despised. But telling Belford that, or telling him what an arrogant, small-minded fool he was, wasn't worth the breath.

James ate another canapé at his leisure before he replied. "Incredible. It really is the only word to describe it."

Satisfied by the answer, Parker and Belford moved on to a discussion of the real estate market.

James wandered a few feet away, poured himself a glass of cold dry white Riesling. At least his host had good taste in wine, he thought, the aged oak flavor of the alcohol lingering on his tongue.

What were they serving at Ivy's party?

She'd better not be drinking. She wasn't even legal yet.

Remembering her age and the unwelcome physical reaction he'd been having to her lately, he refilled his glass.

The party was proceeding at full tilt, the music a loud syncopated backbeat as couples swayed together in the center of the room

"Why don't you let me trade in that soda for a margarita? One won't hurt you." Fred reached for Ivy's empty glass.

She shook her head and glanced over at him from her place on Neil's lumpy plaid sofa. "I already had a beer tonight, remember? One's my limit."

And obviously not his. Fred, she suspected, had imbibed a bit too much.

"One beer?" he complained. "Come on. Live dangerously. It's a party."

"Really, I can't." She checked the clock on the nearby DVR. "Besides, it's nearly midnight. Time for me to be heading home."

"You can't leave yet; it's early." He slid closer and stretched an arm out behind her along the top of the sofa. "We've hardly had a chance to get to know each other, not after Neil and then Lulu dragged you away."

"She took pity and introduced me around. Lulu's a dear. She really made me feel welcome."

He gestured to himself with his thumb. "And I haven't?"

"Sure, but not the same way."

He smiled. "Time for a dance!"

She gasped out a laugh as he yanked her to her feet and pulled her into the crowd.

Hey, can't talk right now. Leave me your digits. You know the drill.

James cut off the message with an impatient jab of his finger. One in the morning and Ivy wasn't answering her cell.

Where in the hell is she?

He slipped his ultraslim cell phone into his suit pocket.

"Who was that, darling?" Parker asked, returning from her visit to the guest bath.

His head whipped around. "What?"

"On the phone. Who were you talking to?"

"No one. Just checking my voice mail."

Parker *tsk*ed. "Working even on a holiday? You should slow down."

He gave a noncommittal grunt. "Are you about ready to leave?"

"Hmm. Let me thank our hostess; then we'll go."

He waited until she'd crossed to the opposite side of the room and had fallen into conversation with Arlene Belford before he tried Ivy's number again.

And got her voice mail again.

With a muffled curse, he hung up.

Where is she?

Was she home and just had her cell on mute? Or had she gone to that party?—the one he'd told her not to attend. The neighborhood where her friends lived might be showing signs of improvement, but it could still be a dangerous place, especially at night.

He was about to call her one more time when Parker exchanged air kisses with Arlene and headed his way.

Inside the car minutes later, he sensed Parker watching him.

"Is anything the matter?" she asked in a quiet voice.

He slowed for a red light. "No. Everything's fine."

"You're so quiet. I just wondered."

"It's late, that's all."

"Hmm, but not that late." She reached out and laid a palm on his thigh.

He covered her hand to prevent it from straying, stroked his thumb over the top.

The light changed to green.

He returned her hand to her lap, stepped on the accelerator. "Would you be terribly hurt if I didn't come in tonight?"

She crossed her arms. "I thought we were celebrating the holiday. It's been weeks since we made love."

"You were away," he hedged. "I've been busy and our schedules just haven't meshed. And tonight . . ."

She shifted in her seat and glared at him. "Yes? What about tonight?"

"I'm . . . well, actually, I'm not feeling well."

"Not feeling—oh, you poor baby." She settled her palm across his forehead, then his cheeks, checking for fever. "I knew something was wrong. Why didn't you tell me?"

"I didn't want to spoil your evening."

"Don't be silly. You should have said something. If you're sick, you need to be in bed."

He couldn't help feeling guilty. "You're right. As soon as I drop you off, I'll go straight home and climb under the sheets."

"Why don't we save time and go directly to your place? That way I can mother you a bit."

He shook his head. "You know I hate being fussed over."

At least that wasn't a lie, he thought. Since childhood, he'd detested people hovering over him when he wasn't feeling well.

"You won't be able to do anything but watch me sleep," he said. "I'll be fine on my own."

She hesitated. "Well, if you're sure?"

"Positive. It's probably just a touch of food poisoning. Queasy stomach. You can't be too careful these days, especially with shellfish."

"You're right about that."

He slowed the car and doubled-parked in front of her brownstone.

She sat without opening the car door. "You'll call if you feel worse? Food poisoning can be very serious, you know."

"I'll phone you in the morning."

She leaned over and brushed her lips against his. "Feel better."

He waited to make certain she made it safely inside her building, then pulled away from the curb.

Since when, he asked himself, had he started lying to women?

Lately, he seemed to be making a habit of it. If there was one thing he prided himself upon, it was his honesty. Yet tonight he'd blatantly deceived Parker, a woman who trusted him.

He didn't like the feeling.

But he couldn't tell her the truth. If he'd mentioned Ivy's name, she would have worked herself into a snit and drawn all sorts of erroneous conclusions.

Dialing Ivy's number again, he listened as the familiar message played one more time.

He scowled. This just wasn't like her.

With a curse, he disconnected and called the security desk at his building.

"Did Miss Grayson go out tonight?" he asked the guard once he'd identified himself.

"Just a moment, Mr. Jordon. Let me check the logs. Yes. Looks like she left around six."

"And has she returned yet?"

"No, sir. Not yet. Is there a problem?"

"No, no problem." At least not one the guard could resolve.

Disconnecting, he tossed his phone onto the empty passenger seat. At least he'd had the good sense to ask exactly where her friends lived.

Hooking a left onto Lexington, he headed south.

"Look, this has been fun, but I've really, really got to get going," Ivy told Fred a couple of dances later. She glanced around, wondering how she'd ended up on the wrong side of a large potted palm in a secluded corner of the living room with him.

Fred planted a forearm against the wall next to her head. "Not yet, babe. There's still a lot of party left to go."

If he hadn't been drunk before, he was now. In between dances, he'd procured more than one round of drinks. While she'd taken only occasional sips of hers, he'd emptied each of his own.

"It's late," she said. "I think people are starting to take off. Anyway, don't you have dance class in the morning?"

He nodded. "I always have dance class. A *danseur* has to keep his muscles strong and limber. Of course, there're other ways to keep in shape." His voice deepened, eyelids drooping, as he lowered his head toward her.

She held him off with a hand. "Sleeping, for one. Can't be at your best without enough sleep. If I have any hope of being more than a zombie tomorrow, I need to get some rest."

"Sleep here."

She shook her head. "I'll sleep better in my own bed."

"Sure, we can use your bed," he said with a drunk's logic. "I'll take you home."

"*Neil's* taking me home."

Fred glanced over his shoulder. "Neil looks busy."

"Josh, then."

"Josh looks busy too."

She glanced past Fred's broad shoulder and spotted the two men wrapped in each other's arms, slow dancing. "Fine. I'll take the train."

Fred scowled. "You can't go out this time of night, not alone. You need an escort. Someone strong to protect you, like me."

"You," she said emphatically, "aren't in any condition to go anywhere except to bed."

She tried to spin him around and point him in the right direction, intending to give him a good shove. But he was immovable, a mass of solid muscle.

Misinterpreting her touch, Fred wrapped his arms around her. "Yeah, my bed. Let's go, babe."

He leaned in for a kiss.

She turned her head so that his lips landed on her neck. "No, Fred. Wait." Perhaps a bit of trickery was called for, she thought. "Why don't you go on ahead to your room? I'll follow in a minute. I need to make a detour first. Bathroom break."

He smiled. "Oh, okay. But you won't be long, will you?"

"Barely an instant."

"Promise?"

"Definitely. Now, let me go."

"Yes," said a hard, male voice. "Let her go."

She and Fred both turned their heads.

"James!" she said on a squeak.

Meeting his eyes, she saw a look burning within them that she'd never seen before. A mixture of surprise, fury, and worst of all, contempt.

He inclined his head. "Ivy."

She'd always loved the sound of her name on his lips. Hearing it now sent a chill down her spine. "What are you doing here?"

"You weren't answering your cell. It's late, so I came to find you. I was worried." He swept a condemning glance over her and the man in whose arms she still stood. "Perhaps I shouldn't have been."

"He's drunk."

"I can see that."

She swallowed, feeling unaccountably guilty. With clenched fists, she gave Fred a hard push.

Fred was distracted enough to release her. "You know this guy?"

"Yes, I know him."

Fred's cocky attitude returned. He draped an arm over her shoulders. "Yeah? Well, whoever you are, F off. I saw her first."

James pinned the other man with a scornful look. "I sincerely doubt that, unless you were around to change her diapers."

"Huh?"

Ivy shrugged out from under Fred's embrace. "Stop it, both of you."

James turned on her. "You want to stay with him?"

"No."

"Let's leave, then, while I still have a car. Assuming it hasn't already been boosted for parts."

"I need my purse."

"Get it."

"Hey, who are you to give her orders?" Fred demanded, swaying with a grace only a drunken ballet dancer could muster. He tossed Ivy a sappy smile. "Don't you listen to him, sweet thing. I told you before—there's hours left of this party."

James visibly ground his teeth. "Ivy. Your purse."

Neil suddenly appeared, Josh in his wake. "Hey, what's going on? We sensed a little tension emanating from this side of the room. Problem?"

James swung slowly around. "No problem. I came for Ivy. And you are?"

"Oh, I'm Neil. Neil Jones. This is Josh Moran." He nodded toward his partner, who waggled a set of fingers. "I guess you've already met Fred Pike."

Fred reprimanded him with a loud shushing noise.

Neil rolled his eyes and cleared his throat. "I mean Frederick Picarovsky. This is our place."

"Ah, the roommates," James drawled as he surveyed the apartment and its party-pleasured occupants. "Thank God she was spared from taking up residence in this dump."

Neil's friendliness disappeared. "Hey, where do you

get off making comments like that? Who the hell are you anyway?"

Josh jumped in. "It's for sure you weren't invited to this party."

James raised a superior brow. "Lucky me."

"If you don't like our place, then get the fuck out," Josh said. "Here. We'll help you leave."

Taller by several inches, James glared down at him, his stance intimidating. "Touch me and you'll wish you hadn't."

The other men bristled at the challenge, fists clenched.

Ivy stood, stunned by the brief, nasty exchange. She'd never seen James act in such a snide, arrogant way. What on earth was the matter with him?

She planted herself in front of James and held out a hand. "Don't! There will be no fighting. All of you, stay where you are."

"Let me knock him around," Fred urged. "I'm trained in judo." With a bloodcurdling scream, he leaped into the air and twisted, nearly kicking over a lamp. He stumbled on the way down, but caught himself at the last minute. Miraculously, he regained his balance, no harm done.

"Ivy, who is this guy?" Neil demanded, jerking a thumb toward James. As Neil glared at him, his expression abruptly changed. "Jesus, he's not your dad, is he?"

"No!" she and James exclaimed in horrified unison.

"Your brother, then?"

James glowered. "I'm not her brother either. I'm her friend. An old family friend."

Josh snorted. "Old's certainly right."

She stood her ground, determined to make sure there was no bloodshed. "James is my friend. Just as the rest of you are my friends. And I want my friends, *all my friends*, to get along. Do you gentlemen think you can do that?"

James crossed his arms over his chest.

The other three looked away; Josh actually shuffled his feet.

Neil was the first to speak. "Yeah, all right. If it'll make you happy, Ivy."

She gave him a grateful smile. "It will. Thank you."

Josh and Fred mumbled like a pair of boys caught brawling in school, forced to shake hands and make up.

James remained silent.

She prompted him. "Don't you have something to say?"

"Yes. It's late. Let's go." He placed a hand on the nape of her neck, curling it there in a possessive grip.

Neil frowned, eyeing her and James for a moment before unexpectedly reaching out to pull Ivy into his arms for a hard hug. "I hope you had a great evening, cupcake." Under the cover of kissing her cheek, he whispered, "You sure you're safe with that one?"

Her eyes widened. "Of course. I couldn't be safer."

He studied her for another long moment, then nodded. Rather than return her to James, he passed her on to Josh, who hugged her with the same defiant exuberance as Neil.

Then it was Fred's turn.

Ivy waylaid him by holding out her hand. "Tomato juice, Tabasco, and a raw egg in the morning. My brother swears the combination works miracles."

He clasped her palm between both of his. "Sounds nauseating."

"It's supposed to. Sleep it off, Fred. I mean *Frederick*."

He grinned crookedly. "Sure you don't want to help me? It's not too late to change your mind."

James grabbed her free hand, tugged her away. "Let's find that damned purse of yours and go." As an afterthought, he nodded. "Gentlemen."

As soon as her purse was in hand, James towed her along behind him, forcing her to trot to keep up.

"James, slow down."

He kept walking.

Shocked, she realized he was furious. James was never furious. In all the years she'd known him, he'd never so much as raised his voice. He could be annoyed, irritated, even grudgingly angry upon occasion, but she'd never seen him like this.

Blazing mad.

CHAPTER SEVEN

On the drive home, Ivy began to suspect Fred wasn't the only one who'd had too much to drink this evening.

It wasn't James's driving that clued her in—his reflexes appeared as sharp as ever. No, it was the glitter in his eyes that caught in the reflection of an occasional passing streetlamp.

She remembered a New Year's Eve more than a decade ago when he'd drunk the entire Grayson clan—hollow-legged Scotsmen every one—straight under the table. She'd been young and wasn't supposed to know anything about it, but long after her bedtime that night, she'd snuck out of her room to watch the spirited goings-on from a stealthy vantage point on the stairs.

With plenty of empty bottles to attest, James had pushed away from the table the winner, rock steady on his feet, acting no different than usual. But when he'd come out into the foyer to don his coat to leave, she'd glimpsed a feral, overbright gleam in his eyes.

The same look he wore now.

They completed the trip home in silence. He parked; then they walked, still not speaking, through the dark to the entrance. In the elevator, he twisted his key in the panel and sent the car racing upward. He hadn't punched the button for her floor, she noticed.

Once inside his penthouse, he slammed the door, then slammed his keys onto the entry table, a lovely old French provincial piece worth a small fortune.

She winced as he rounded on her.

"What in the hell was that tonight?" he demanded.

Her fingers cold from nerves, she set her purse on a small Louis Quatorze chair, then drew a breath to compose herself. "What do you mean? Why are you so upset?"

"Why am I upset? It's"—he broke off to check the face of the grandfather clock stationed just outside the study door—"two forty-five in the morning and you want to know why I'm upset?"

Without waiting for her to reply, he marched down the hall into the wide expanse of the living room. Reluctantly, she followed.

"I'm upset because I had to drive all the way to Brooklyn and pull you out of that crack house."

"Crack house!" she repeated, her eyes wide. "That's the most ridiculous thing I've ever heard you say. There weren't any drugs at the party. Neil's very strict about that sort of thing."

"Oh, is he? And what about the booze? He clearly doesn't take issue with that drug of choice."

"I wouldn't be too critical on that score if I were you, not in your present condition."

He froze. "What condition?"

"Your inebriated condition."

"You think I'm drunk?" He laughed. "I don't get drunk on a few glasses of wine."

She held her ground. "Well, you're not sober. I know that much. And as for *having* to drive to Brooklyn to find me, you didn't *have* to do anything."

"What else am I supposed to do when you don't answer your cell and I find out from the guard desk that you've been out all evening and haven't come home? It was either look for you at that damned party or start calling hospitals."

"You called the guard desk about me?" she said, stunned.

"You bet your sweet ass I did."

Anger burned in her chest. "Well, as you can plainly see, my ass is fine. And not that's it's any of your business, but I was about to leave for home when you showed up."

"Yeah, I could see how much progress you were making. Wrapped up like a present in the grip of that ten-armed ape."

"You mean Fred?" It was her turn to laugh. "*Please.* He's harmless."

"You think so?" James sneered. "I doubt you'd have found him so harmless once he had you pinned under him on his bed."

She squirmed for a moment, since that's exactly what Fred had been trying to do. "That wouldn't have happened," she stated. "I had the situation well under control."

"Oh, I saw the kind of control you had, like a kitten caught inside a sack. Maybe you'd have gotten lucky and escaped, maybe not."

She rubbed her arms, chilled in her sleeveless sundress. "Fred would have respected my wishes."

"I saw the way he was *respecting* you."

"He would have let me go or else I'd have gotten away."

He reached out and yanked her close, his arms fastening at her back, strong as steel bands. "Try to get away from *me*," he challenged.

She laughed but without humor. "What do you think you're doing?"

"Testing your theory. I'm a man. Get away from me."

"It's not much of a test, since I know you'd never hurt me."

"You didn't think Fred would hurt you either."

"And he didn't."

"Because I stopped him."

"You had nothing to do with it," she said. "He was ready to follow my lead and toddle off to his bedroom, supposedly to wait for me, when you interrupted. If you hadn't, he'd have been in his room, sound asleep, and the morning sun would have been streaming through his window before he realized I'd never shown up."

"Oh, he'd have been in his room, all right, and you'd have been in there with him." His eyes gleamed an intense blue. "You've always been far too willing to trust people, to believe the best of them whether they deserve it or not. The sort of behavior that's bound to get you into trouble one of these days."

She trembled with a rush of nerves. "That's absurd. Just because I'm nice to people doesn't mean one of them will eventually hurt me. Despite what you think, I'm not naive. I'm more than capable of looking after myself. Now, let me go."

"What are you going to do about it if I don't?" he taunted.

"Cut it out, James. I mean it. This is stupid."

"Would it seem so stupid if I were Fred or a stranger?"

"This game is ridiculous, and I'm not playing along."

"Fine. Admit I'm right and I'll let you go."

She wasn't used to being pissed off with James, but boy, he was really pushing her buttons tonight. She could see the smug confidence on his face, knew he expected her to knuckle under.

Giving in would be the easy way out.

Well, damn the easy way.

Without any warning, she lunged forward, giving him a hard shove and an elbow dig in the ribs. She twisted her hips, hoping the momentum would be enough to break free. For a split second, his grip loosened and she thought she'd done it. But just as quickly, he recovered, cinching up the slack to haul her close again.

She gave a frustrated shout and tried again, feet shifting in an odd sort of dance as both of them struggled to gain the upper hand. She lashed out with one foot, then the other, trying to overbalance him with a clever hook behind his ankles.

But James was entirely too fast, entirely too strong. He countered, planting his legs on either side of her own, trapping her thighs in between. With carefully controlled strength, he forced her arms behind her back and gathered her wrists into his hands.

She could barely squirm and wondered whether this was how a turkey felt, trussed and helpless as it waited to have its feathers plucked for Thanksgiving dinner.

Their faces were close. So close she could see the tiny creases that fanned out at the corners of his eyes. His short eyelashes, so pale they looked nearly white. And the color of his irises darkened to a deep, rich indigo.

Their bodies were fitted together as tightly as a pair of hibernating minks, every millimeter touching.

Torso, belly, thighs.

Her nipples tightened as her breasts rubbed against his firm chest, up and down while she fought to catch her breath.

Hot.

His body seemed to radiate warmth. His heat, his scent, pouring over her, seeping through the thin cotton of her dress. Goose bumps rose on her skin at the vivid contrast between him and the air-conditioned coolness of the room.

Her muscles trembled from the strain, her spine bent back in an awkward arch. She bucked and twisted in a final bid for freedom, grinding pelvis to pelvis. She stilled when she realized what she'd done. Against her, she felt the hard evidence of his arousal. An accompanying ache sprang to life in her, igniting an intimate pulse of want that beat deep within.

Her mouth opened on a soundless gasp.

Neither of them spoke; neither of them could.

Air rushed in and out of his lungs, his eyes locked on the parted fullness of her lips.

Then his mouth was on hers—or hers on his—since she had no idea which one of them had actually moved first.

He caught her lower lip between his teeth and gave it a gentle bite. His brief nip shot straight to her core. She whimpered when he took her deeper, sucking her tongue into his mouth to kiss her in a way she hadn't known anyone could.

Caught in an agony of longing, she writhed against him, struggling to free herself from his relentless grip, desperate to wrap her arms around him and cling.

Instead, he held her captive, arching her even tighter against his body. If not for his formidable strength, she knew she would have fallen. He ground his erection against her, pressing her hands into the small of her back as he made love to her through the barrier of their clothes. His fingers stretched to link with her own, clasping, clutching. She threaded hers tight in return.

His lips fell upon the curve of her neck and burrowed there with erotic intent. She moaned as he kissed and laved her tender skin in a way that was certain to leave a mark.

Then suddenly she was free, as he released her wrists to shift position—not to stop but to gain fuller access. She understood his need without the necessity of words, knew he wanted more.

She wanted more as well.

His hands cupped her breasts.

She raised her arms to touch him, to hold him as she'd been longing to do. She stopped, crying out as a sharp spasm of pain jabbed through her right shoulder.

James blinked and stared, her distress shredding the passionate haze around him as nothing else could have done. "What's wrong?" he asked, his voice little more than a harsh croak.

"Charley horse." She massaged the cramped muscle. "It's not so bad." She grimaced and lifted her arm into the air to stretch.

James's eyes went immediately to her breasts, watching them shift beneath the bodice of her dress. He turned away, scrubbed a hand over his face.

Dear God, what am I doing? What have I done?

Trembling, he raked his fingers through his hair.

His behavior was appalling. Inexcusable. Vile. Never in his life had he handled a woman so roughly, so thoughtlessly. To know he'd treated Ivy—his dear, sweet, little Ivy—in such a way, made it all that much more reprehensible.

How would she ever be able to speak to him, look at him in any sort of a normal way again?

Yet even now, overwhelmed as he was by guilt and regret, he couldn't stop wanting her. "Ivy, I'm sorry."

She paused, a hand on her elbow as she flexed her arm. "I'm all right now. No pain." She lowered the strained limb to her side, wiggled her fingers. "See?"

He stepped away, not trusting himself to touch her, even in an innocent way. "Go home, Ivy."

"What?"

"Go home. Let yourself out and lock the door behind you." He turned and headed up the staircase toward his suite of rooms.

He didn't look back.

Upstairs, he plunged his head beneath the punishment of a cold shower spray.

Sleep was next on his agenda, assuming he could sleep. At least tomorrow was Sunday, so he wouldn't have to worry about rolling out of bed at his usual early hour.

He lowered the water temperature another notch. Shivered as he leaned his forehead against the slick white tile wall of the shower enclosure, his mind as tortured as his body.

Five minutes later and about three-quarters recovered, he toweled himself dry and slipped on a pair of loose-fitting, navy blue cotton boxers. He scrubbed his teeth with a minty-tasting toothpaste, drank half a glass of water, then snapped off the lights before exiting the bathroom.

The lamp next to his bed cast a weak amber glow that left most of the room in darkness. When he'd walked in earlier, he'd paused only long enough to switch it on before flinging his clothes haphazardly to the floor. He was halfway across the room before it dawned on him that the clothes were gone.

Ivy drifted out of the shadows. "I put your things in the hamper in your dressing room. I hope that was all right."

His head jerked in her direction, the shock of finding her there sizzling along his nerve endings. "I thought you'd left."

She shook her head. "I locked up like you asked me to, but I couldn't go, not after what happened."

He scowled. She shouldn't be here. Didn't she know that? This was no time to talk. No place to talk either. Hell, even if it were, what would he say? What could he say?

"If you've come looking for an apology," he told her gruffly, "it'll have to wait. It's been a long day, and I'm tired."

God help me, she has to leave, he thought.

For both their sakes, couldn't she see she had to go?

"I don't want an apology," she said, her voice soft and melodic.

He crossed his arms over his chest, wishing he'd put on a robe. "What do you want, then?" His voice deepened, rough with frustration and remorse. "It's done, Ivy. I can't take it back."

Graceful, she glided toward him, halting only inches away. "I know that, and I'm so glad you can't."

He blinked, his arms falling to his sides. "What?"

She caressed him with her eyes. He couldn't mistake the look for anything else as it roved over his skin like a violinist admiring a prized Stradivarius.

"You asked me what I wanted," she murmured, stretching out a hand. Her fingers trembled as she laid them against his bare chest. "What I want is you. I always have."

He tried to swallow, his throat dry. Her touch was warm and smooth and seared him to the bone. "I thought you'd gotten over your infatuation with me long ago."

"Letting you believe that seemed easier." Undeterred, she stroked her other hand over his shoulder, fingers playing like silken ribbons against his skin.

His cock hardened again inside his boxers. "Ivy, don't. We can't do this."

"Why not?" She bent forward and pressed her lips to his neck, zeroing in on a particularly sensitive spot just under his chin. "I'm not fifteen anymore."

Blood beat in his temples, slowed and thickened in other places. "Even so, it—wouldn't be right. We—the two of us—we shouldn't be together, not like this."

Her free hand stayed busy, roaming over him while her lips scattered kisses across his collarbone. "We were together downstairs," she whispered. "I thought we fit together perfectly."

"What happened downstairs was a mistake. I didn't mean to kiss you. I—well—it all got out of hand."

"Hmm, didn't it, though?" She kissed his cheek, then sighed into his ear. "Let's get out of hand again."

He fought the red haze that rolled through his brain.

Show some restraint, he thought. *Have enough will-power to do the right thing.*

"Ivy, no." He untangled himself from her and stepped away. "Stop. I mean it."

She pinned him with a smoldering look, her eyes brilliantly blue. "I mean it too. You want me. Why deny what both of us want?"

"Because it'll change our relationship. If we do this, nothing will ever be the same between us again."

"It'll never be the same no matter what we do tonight," she said. "These feelings on both sides are in the open now and can't be taken back."

She was right.

Never again would he be able to look at her, think of her, in the way he used to.

She wouldn't ever again be the child who'd once solemnly held out her shoes to him, laces dangling, to ask if he'd teach her how to tie a bow.

Or the shy adolescent who'd phoned him the first time she'd ever stayed home alone, then talked with him for more than two hours, until her parents came home, so she wouldn't be afraid.

Or the teenage girl whose cheeks had bloomed with innocent delight when he'd placed a strand of cultured pearls around her neck as a gift on her fifteenth birthday.

As she'd reminded him, she wasn't fifteen anymore. The girl she'd once been was gone, a memory of the past. She was a woman now and no longer an innocent; her bold actions tonight assured him of that. Still, that didn't mean he had to take advantage of her.

He shook his head, denying himself as much as her. "All the old reasons against our being together still apply. There's too much history, too many years. I'm too old for you, Ivy."

"Your mind only thinks you are." Pointedly, she skimmed her eyes downward. "Your body doesn't seem to agree."

Dressed as he was, there was no disguising his erection. "What my body thinks doesn't matter."

She drew a breath, then reached for his hand. In silence, she carried it across the space between them and placed it over her breast. "Doesn't it?"

His palm cupped the warm curve of her pliant flesh as though fashioned for that express purpose. He fought to yank his hand away. Instead, as if controlled by a will of its own, his thumb slid sideways, brushing across her nipple.

The sensitive tip peaked beneath his touch.

Her lips parted, eyelids growing heavy.

His thumb moved again.

And again.

A flush raised bright flags of color in her cheeks. She shivered once, then took his hand, slipped it inside the bodice of her dress, fitting his palm around the warm softness of her naked breast.

He held himself rigid as he fought one last battle, as he tried to gather the will to resist.

You can't, he ordered himself.

It would be a mistake, he warned.

There will be regrets, pain, recriminations, and loss.

But his aching body cared for none of those things.

He hungered for her in a way he couldn't remember ever hungering before.

With a shudder, he buried his face in the sweetness of her hair and let himself be lost.

Ivy gasped when his hand moved, kneading her flesh with a skill that drove the breath from her lungs. He reached around and unfastened the buttons on the back of her dress. She closed her eyes and let the sensations wash over her, better than anything she'd ever imagined.

She didn't know where her daring came from tonight. Seducing him, enticing him with the confidence of a woman far bolder, far more experienced than herself. Of course, nearly any woman was more experienced than she, Ivy thought wryly.

Hormones and adrenaline, she decided. That must be the source of her confidence. An explosive combination that had fueled her system with a strength of purpose she hadn't known she possessed.

When he'd left her downstairs, she'd been a mass of seething emotions, desire flooding through her like a storm-swollen river. She'd been kissed before but never the way he'd just kissed her.

For a long while after, she'd stood, half dazed, her lips throbbing, her blood humming, and she'd known she couldn't leave. So instead of letting herself out of the apartment and heading for her own, she'd followed him up the stairs.

Her limbs quivered as his hand slipped beneath her panties to caress the fleshy curves of her buttocks, the upper edges of her thighs. She whimpered and leaned against him, suddenly aware she was naked, her dress ringed in a colorful pool around her ankles.

When had that happened?

Coherent thought fled as he kissed her, ravaging her mouth, his scent and taste both dark and delicious. She looped her arms up over his shoulders, bare breasts rubbing against the silky hair covering his chest in a most tantalizing way. She ran her hands down the long supple warmth of his back, her fingertips tingling at the sensations.

His hand, the one that had been roving over her bottom and thighs, made a sudden downward turn. He parted her legs and cupped her intimately. Before she fully guessed his intent, he dipped his fingers into her, slow and easy. First one, then a pair, easing them up inside where she was most vulnerable, most female.

Her eyelids slid closed, breath panting from between her parted lips. She moaned and clung harder, her nails curving against his skin as he built the pleasure inside her, each stroke better than the last.

His thumb moved, finding and flicking a spot that made stars spin behind her eyes. She shuddered, helpless against the delight as he kept on.

When the climax hit, it rocketed through her with a force that shook her to her toes. She cried out, hanging limp and lax against him as she waited for a hint of sanity to return.

But she didn't have a chance to recover before he was kissing her again, deep and demanding, his arousal pressing insistently against her stomach. He locked an arm around her waist, pulled her with him to the bed.

Her muscles were as wobbly as Jell-O and she nearly

stumbled on the way. But it didn't matter, as they fell upon the mattress, entwined.

He stripped off his boxers, then covered her. His long, muscled body lay heavily against hers despite the weight he was careful to keep on his forearms and knees. Suspended above her, he captured her mouth in an intense mating of lips and tongues and teeth.

She was panting, low moans coming from her throat, when he slid downward to suckle her breasts. First one, then the other, using a delicious suction as he swirled his tongue around each tender tip until they were tight and aching. She arched, assailed by a rush of new sensations. Fresh desire gathered deep within, weeping anew between her legs.

She threaded her fingers into his hair, stroked his face and neck, then down his shoulders and back. He moaned as she touched his hips and buttocks, stroking his skin the way he'd stroked hers earlier.

He levered himself upward, centered himself between her thighs. Then, pushing them wider, he thrust forcefully inside.

She cried out, stiffening involuntarily against an intense stab of pain.

A single teardrop leaked from the corner of her eye as she forced herself not to fight the intrusion, the feeling of being stretched too tight, too full. She'd known it would hurt the first time, but not like this. Somehow, she'd always thought her height would compensate for such things.

He froze, meeting her eyes in the low lamplight. He clenched his teeth, muscles quivering. "Why didn't you tell me you were a virgin?" His breath fanned her cheek, hot with strain and suppressed need.

"You might have said no," she whispered. "I couldn't bear for you to say no."

"Christ, Ivy." He hung his head. "Jesus H. Christ."

Trying not to move, she smoothed a comforting hand over his back. "Don't be angry. Please. It had to be someone, sometime, and I wanted it to be you. I needed it to be you."

"Shit."

A second tear leaked from her eye.

"Shh. Don't cry," he pleaded, kissing her damp cheek. "I can't bear to see you cry." He touched his lips to her temple and stroked her hair. "It'll be all right, sweetheart. I'll stop."

"No!" She locked her arms around his neck and raised her legs to hold him in place. Her breath caught as her movements pulled him deeper. "Don't stop. It's not so bad now."

As soon as the words left her mouth, she realized they were true. The pain had diminished considerably, her body beginning to accommodate him.

He closed his eyes, sweat beading his forehead. "Still, I—"

"No." She shifted her pelvis again, squeezing tighter. "Please, James."

He groaned and muttered another curse under his breath. Taking her hips in his hands, he started to ease back.

She held on. "Don't stop."

His muscles bunched, and he gave a shaky laugh.

"With all that wiggling you're doing, I don't think I could stop now if I tried." He kissed her again, tender and unbearably sweet. "Relax, and I'll show you."

Trusting him implicitly, she lessened her hold and allowed him to start moving inside her. He slid his hands under her hips to position her as he wanted, quickly establishing a rhythm that made her yearn and yield.

Her toes curled, her heart pounding at a wild clip as her pleasure increased, the last of her discomfort easing until she forgot there'd ever been any pain at all. Until there was only heat and motion and the most exquisite delight she'd ever known.

A new ache formed—an ache of want, of hunger so fierce she trembled beneath its force. The deeper and faster he plunged, the more she craved, until she didn't think wanting more was possible.

Her head rolled back and forth across the comforter, her hands grasping his wide shoulders as he pistoned in and out. She forgot everything but him, utterly lost, utterly without control, her breath coming in ragged, needy gasps.

Suddenly she crested, calling out his name as bliss spread through her.

He found his own satisfaction moments later, giving a hoarse shout as he followed her across to the other side. He buried his face against her neck, damp with perspiration, lungs pumping as if he'd just run a race.

She held him, awash with happiness and love.

Sometime after, he rolled them over so that he lay on his back. Smiling, she snuggled against his chest and drifted to sleep.

CHAPTER EIGHT

James leaned back against the sparklingly clean kitchen countertop made of black-and-white-flecked granite and waited for the coffee to finish brewing. God knew he needed a cup, even if it was two o'clock in the afternoon—well past any conventional breakfast hour. Hungry, he considered fixing himself some eggs and toast, then decided he'd wait for Ivy.

He'd left her sleeping, curled snug as a kitten beneath the covers. Not even the dull roar of his shower had penetrated her slumber. While he dressed in a pair of navy slacks and a button-down white cotton shirt, he'd studied her. The way her hair spread across his pillows like long rays of golden sunshine. How her cheeks glowed, dusty pink with warmth. The faint smile that curved her sweet lips.

Young, he'd thought, as he'd fastened on a wrist-watch he'd owned for more years than she'd been alive. *She is so young. Much too young for me.*

A shroud of guilt settled over him.

Until last night, she'd been innocent. No matter what she'd said she wanted, he'd taken that away from her. By making love to her, he'd crossed an invisible line. No longer her friend and protector but the man who'd corrupted her.

And who wanted to go on corrupting her.

The coffeemaker gurgled, hissing pungent steam as it finished filling the glass pot. He poured himself a cup and had just taken a first sip when the door chime rang. Mildly irritated by the interruption, he set down his cup and left the kitchen.

He discovered the last person he would ever have expected to see waiting on the other side of his front door.

Madelyn.

With hair the color of a fiery sunset, eyes deep and blue as a sunlit sea, Madelyn Grayson was more beautiful than ever.

Madelyn *Douglas*, he corrected himself, remembering she was married now—to the man she'd jilted him for more than five years before.

She'd added an extra pound or two at the hips and bust, he saw—no doubt weight from the babies she'd given birth to. But the extra inches only made her lovelier, adding a lush maturity to curves no man could possibly find lacking. She'd shortened her hair, coppery curls bouncing around her expressive face in a sassy chin-length bob. She looked the part of a married suburban professional with an extra day off for the long weekend.

She was dressed in butter-colored chinos, leather loafers, and a peach T-shirt. He noticed a smear of something that looked suspiciously like strawberry jam on her sleeve.

She met his eyes with a cautious smile. "James, hi."

"Madelyn."

She rubbed a hand down the side of one thigh as if her palm were perspiring. "Sorry to drop by with no notice. I wasn't sure if you'd be home. I . . . uh . . . decided to try my old elevator passkey. Imagine my surprise when it still worked. "

Many years ago, she'd been one of the first people he'd added to his small list of visitors granted unlimited access to his floor. He'd meant to remove her name and decode her key. Somehow he'd just never gotten around to it.

Abruptly remembering his manners, he stepped back. "Would you like to come in?"

Awkwardness hung between them, heavy as a thick pane of glass. Sad, considering the staunch friendship they'd once shared.

"All right," she agreed, "but only for a minute."

She followed him inside, looking around as they went. She paused for a quick sniff at the bouquet of fresh flowers Estella kept arranged in a Meissen vase on a stand in the hall outside the dining room. This weekend's arrangement contained red and white roses mixed with blue hydrangeas, their perfume dewy sweet.

"You haven't changed anything, I see," she remarked.

"No. It's all exactly as I like."

She shot him a look.

He continued on into the living room. "I'd offer you coffee, but I know you don't like the stuff. Something else perhaps? Tea? Juice? A cocktail?"

"No, no, that's all right." She twisted her fingers together in a nervous gesture. "I can't stay long. I wouldn't have stopped by at all except . . . Well, I wanted to ask you . . ."

He frowned at her distress. "Ask me what? Is something wrong?"

"It's Ivy," she blurted. "I called her late last night and several times again today, but she isn't answering her cell. She's not at her apartment either. I just came from down there. Zack and the girls dropped me off up here, then went back down to her place in hopes that she'll show up. I'm probably worrying for nothing. I was wondering if you have any idea where she might be. James, have you seen Ivy?"

Her words hit him with the stinging crack of a whip.

My God. Ivy!

He'd forgotten all about her.

Disloyalty crept over him at the realization. After last night, how could he have forgotten Ivy, even for an instant? Apparently, finding her older sister—his ex-lover—on his doorstep had retarded more than a few of his higher brain functions.

Did he know where she was?

Hell yeah, he knew. Upstairs, asleep in his bed, where he prayed she'd remain.

I can't let Madelyn find Ivy here.

Lord, what had he been thinking, inviting Madelyn in?

She had to leave, and leave now.

"Ivy went to a party with some friends last night, I think," he said hastily. "Maybe she decided to stay over with them."

Madelyn wrinkled her forehead, considering. "I suppose, though it doesn't seem like something she'd do. Ivy's not much for impromptu sleepovers."

Madelyn obviously had a lot to learn. Ivy's sleepover with him last night had been about as impromptu as they came.

"Even if she did stay overnight with friends, she ought to have checked her phone and at least texted me back." She glanced at her watch. "It's almost two thirty in the afternoon. Surely she should be back home by now."

"Oh, I don't know. It was the Fourth last night, so she probably slept late and decided to stay for lunch. Or maybe she's out sketching. You know how preoccupied she can get when she's working on her art. You two've probably just missed each other. I'm sure she's fine."

"You think so?"

"I'm positive. And you know how bad she can be about answering her phone, especially when she's painting. She probably put it on mute and forgot to turn the ringer back on."

"That's true. She does tend to ignore calls when she's in the zone, as she calls it," Madelyn said.

"Exactly. So why don't you join"—he broke off, finding the casual use of Zack Douglas's name distasteful even now—"your family down at Ivy's place. She's bound to turn up soon." With a gentle hand on Madelyn's elbow, he began to steer her toward the door.

She took a couple steps, then stopped. "I suppose you're right. Trouble is, we don't have a key to Ivy's apartment. I can't leave the girls sitting out in the hallway for hours."

"Don't worry. I'll call the guard's desk, explain the situation, and ask them to come up and let you in."

"Okay. If you're sure you don't mind?"

"I don't mind at all." He stretched out an arm to herd her in the right direction. "Why don't you go ahead in case she's already there, while I make the call?"

"All right. I—"

The door chime rang.

Holy Mother of God, James silently cursed. *Who is it now?*

Before he took a step, Madelyn headed for the door.

Moments later a child's high-pitched squeal rang out, followed by the drumming of tiny feet.

A toddler raced around the corner, then stopped dead the instant she saw him. She tipped her head back as far as it would go, her hair a mass of silky black ringlets silhouetted around her cherubic face. She met his eyes, her own a brilliant shade of green. They widened to the size of moons as she stared.

He'd never seen one of Madelyn's children before. Not much resemblance to her, he decided, the small girl's beautiful features a feminine version of her father.

Except for the stubborn chin. That he recognized as pure Grayson.

Yet aside from the child's dark coloring and another man's features, he couldn't help but think, *She should have been mine.*

If life had worked out right, she would have been mine.

Forcing away such useless thoughts, he smiled at Madelyn's daughter.

The girl turned and ran straight to her father, who'd just walked into the room. Seeking his protection, she wrapped her pudgy arms around his sturdy leg. Safe again, the child darted a shy peek up at James, checking to see if he was still watching.

He smiled at her again, then lifted his eyes to meet his former rival's shrewd green gaze. He gave a curt nod. "Douglas."

Zack returned the gesture with an equal lack of enthusiasm. "Jordan."

"I see you've met Hannah," Madelyn remarked, coming up next to her husband.

Another child—identical to the first—clung to Madelyn, her tiny little arms locked around her mother's neck. The girl rested her cheek against Madelyn's shoulder and watched him out of a second pair of startlingly clear green eyes.

An uncomfortable wave of melancholia hit him. "They're beautiful, Meg," he said, unconsciously using his old nickname for Madelyn. "You should be proud."

Madelyn smiled, obviously touched by his words. "I am." She bounced the girl she held in her arms. "This is Holly."

"Hello, Holly."

The baby stuck her thumb in her mouth and turned her face into her mother's neck.

Hannah, not to be upstaged, swung around to face him but kept a fistful of her father's jeans held tight in one little hand.

"Hello, Hannah," James said, trying again.

She giggled.

"They refused to stay downstairs," Zack informed Madelyn. "Insisted I find Mommy. What could I do? I was outnumbered. Lucky for all of us, you gave me the passkey so we could come to get you."

James promised himself to make updating the passkey list a priority.

Somehow he doubted the idea to find Madelyn had originated with the children. James hadn't exchanged more than a few words, and some choice sneers, with Zack Douglas over the years. And James was an astute enough judge of people to know that letting Madelyn come up to his penthouse alone must have been driving the other man insane.

She adjusted Holly on her hip. "James thinks Ivy may have stayed over with friends last night and is having a late lunch with them. Or that she went out with her sketch pad to do some drawings. I have to admit it sounds like something she might do. Both of you are probably right, and I shouldn't be so worried."

"Not yet anyway." Zack reached down for Hannah, who'd decided she wanted to be held like her sister. "Maybe we should have a late lunch ourselves. I didn't get to eat peanut butter and jelly crackers and apple slices in the car like these two." He lifted his daughter's hand, pretending to bite it. Delighted, she screeched and then laughed. "We'll stop back afterward. Ivy'll probably be home by then."

"Oh, well, I suppose we could, but James was just about to call down and have one of the guards let us into Ivy's apartment."

"Really?" Zack shot him a look. "Guess there're a few perks to owning the building, such as bypassing security protocols."

James stared back, refusing to take the bait.

After a minute, Zack broke off the staring match and turned to his wife. "All right. We'll go to Ivy's instead, since I know it'll make you feel better. We'll raid her fridge. If it's bare, I'm calling for takeout."

Relieved they were finally leaving, James did his best to shepherd them toward the door.

"He's right," James prompted. "You all go on and I'll make the call. The guard will be there in less than five minutes."

Madelyn paused. "Maybe I should phone her one more time. With luck, she'll pick up this time and you won't need to bother the guards."

A sudden image of Madelyn calling her sister and Ivy's phone ringing from inside Ivy's purse here in the penthouse popped into his mind.

"No!" he said quickly. "No need to do that. It's no bother, none at all. It'll give the guards something interesting to do on a lazy Sunday afternoon. Now, go on. Won't be but a minute."

Madelyn frowned, confused. "Well, all right. If you're sure—"

"*Hell-o,*" called a cheery, singsong voice. "James? It's me." High heels clicked on the entry hall's polished cherry floors.

Parker.

Fuck me. Not her too! he thought.

She rounded the corner, halted abruptly when she saw he had company.

"Oh, hello." She nodded a greeting at the Douglases and then looked at James. "Did you know your door's open, darling? Is everything all right?"

"Everything's fine. Actually, we were on our way out." He took Parker's elbow and tried to turn her, stretching his other arm wide behind Madelyn and Zack and their little girls as if he could force them onward.

Madelyn stood her ground, tossed him another puzzled look. "But you were going to call."

"Yes, yes, of course I was. I am. I mean . . . I just . . . That is, when I said *we,* I meant all of you. And then me, since I thought I'd come downstairs . . . after I call, you know, to make sure everything's okay. Okay?"

Madelyn frowned. "Is something the matter, James? You're acting weird."

"Maybe he's been drinking," Zack quipped in a caustic aside.

"He's sick." Parker pulled out of James's grip and reached up a hand to check his forehead for fever. "Poor baby came home quite ill last night. Are you still nauseous?"

Actually, he was beginning to feel a little sick.

Madelyn reached out, set the back of her hand against his cheek.

Zack shot her a black scowl.

She ignored it. "You should have said something if you aren't feeling well," she told James.

"Actually, I'm feeling much better today. Really. Now, why don't we all go on downstairs?"

Madelyn shook her head. "Even so, if you've been ill, you shouldn't push yourself."

"Exactly," Parker agreed. She lifted up a small brown paper sack. "I brought chicken soup from the kosher deli, if you're up to it."

"I am not hungry," James stated, the volume of his voice increasing with each word. "And I am not sick. Now, let's go on before—"

"Who's sick?" A soft, distinctly feminine voice cut through the conversation, carrying with the force of a rocket-propelled grenade.

Parker, Madelyn, Zack, even the twins, looked toward the upstairs landing.

James closed his eyes.

Madelyn found her voice first. "*Ivy?*"

"Malynn? What are you doing here?"

"Looking for you. We were worried."

"You were? Why?"

"We've been trying to call you since last night. We stopped by your apartment, but you weren't there."

"No, sorry. I went to a party last night and it was really late when we got back. I just woke up and didn't think about checking my cell for . . ." Her words abruptly trailed off as she apparently realized what she'd just revealed. "Messages."

James winced and reluctantly opened his eyes.

Looking up, he found her standing at the railing outside his bedroom. Barefoot, she wore her badly wrinkled party dress from the night before, her long hair hanging in hastily brushed waves around her shoulders. She looked rumpled and rosy and well satisfied from a night of pleasurable sex.

"I see," Madelyn murmured with an odd-sounding squeak to her voice.

"So do I." Hissing like a snake, Parker turned on James. "You . . . you lying, deceitful, conniving bastard."

She pointed an arm toward Ivy. "Is that your little *friend*? The one you've been spending so much time with lately? The *little sister* you would never, ever think of fuc—"

"*Parker*," he interrupted, cutting her off.

She growled. "Don't you *Parker* me. To think I believed you. All that BS about her being like family. 'My God, Parker,'" she mimicked, "'she's only twenty years old. Do you really think I'd be interested in a twenty-year-old?' Ooh, it's so typical. The younger they are, the more men just have to screw them."

"Excuse me. There are children present," Madelyn interjected.

Parker ignored her, still raging at James. "Friends, ha! I see what sort of *friends* you are. The sort that lie and cheat and sneak around behind other people's backs."

"It isn't like that," James defended.

"Isn't it? Then tell me you haven't slept with her."

He opened his mouth, but the words wouldn't come. Desperately, he looked around.

Accusing eyes bore into him from every direction. He knew then how it must feel to be a condemned man on trial—and to hear the verdict: guilty on all counts.

He shut his mouth.

Unshed tears glistened in Parker's eyes. "I thought you were different, decent, but you're just like all the other selfish bastards out there. Enjoy your hot little Twinkie. She'll get tired of you soon enough when she realizes just how old you really are."

She whirled away, then stopped and marched back. She smashed the sack she carried against his chest. "Here's your soup!"

James caught it. A large, wet, greasy stain soaked through the brown paper bag, as warm soup leaked onto his shirt. The aroma of chicken drifted into the air.

Parker stormed out, slamming the door behind her.

"Bet you feel pretty sick now," Zack murmured to him under his breath.

James glared at the other man and then stalked across the room. He dumped the dripping sack of soup in the wet bar sink.

Disgusted with himself, with the whole terrible, hurtful scene, he turned on the water to wash his hands clean. If only he could clean up the rest of this mess as easily.

He daubed ineffectively at the greasy stain on his

shirt with a napkin. His efforts did little to remove it, spreading water in a massive spot across the fabric.

Ivy appeared at his elbow. "You might as well give it up," she murmured softly. "It'll never come out that way. You're only making things worse."

He cursed and tossed the sodden napkin aside. "I don't see how things could be worse."

She met his eyes, gave him a wry smile. "My parents could be here."

He sighed. "Thank heavens for small miracles."

"Here," she murmured. "I brought you a fresh shirt."

"Sorry to interrupt your little confab, but I want to know if it's true. What she said, that Parker woman," Madelyn demanded, her question sharp enough to slice glass.

He and Ivy froze, then slowly turned their heads.

"From the way you two are behaving, I suppose it must be, though I still can't believe it." Madelyn drew in an audible breath, as if the air would give her strength. "Did you sleep together?" When neither of them answered immediately, her tone grew shrill. "Well, did you?"

James tucked his hands into his pockets and faced her. "Yeah, we did."

Madelyn sagged, her face pale with shock. Her arms tightened around her daughter, hugging her close.

Too close for Holly apparently, who, despite remaining quiet throughout the turmoil, now began to wail. Tears spurted from her eyes like a fountain. Hearing her sister's distress, Hannah joined in a moment later.

Zack touched his wife's shoulder. "Here, let me take her."

"What?" Madelyn mumbled, clearly unsettled.

"Let me have her. I'll take these two watering pots for a walk. Some fresh air should calm them down. We'll meet you in the lobby when you're ready."

She transferred the bawling youngster to Zack. "Yes. All right. Thanks."

"Hey, that's what I'm here for." He gave her a reassuring smile.

Arms overflowing with sobbing babies, Zack glanced at Ivy.

His green eyes twinkled.

He winked, then shook his head at James with a "Man, what were you thinking?" look in his eyes.

The room grew unnaturally still and quiet once Zack and the twins departed.

An entire minute passed; no one said a word.

Madelyn crossed her arms, shifted her feet. "How long has this been going on? The two of you involved as"—she paused, spitting out the last word with obvious distaste—"*lovers*."

"However long it's been is between Ivy and me," James stated in an implacable tone. "I'm not going to discuss it with you, so leave it alone."

Madelyn gasped. "*Leave it alone?* I don't think so. She's my sister, my *baby* sister, and you were supposed to be her trusted friend. A reliable older man. Someone who would watch out for her, not take advantage of her. Not seduce her."

"He didn't seduce me." Ivy jumped in. "I seduced him."

"Ivy!" Madelyn said, shocked.

"I did, and I'd do it again." Ivy laid a fist against her chest. "What James and I shared was beautiful, and I won't have you twist it into something sordid. I won't let you turn this against him. He didn't do anything wrong."

"Didn't he?"

"No."

Ivy's impassioned defense warmed him, however little he deserved her loyalty. He didn't move as Madelyn pinned him with a baleful look.

"You lied to me," she said, hurt resonating in her words. "I've known you since we were kids, and in all that time, you've never tried to deceive me. I remember when we were dear friends without any secrets. Now I feel like I don't even know who you are."

She cupped her hands around her elbows. "I came here today, asking for your help, worried about Ivy, wondering if she's hurt or in danger, and you make up stories. You feed me lies, one after another, knowing all the time she's upstairs in your bed. I'm surprised you let me in here at all."

"If I'd been thinking straight, I wouldn't have," he grumbled. "As for the lying, I apologize. It was beneath me. However, it wasn't solely up to me to tell you Ivy's whereabouts. I wasn't sure she'd want you to know, under the circumstances."

"I'm her family. I have a right to know."

"Not everything," he said. "Not that. If she wants to discuss particulars with you, that's up to her. But I won't let you bully her over this. Do you understand?"

Moisture sparkled in Madelyn's eyes. "*Bully* her? I've never bullied her in my life. What a dreadful thing to say. When have I ever bullied anyone?"

"You haven't, Malynn," Ivy interceded. "You've always been a wonderful, caring sister. The best anyone could want." She shot a telling glance at James, who raised a single unrepentant eyebrow in reply.

"We're all on edge," Ivy said. "Why don't we put this aside for a few minutes and find something to eat in the kitchen. I, for one, am starved."

"I can't." Madelyn crossed her arms. "Zack and the twins are waiting for me downstairs, remember?"

"Invite them back up."

She shook her head, her shoulders stiff. "We need to be starting for home. This detour to find you has already taken up more of the day than I'd anticipated."

"Why were you trying to get in touch with me anyway?" Ivy asked. "When we talked last, you didn't say anything about stopping by to see me on your way home from Mom and Dad's."

A new seriousness swept over Madelyn, a gravity of spirit that darkened her eyes. "We weren't. There's news about the family. I can't believe I nearly forgot. Obviously, the shock of finding you two . . . Well, never mind that."

"What news?" Ivy prompted. "From your expression, I take it it's not good."

"No, it isn't. And there's no way to pretty it up, so I'll just say it straight. Caroline's ill. She has cancer."

"*No.*" Ivy covered her mouth with a hand.

James gave a low curse. "How bad is it?" he asked after a moment.

"Bad," Madelyn said. "Bad enough that we all noticed as soon as she and P.G. and the kids arrived for the party. She tried to put a good face on it, but you can tell. She looks tired just sitting in a chair. And thin. My God, she's so thin—bones really. P.G. wanted her home—I overheard them arguing—but she refused to go. She wanted to see the fireworks, she said."

"How far along is it? What's being done to treat her?" he demanded.

"She and P.G. wouldn't say for sure, but it has to be fairly advanced. They've been hiding it, for months I guess. She had surgery and an entire round of radiation and chemotherapy. It's uterine cancer. Mother was furious when she found out they'd been keeping it secret." Madelyn wiped a tear from the corner of her eye. "Maybe we could sit down. Do you mind?"

"No. No, of course not." He gestured her toward a comfortable armchair. "Would you like some water?"

Madelyn shook her head, then sat.

"Ivy?" he asked.

She refused as well, took a seat on the wide leather sofa.

Ivy waited for James to join her. Instead he crossed to a chair opposite, obviously wishing to place some distance between them.

His gesture stung. She shook off the hurt, telling herself he was just uncomfortable displaying their new relationship in front of Madelyn. After all, the two of them hadn't even had a private moment to talk about their night together.

"Do you know why Caroline and P.G. tried to hide her condition?" Ivy questioned.

"He said they didn't want to worry everyone. But there must be more to it. You know how they sent the kids to stay with Mom and Dad after Christmas last year while they went overseas? A special trip to Europe, they said. Now that I know about Caroline's illness, I realize she must have been undergoing some sort of procedure. Poor Caroline. Poor P.G."

"Perhaps they hoped they'd beat it without telling anyone," James suggested. "Perhaps they didn't want people, not even family, treating them differently. Once the C word gets out, it's the only thing some people see. I remember when my grandfather was stricken with emphysema. He said he hated the pity in people's eyes worse than he hated the disease. Maybe that's how Caroline feels."

"Maybe so." Madelyn sighed, looked at Ivy for a moment, then looked back at James. "I think you should go see her. She can use all the moral support she can get right now."

"Of course we'll go see her," he said. "I've always liked Caroline."

"Everybody likes Caroline," Ivy said, knowing it to be the truth.

Sweet and warm and giving, Caroline was the kind of person you couldn't help but like.

And love.

Ivy's heart ached to know she was ill. "How are P.G. and the children doing?"

"Holding up. The kids are quieter than usual, especially Brian. Heather's only four, too young to really understand. All she knows is that Mommy's sick."

"And P.G.?"

"Stubborn. Determined. Trying to be a rock for her when I know it must be tearing him apart inside. I've never known anyone with a happier marriage than theirs. She's the love of his life. I don't know what he'll do if she dies."

A heavy pause hung in the air. "He'll go on," James said. "When you lose someone you love, what other choice do you have?"

Something in his tone made Ivy pause.

Was he speaking only of P.G.? Or was he talking about himself as well? Was he talking about Madelyn? There were more ways to lose someone you loved than through the finality of death.

Ivy curled a hand in her lap. *Oh, why did Madelyn have to show up today of all days?* she thought.

Last night had been so glorious, so wonderful, the culmination of everything she'd dreamed of for such a very long time.

James wanted her. Finally, he desired her as a woman.

And now that he did, might it not be possible for him to want more? To want her, to love her, for always?

They could have spent the day together, lying in each other's arms, talking and making love. Instead, he sat across from her, his reserve back in place. All the accusations Madelyn and Parker had thrown at him no doubt running through his head.

She listened as he and Madelyn continued to talk about Caroline.

How horrible of me, Ivy thought. Fretting over her own selfish concerns instead of concentrating on her sister-in-law.

She shifted in her seat, suddenly feeling rather low and petty.

Madelyn's words slowed as she began to run out of new information to share. She checked her watch. "I should be leaving. I . . . well, we have the drive home, and Zack wants to grab a bite here in the city first. This time of year the restaurants are all sure to have extra-long lines."

"You're welcome to eat here if you'd like. All of you," James offered, grudging but polite.

"No. I think it would be best if I just left." She stood, looked toward her sister. "Ivy? Shall we ride down to your floor together?"

She met Madelyn's expectant look, shook her head. "I'm staying here with James."

Her sister's lips tightened, her disapproval clear. "Then perhaps you could see me out, at least?"

"All right." Ivy rose from the couch.

"I'll take that shirt now, Ivy." James stood, extended his hand.

"Oh, of course." She'd nearly forgotten about the garment still draped over her arm. She passed him the clean shirt, vibrantly aware as their hands brushed. "Need any help?"

The corners of his lips edged upward. "I think I can manage on my own, but thanks."

His expression neutral, James turned to Madelyn. "Safe trip home."

She raised one sharp red eyebrow, then lowered it without saying whatever had been ready to emerge. She nodded once. "Bye."

She preceded Ivy into the hallway. Once they were out of earshot, Madelyn stopped and turned. "What in the world do you think you're doing?"

"About what?"

"About James. What else would I be talking about? A relationship between the two of you is completely out of the question."

Ivy folded her arms over her chest. "Why?"

"Well, for one thing, you've known him forever. My God, he used to play patty-cake with you. He used to give you piggyback rides on his shoulders."

"I barely remember."

"Of course you don't—you were too young. You're only twenty. You should be out enjoying yourself, having fun."

"I am having fun." Her lips curved. "I hope to have a lot more fun very soon."

Madelyn ignored the innuendo. "I meant with people your own age. James is even older than I am."

Ivy snorted. "By all of eight months."

"And I'm older than you by *fifteen* years."

"I know how old all of us are. His age doesn't matter to me."

"Well, it ought to." Madelyn threw up her hands.

"What will everyone think? Our friends, our family, our parents?"

"I would hope Mom and Dad will be happy for me, for James. They've always loved him. I love him."

Madelyn's tone softened. "And does he feel the same?"

Ivy lowered her eyes. "I don't know. But if he doesn't now, I plan to do everything I can to convince him he does." She looked up and took a breath. "What's the problem, Malynn? Are you really so concerned for me, or are you just upset for yourself?"

Madelyn's eyes narrowed. "What's that supposed to mean?"

"He was yours once. We all know that. Because he was yours, you don't want me to have him."

"Don't be ridiculous. You make it sound as if I'm jealous, which I'm not. I'm a very happily married woman. James can have any female he likes."

"Just not your sister."

Trapped by Ivy's unassailable logic, Madelyn sputtered.

"You didn't want him," Ivy continued. "But I do. I've loved him for as long as I can remember. I loved him when I didn't think there was a hope in this world he'd ever look my way. Even when his heart belonged completely to you. When you refused him, I cried. I mourned for him and for his pain."

Ivy took a breath. "But I have a chance now. Please don't deny me that. He's the only man I'll ever want. The only one I'll ever love. You love Zack; you must understand how I feel."

Madelyn laid a hand on Ivy's cheek. "I think I'm beginning to. I always knew you had a crush on James. I just never realized how deep your feelings really went." Madelyn sighed. "I only want you to be happy."

"I am. I will be. With him. Can't you be happy for me back?"

Madelyn lowered her hand. "I'll try. Getting used to this is going to take some doing." She glanced up at the crown of Ivy's head. "I'm still getting used to the fact that you're several inches taller than me. Give me some time, okay?"

Ivy smiled. "Okay." She reached out and hugged Madelyn. "I love you."

Madelyn hugged her back. "Same here, kiddo. Take care of yourself. I'll call. And turn on the ringer on your phone for a change."

Ivy laughed and agreed.

They exchanged one more hug; then Madelyn let herself out the door.

CHAPTER NINE

vy found James in the kitchen drinking coffee out of an oversized white ceramic mug.

He looked up as she entered. "Still alive?"

"Of course." She went to the cupboard where he kept the mugs and took down one for herself. "We talked. There were a few sticky moments, but Malynn and I are okay again."

He lifted the coffeepot and filled her cup. "So did you promise never to see me again after today?"

She turned earnest eyes upon him. "You know I would never promise that."

He was silent for a long moment. "Maybe you should." He pushed away from the countertop where he'd been leaning, crossed to the refrigerator. "You want something to eat?"

Uneasy surprise rippled through her. "Yeah, but not until you tell me what you meant by that last comment."

"Eggs and bacon or French toast?" He pulled out a carton of eggs. "Estella taught me a recipe that's gotten me through many a hungry Sunday morning."

"James, tell me what you meant." She reached out and wrapped a hand around his arm. "You're avoiding my question. Why?"

She swallowed, dread settling in her belly.

He set the eggs and a stick of butter on the counter, then closed the refrigerator door. He thrust his hands into his pants pockets, a sure sign he felt uneasy. "Ivy, last night was . . ."

"Yes, what was it?" she murmured.

"Special. Amazing. Utterly unforgettable."

He looked up, met her eyes, then pulled in a sharp breath. "But it was wrong. Last night was a mistake that should never have happened."

A fine tremor ran just beneath her skin. Was he breaking up with her after only one night? *No. Impossible.* He couldn't be, not after saying such lovely things at the start.

But as she searched his face and read the remote expression in his blue eyes, the dread in her stomach turned to stone.

My God, he is breaking up with me.

She grabbed his arms, pressed herself against him. "It wasn't wrong," she pleaded. "It was wonderful. Don't let Madelyn and that . . . that unfortunate scene with that other woman you've been seeing make you regret what we shared. I don't regret it, not for an instant."

"You should," he said, his voice as cool now as his

eyes. "Madelyn's right. We've got no business being together, sleeping together."

Gently, he pried her hands loose and took a step back. "My God, Ivy, your father and brother would beat me bloody if they knew what I'd done. And I wouldn't blame them. I was supposed to look after you, not seduce you. I took advantage, took your innocence, to my everlasting shame. I can barely stand to look at myself in the mirror."

"You didn't take advantage of me," she said with a shake of her head. "What we did last night was *my* choice. My innocence, as you call it, was mine to give. Why, I practically pleaded with you last night to make love to me. James, if anyone took advantage, it was me. I'm the one who seduced *you*. I'm the one who's been seducing you for weeks."

His golden brows furrowed. "What's that supposed to mean?"

"Well, I . . . You see . . . Ever since I moved to the city, I've been trying to get you to notice me. The bathing suit I wore in your pool, the impromptu visits, the picnics, they've all been my attempt to make you see me as a desirable woman. I even kissed you once while you were asleep."

"You mean that wasn't a dream?"

Her cheeks warmed at the memory. "No. I didn't know whether or not you realized. I just couldn't help myself that night. You looked so beautiful lying there on my sofa. I simply had to kiss you. So you see, you are not to blame for any of this, and you don't need to feel responsible. You are what I want."

She slid her palm over his smoothly shaven cheek, gazed into his eyes. "You are what I will always want."

Reaching up, she looped her arms around his neck, tugged his head down, and crushed her lips to his. For a moment, he stiffened and tried to pull away. But she wouldn't let him go, kissing him harder, as she poured all the passion in her soul into the embrace. She traced the tip of her tongue over his lower lip and felt his response.

Suddenly he was kissing her, pressing her mouth wide for a fiery mating of lips and tongues and teeth. Blood hummed in her veins as she tunneled her fingers into his hair and hungrily waited for him to take more.

Abruptly, he pulled away, paced across the kitchen. "This can't go on, Ivy. It's wrong. We shouldn't have these feelings for each other."

"Why not?" she asked, her voice husky from their kiss. "We're both single. We both want each other, like each other. Where's the harm?"

He thrust his hands into his back pockets as if he didn't quite trust himself not to touch her again. Then he sighed. "You saw the reaction today. Everyone's horror at the idea of the two of us intimately involved. Your sister won't be the only one who feels that way; there'll be the rest of your family, especially your parents. What am I going to say to them when they find out that I'm sleeping with their underage daughter— the girl they asked me to watch over while she's here in New York?"

"I'm not underage. I'm an adult woman."

"Yeah, so adult you're not even allowed to drink legally."

"Only for a few months more," she defended softly. "Then I'll be twenty-one."

"That old, huh? Twenty? Twenty-one? Do you think that will make any difference to my friends and business colleagues? Just imagine their reaction if I showed up with you on my arm. There'd be no end to the crude jokes and snide comments."

She cringed. "So I embarrass you. Is that it? You'd be ashamed to be seen with me in public?"

He dragged a hand through his hair, ruffling it. "No, you don't embarrass me. But other people wouldn't be kind if they knew we were lovers, and you deserve better. You deserve to be treated with respect."

"What if I said I didn't care? What if I said I loved you? Would it matter then?"

He gave her a long look, then shook his head. "You don't love me; you just think you do." He waved a hand, dismissing her declaration. "You've always looked at me with a bit of hero worship in your eyes. What you're feeling is infatuation, pure and simple."

"It didn't feel like infatuation last night or again this morning when you woke me up for a couple rounds of predawn nooky."

He blanched. "Don't be crude."

Temper began to simmer in her veins. "And don't tell me what I feel and whether or not it's real."

"Stop acting like a spoiled child and I won't."

She gasped, his words hitting her like a slap in the face. "Spoiled child?"

"That's right. You say you love me, but what do you know about relationships, about commitment, about real life? You've barely experienced any of them for yourself. My God, you've never even held a real job. You were in school until a couple months ago, and now you're out trying your hand at painting. That's great. That's wonderful, but it doesn't mean you're mature."

He walked over and leaned back against the countertop, gripping the edge. "You're young, twenty years old, just like you said. People change a lot in their twenties, Ivy. Who you are now isn't who you're going to be in another ten years, twenty years. You think you want me? You think you love me? You have no frame of reference to be sure."

Unshed tears burned in her eyes, her voice sounding thick to her own ears. "Did you have a frame of reference when you fell in love with Madelyn? You were barely in high school, weren't you? Far younger than me. And yet you were thirty years old by the time the two of you got engaged."

She drew a quick, hard breath. "Had anything changed in all those years? Did screwing a bunch of other women during the years you were apart help you decide she really was the right one for you? Is that what I need to do? Go out and screw a bunch of men to prove I love you?"

His face grew thunderous.

"Because there're plenty of men who want me," she said. "Fred, to start with. He'd be happy to further my education."

"*Ivy.*" he growled in warning.

"But that isn't what all this is about, is it? It isn't about me; it's about Madelyn. About the fact that you adored her and she ripped out your heart. It's because you can't trust anyone, especially not me, her sister. I told myself it didn't matter if you still loved her. I told myself I'd take you no matter the price and damn the cost. But the truth is, you won't let me close enough to even worry about giving up my pride. You've decided to push me away before we've even had a chance to begin."

She wiped a tear from the corner of her eye. "So you can breathe a sigh of relief. You want me out of your life, then I'll get out."

"I don't want you out of my life," he said, raking his fingers through his hair again. "I just want things back the way they used to be. I just want us to put all this in the past and be friends again."

She looked at him out of bleak eyes, her chest heavy and aching. "Last night you said our making love would change everything, and it has. Nothing between us will ever be the same again." She released a despondent sigh. "I'll always be your friend, James, but I won't ever again be your little sister. I love you, as a woman, whether you choose to believe me or not. If you ever decide you want something more between us, come and see me."

Then, before she broke down completely, she spun from the room, hurried through the penthouse, and went out the door.

Ivy cried for three days straight.

She couldn't believe their love affair had started and ended in less than a day. She thought about those hours over and over again, replaying each word, every touch and sensation, wondering whether there was anything she might have done differently.

Finally, she forced herself out of bed, dried her eyes, and took a long, hot shower.

So James thought she was too young, did he? Too inexperienced to know what she really wanted. Well, she *was* young, and she supposed she didn't have a great deal of real-world experience, but she could change that.

She *would* change that, she vowed.

She couldn't help her youth; only time could correct that flaw. But every day she would get a little older, a little wiser and more mature.

He wanted a woman who knew her own mind? A woman able to stand on her own two feet? She'd show him she was that woman. If finding a job and proving she could succeed on her own terms were what it took to gain his respect, then she'd do it. Her parents had given her a safety net, a comfortable cushion on which to land should she falter, should she fail. Well, she was going to give up the net and go solo. She was going to walk the wire alone and fight for every inch; failure would not be an option.

He said she didn't really love him, that her feelings were still nothing more than a passing infatuation. She'd show him he was wrong about that too. She didn't know how, but she'd find a way to convince him her love was enduring and true. She'd show him she wouldn't change her mind, that she wasn't her sister.

Of course, it might all be for nothing, since it was clear he wasn't in love with her.

Not yet.

But he wants me, she reminded herself.

He hadn't been able to control his desire for her the night he'd taken her to his bed. And she knew he'd still wanted her the next morning, there in his kitchen, even after he'd pushed her away. She'd felt the aching need in his kiss, the raw hunger in his body. Despite his words, he felt more for her than he wanted to admit.

And as long as that spark of desire remained, she wasn't going to give up.

Two days later she rented a car—a shiny blue Honda— and made the three-hour trip into Connecticut to visit Caroline and P.G.

She'd called the day before to tell them she was coming, then phoned her parents to let them know she'd be spending the night at home. Her mother was delighted, saying she and Ivy's father couldn't wait to see her.

But Ivy knew they would be less delighted when she broke the news about her decision to move out of her plush Upper West Side apartment and in with the guys in Bushwick, as she'd originally planned.

She'd already phoned Neil. He'd laughed and said the extra room was still hers whenever she wanted it. He'd even offered to waive her share of the rent until she found a job and got on her feet.

She was prepared to withstand all of her parents' arguments and persuasions; she knew there would be plenty. This time she would stand firm against them. She'd moved into James's building because of James, and ironically, he was the reason she was moving out—

not that she planned to share that tidbit of information with her parents.

As she neared her brother's house, the woody hills burst forth in mantles of rich, leafy greens and dark, earthy browns. She turned onto a two-lane road and rolled down her windows to enjoy nature—the birds trilling, the bees humming, and the sweet scents of honeysuckle and lavender drifting in the hot, humid air.

She turned again, this time onto a wide residential street that led to P.G. and Caroline's home. Their spacious, five-bedroom Victorian soon appeared, painted in cheery hues of pastel blue and yellow. The driveway was long and welcoming, shaded by stately elms and gracious two-hundred-year-old oaks.

An architect of national standing, her brother, Philip George Grayson III—shortened as a youngster to P.G. to distinguish him from his father—had originally planned to design and build a sprawling contemporary home for himself and his young bride.

Instead, Caroline had found the Victorian, a gracious old lady in need of care and attention. For Caroline, the house had been love at first sight, and P.G. hadn't had the heart to tell her no.

Over the next fourteen years, they'd sweated and slaved, poured heart and soul and a bundle of money into changing what P.G. indulgently called "the old pig's ear" into the glorious silk purse it was now.

He and Caroline had filled the house with love and laughter and babies. It didn't seem right its occupants should now know sickness and tears.

Ivy parked the car and studied the house and the two acres that surrounded it. Heirloom trees and mature bushes graced the grounds. Leather-leafed hydrangeas festooned with dish-sized mop heads of snowy white and pastel pink surrounded the house while masses of lilacs, forsythia, and nose-sweet mock orange carried a glory of texture and fragrance into the yard beyond.

A plain shell path wound through the yard like a foamy white ribbon cast adrift in a sea of color. Flowers of every height and variety, hundreds of delicate blooms, lifted their velvety faces to the sun. Toward the west, neat rows of vegetables thrived on hearty green vines sprung from the black fertile earth: pole beans, tomatoes, squash, eggplant, and onions, each ripening in their own way and time.

In the heart of it all stood Caroline—a wraith dressed in a floppy brimmed straw hat and a gauzy pink dress, her skin as pale as the path on which she stood. Caroline lifted a gloved, soil-stained hand to shade her eyes as Ivy stepped from the car.

Ivy was glad Madelyn had warned her what to expect. Her face would surely have given her away, so shocked was she at the dramatic changes the past few months had wrought in her sister-in-law.

Ivy lifted a hand and waved.

Caroline waved back, a smile of welcome curving her pretty bow-shaped mouth. She dusted garden loam from her gloved fingers, drew off the gloves, then stepped forward. "You're here. How was your trip?"

Ivy joined her near a massing of tall, cinnamon-tipped orange daylilies and purple coneflowers. "Great. It's a nice day for a drive."

She wrapped her arms around her sister-in-law, finding hard-edged bone where there should have been the soft give of flesh. She willed herself not to stiffen, continued the hug an extra second in unspoken apology.

When she pulled away, she glimpsed the thin, dull wisps of tawny hair Caroline had tucked up underneath her hat—hair that had always been glossy and thick, her one true vanity.

How it must pain her to watch it come out in clumps in her comb, Ivy thought.

She met Caroline's eyes, finding them the same as ever, soft and sweet as warmed caramel. She smiled and took Caroline's hand to give a loving squeeze. "How are you?"

"Not dead yet."

Ivy felt her eyes widen.

Caroline relented. "Sorry. Cancer humor. P.G. doesn't care for it either. A bad habit I've picked up recently at the hospital when I go in for my treatments. You get to know the other patients, and some of them are pretty blunt."

"That's okay. I, for one, am glad you're not dead yet."

Caroline laughed, the tension broken.

Ivy stepped back to survey the yard. "The place looks wonderful. Anything ripe yet in your garden?"

Caroline looked over her shoulder with obvious pride. "A mouthful of beans and some tomatoes, I think. The rest is still coming on. I'll pack a basket for you to take back."

"Oh, now, don't go to any trouble."

"It's no trouble. You know how I love the garden. Any chance I get to work in it is a pleasure. Besides, it takes my mind off things."

Ivy paused, unsure whether to pursue the opening. "So where are the kids?"

"At the grocery with P.G. and Laura. I don't do much of the marketing anymore." She laid a hand across her stomach. "The chemo makes me too nauseated to get in and out of the store in one piece." She glanced down the driveway as they strolled toward the house. "They should be back soon. Would you like something to drink?"

"Sure. It's hot out here under the sun. But let me get it. I've been in your house often enough to know where things are."

They mounted the steps to the covered wraparound porch. Ivy motioned Caroline toward a grouping of comfortable outdoor furniture. "Sit in the shade and I'll be right back."

"Okay," Caroline agreed. "Just a little cool water for me."

Ivy returned shortly, carrying two tall glasses of chilled water. Caroline's eyes were closed, an expression of weariness on her face.

"Here you go," Ivy said with false brightness.

Long moments passed as they sipped their drinks, listened to the rhythmic rise and fall of cicadas humming in the underbrush.

Ivy set down her glass, which was beaded with condensation from the heat. "So, how are you really?"

Caroline met her look. "Not so bad. The doctors think this second round of chemotherapy and radiation should do the trick. Only a few more weeks; then I can start to feel like myself again. Start eating again, hopefully in time to enjoy a little of the produce I've been working so hard to grow."

Ivy listened to her words but saw the shadow in Caroline's eyes, suspected she felt far worse than she let on. "You should have told us, you know," she reproved gently.

"Don't you start in on me too. I've already received a thorough scolding from your mother." She sighed. "I didn't want you worrying, the way you're all doing now. Even if I'd told you, what could you have done?"

"Been there for you, to help you in any way you needed."

"But you're always there for me," Caroline said with a gentle smile. "You always have been. That's the great thing about this family. We all stick up for each other."

Ivy nodded. "Yeah, we do."

Caroline reached out and wrapped her fingers around Ivy's wrist, her voice serious. "Ivy, there is one thing. If I don't make it. If I—"

Ivy cut her off before she could finish. "Don't talk that way. Of course you're going to make it. You're only thirty-four. You've got lots of years left."

"I pray you're right, but if you're not and the worst happens, promise me you'll look after P.G. and the children. Oh, not all the time," she amended at Ivy's obvious look of dismay, "just often enough to see they're getting on with their lives, finding some happiness along the way."

Caroline's eyes gleamed bright with intensity. "Especially P.G. Don't let him grieve forever. The children are young. They'll need a mother. A woman who'll love them as if they were her own. And P.G. will need a wife. He's the kind of man who's better off in a comfortable, settled relationship."

"Which he already has with you."

Caroline ignored her, released her grip. "He's stubborn as all the rest of you, and I worry he'll cut himself off, crawl into his work, and withdraw in a way that isn't healthy." In her lap, she began to clench and unclench her too-thin hand. "He deserves to be happy. He deserves to be loved."

"And he will be, happy and loved. By you. Because you're going to be here with him. With your children, to see them grow to adulthood. You're going to finish out these dreadful treatments and get strong again, healthy again."

Caroline refused to relent. "Promise me you'll do this."

Uncomfortable, Ivy shifted. "Why me? Madelyn's his twin. Wouldn't she be a better choice? Or Brie? She's closer to him than I am."

"That's exactly why. They're too close. You and P.G. love each other as brother and sister, but the years between you force some distance, some objectivity. You'll be able to view things through calm eyes." Caroline drew a ragged breath. "You're a good judge of character. You'll know if the woman he's with is the right one for him. Help me make him happy. Do this for me, Ivy. Promise me you will."

Caroline's making a mistake, Ivy thought. *Why pick me?*

She didn't have any influence over her brother, certainly not in a matter as serious as this. How on earth was she supposed to respond?

Ivy frowned. "I don't know. I—"

Caroline's face fell. "That's all right. I understand. It's too much to ask."

"It *is* a lot to ask." She looked at Caroline—at her friend and sister—who wanted, needed, the comfort of this request. How could she possibly deny her, regardless of her reservations? "All right. If you're really sure, then I'll do it."

Caroline brightened. "Really? Promise?"

"Yes, I promise. Though I still think you could choose someone better for the job."

"There is no one better." Caroline covered Ivy's hand again and squeezed. "Thank you."

They were discussing Caroline's latest book—she'd long ago established herself as a successful children's author—when a wine-colored minivan pulled into the driveway.

The doors slid open, and out scrambled a pair of children, followed by a coal black Scottie dog who raced around the vehicle, emitting a trio of exuberant barks.

P.G. exited next, his wavy russet hair glinting like fire beneath the strong summer sun.

From the passenger's side, Laura Grayson emerged: vivacious, blond, and energetic as ever at fifty-seven.

The kids pounded up the steps.

Heather, the younger one at four, looked adorable in a pink jumper embroidered with plump red strawberries. A crisp matching ribbon was threaded through her silky auburn curls. She leaped at Ivy for hugs and kisses, chattering about the present Grammy had bought her—a stuffed white toy cat.

Long and lanky, Brian hung back, reluctant at seven to participate in any overt displays of affection. Huggy-kissy stuff was for girls and wimps, he would say; everybody knew that.

But Ivy ignored his male stubbornness and pulled him into her arms for a hard embrace. He resisted for a few seconds, then pressed close, winding his slender boy's arms around her waist. Eyes closed, he turned his face into the warmth of her stomach.

She gazed down, brushed a lock of brown hair off his forehead, noting how much he'd grown since they'd last met. He had his mother's eyes, she saw as he tipped back his head—that same warm melting caramel. In them she glimpsed trouble, worry a boy his age shouldn't have to bear.

He knows, Ivy thought. *He understands how seriously ill his mother is.*

She wanted to reassure him, tell him everything would be all right. That the only fear he need face was worrying how far he'd hit the ball the next time he came up to bat in his Little League game.

But she couldn't.

No one could.

Brian pulled away and went to stand next to Caroline as Ivy exchanged kisses with her mother, then hugs with her brother.

Tall and broad-chested, P.G. looked his usual robust self except for the lines across his high forehead, grooves grown deeper with recent worry. They deepened more as he cast concerned eyes over his beloved wife.

"I told P.G. to hurry," Laura said to Ivy, "knowing you must have arrived by now. But the stores were packed and the roads were a nightmare. I've come to make dinner for everyone—baked pork chops with apples and mashed potatoes. I phoned your father. He should be along soon."

Heather wandered up and climbed into Caroline's lap to share her toy cat with her mother. Caroline played with one of her daughter's long curls, listening to the childish prattle, sudden weariness hanging over her like a shroud.

"Need help carrying in groceries?" Ivy asked, stepping toward her brother.

P.G. stood for a moment as if he hadn't heard, then gave a stiff nod. "Thanks. Mom just about bought out the store."

Laura laughed, determined to remain upbeat despite the wrenching byplay they'd all been witness to. "Oh, I left one or two items behind, including that very fine jar of mustard you refused to let me buy. Cruel boy."

P.G. set his hands on his hips. "Fifteen dollars for mustard? Even James wouldn't splurge on that, and he can buy anything on earth."

Ivy jolted at her brother's casual mention of James, making her realize she hadn't thought about him more than once or twice in the past hour. Preoccupied, she nearly missed P.G.'s next remark.

"He's coming up on Sunday for a visit." P.G. opened the rear door of the van, hefted out two bags of groceries. "He wants to treat us all to brunch at the country club, if Caro's up to it." He flicked a concerned glance over at his wife. "Maybe you should stay the weekend, Ivy. Tag along in case Caro and I can't make it. You and James, and Mom and Dad, could take the kids."

Stay and see James on Sunday? Sit through brunch with him in front of her family and endure the agony of pretending nothing had happened between them?

"No, I can't," she blurted before she had a chance to give in to her brother's wishes. "I . . . I've made plans and have to get back. I'm sorry."

P.G. frowned but didn't argue. "Okay. It was just a suggestion. Maybe next time."

She gave a wide, noncommittal smile, then leaned into the van for a bag of groceries.

CHAPTER TEN

James stayed away for a week.

Initially, he'd told himself it wouldn't be a problem having Ivy out of his life. It wasn't as if she'd been around much over the years, certainly not on a day-to-day basis as she'd been this summer.

But as the week wore on, he found himself thinking about her.

At work and at home.

In the morning and afternoon and evening.

Especially in the evening, when he lay alone in his big bed and remembered their night together.

There'd been only the one night, yet he couldn't get their lovemaking out of his mind. Worse, he dreamed about her, waking up aching and stiff with unsatisfied desire. He told himself such inappropriate appetites would fade; all he needed was time.

Spending the day around her family on Sunday didn't help matters. Seeing Caroline so ill made him sad, even after she agreed to visit an internationally re-nowned specialist he recommended.

Entertaining thoughts about Ivy made him feel guilty. And when the conversation at lunch turned in her direction, it became impossible to get Ivy off his mind.

He'd been shocked and displeased when he'd learned about her decision to move out of her Upper West Side digs and in with her slum-dwelling, bohemian friends. As he'd listened to her parents voice their confusion and distress, he'd sat mute and scowling, fully aware that he was the reason Ivy was moving.

He couldn't let her go through with it, which was his excuse today for breaking his self-imposed exile and going to see her.

Her door stood open when he arrived, propped wide with a stacked pair of packing boxes. His jaw tightened as he raised a hand to knock. "Hello," he called.

Moments later, a man appeared in the living room. He stopped and raised an expressive tawny eyebrow.

James remembered him from the party—Neil some-thing-or-other, Ivy's friend.

They stared at each other for a long unblinking mo-ment, like a pair of boxers measuring their best chance to get in a punch.

James cut through the silence. "Is Ivy here?"

Neil's lip curled. "Yeah, she's here." He crossed his arms and moved to block the entrance. "But I don't think she wants to see you."

James stepped forward, looking down from his su-perior height. "Why don't we let her decide that?"

"And why don't you—"

"Neil, who's at the door?" Ivy walked out of her studio, a set of canvases in her hands. She stopped amid the half dozen packing boxes that littered her foyer and living room. A mild sawdust smell hung in the air, big sheets of packing paper lying in a bundle on the floor.

"James," she said, setting the canvases against the wall.

"Hey." He tucked his hands into his pockets and stepped forward, bypassing Neil. "So what's all this about? Looks like you're moving."

"Gee, he's a bright one, isn't he?" Neil quipped.

Ivy turned a reproving look on her friend.

James enjoyed a short-lived gloat before she turned her sights back on him. His instant of satisfaction abruptly disappeared.

Neil eyed the pair of them, then bent to lift a box. "I'll take this one down to the truck. Then I think I'll walk over to Starbucks for a half-caf Caramel Macchiato. You want me to bring you something back, cupcake?"

"No, thanks. I'm fine. Take as much time as you'd like."

Neil shot James a warning scowl, then walked out.

James waited until the other man had gone and folded his arms over his chest. "So? Let's hear it."

She raked a thumbnail over the seam of her jeans pocket. "Hear what? I'm sure my parents have already told you everything."

"They told me enough. They're both quite upset about this move of yours. I wasn't very happy to hear about it either."

She swiveled abruptly, crossed to a display of knick-knacks arranged on one of the living room bookshelves. She moved an empty box into place, picked up a sheet of newsprint, and began to wrap breakables. "Is that the reason you came down here? To talk sense into me?"

"Yes, since you're apparently in need of some."

She shot him a defiant glare. "Then you can turn right around and go home. I already took an earful from my parents. I don't need you ragging on me too."

He worked to control his temper. "I'm not here to *rag* on you. I'm here to stop you from making a huge mistake."

She shoved a paper-wrapped ceramic dog into the box, started on another piece. "My decision to move is not a mistake, and I don't need your advice, however well intentioned it might be."

"Ivy . . . what do you want to do this for? You're comfortable here in this apartment. You're safe and you have the luxury of time to paint. You won't if you move out. You won't if you toss aside your parents' financial help."

"I'll get a job."

"Doing what? Some low-paying retail job that'll eat up all your time and energy? You want to paint. Stay here and paint. Take advantage of your parents' generosity."

She shook her head. "And your generosity as well. I know you had something to do with my living here. I was willing to let it go until now because . . . well, just because." She tucked another paper-wrapped figurine into the box, then turned to face him. "I should never have moved in here in the first place. I should have done what I'd planned—stood on my own two feet without anyone's aid or assistance. You said yourself I need more experience. Well, I'm going to get some."

He stepped nearer, careful to leave a good three feet of space between them. He couldn't risk giving in to the urge to touch her. Whether it was to shake some sense into her or just hold her close, he wasn't sure.

"You don't have to do this because of me, you know," he said, "because of something I said in the heat of the moment."

"I'm not," she declared, her voice filled with quiet conviction. "I'm doing it because of me."

Ivy straightened and set her hands on her hips, suddenly aware she meant every word. She was doing this for herself.

For her pride.

For her self-esteem.

She'd told herself she was leaving because of James, but that wasn't strictly true. She wanted him to be proud of her, wanted him to see her as a woman worthy of his admiration, his love. But more, she wanted to see those things for herself, in herself. She wanted to know she could be the independent, self-reliant woman she'd always imagined she would one day be. She wanted to know she could succeed.

"But you can't leave," he blurted.

A flicker of hope sprang to life inside her. An insane wish that he'd pull her into his arms and beg her to stay because he needed her. That he'd tell her he'd been wrong to toss her aside. That being without her had made him realize how much he truly loved her.

"Why not?" she murmured, her body softening.

He looked at her for another moment, then crossed his arms. "Because I promised your parents I'd watch over you. How can I do that if you're not even living in Manhattan anymore?"

His words struck her like a faceful of ice water.

What a stupid, sappy fool I am, she thought.

She turned away. "I need to finish packing." She reached for another knickknack, barely feeling it in her hand. "I'm only taking a few of my things. The rest will need to go into storage, including most of the furniture. It won't fit in my new place. I'll make arrangements to have it moved."

"The lease is good for a while, so just leave everything. You'll be back."

"No, I won't."

His arms dropped to his sides. "Ivy, what can I do to make you change your mind?"

She met his eyes, reading his frustration and feeling her own in return.

If you don't know, she thought, *maybe there is no hope for us, after all.*

"Nothing," she murmured with an ache in her chest. "Nothing at all."

Her mood melancholy, Ivy strolled along Fifth Avenue, one of the midweek multitude that hurried up and down the city sidewalks. Using a bit of skillful maneuvering, she eased out of the rush and slowed to peer at a window display of elegant leather handbags. A month ago she would have gone inside without a thought and treated herself to one of the store's new collection.

A cute little bag in brilliant cherry red beckoned to her through the glass.

Come in, it whispered.

Take me home, it urged in a seductive, enchanting voice.

But with no job and no income, the expense was out of the question. There were always her credit cards. . . . But no, she'd promised herself she'd use them only for emergencies. A new purse, however gorgeous it might be, was not an emergency.

She turned, forced herself to walk on.

She missed her old Upper West Side apartment; she was honest enough with herself to admit it. The space, the solitude, the amenities—like a shower that didn't run out of hot water halfway through and walls thick enough that you couldn't hear the guy upstairs peeing and flushing every morning at six a.m.

Her new roommates were great though, including Fred, who'd apologized for his drunken behavior the night of the Fourth. He'd told her he'd still like to be more than friends but that he'd keep his hands to himself unless she gave him the go-ahead. The next move, he'd told her with a wink and a grin, was strictly up to her. She'd laughed at his harmless flirting, relieved to know he remained heart-whole and that she wouldn't have to worry about him hitting on her—at least not much.

True to his word, he behaved like a perfect gentleman; they all did. As their first month together passed, her three new roommates did their best to make her feel comfortable and at home. They kept her from moping when the blues got the better of her too.

Which lately seemed to be most of the time.

If only James would quit calling to badger her about moving back. Despite the tough, independent stance she'd taken, she was weak enough to know she'd have tossed it all aside and returned if only he'd say the words she needed to hear.

Ivy, I miss you.

Ivy, I want you.

Please come home.

Instead he spent his time lobbing arguments and questions her way.

Her parents were worried, he'd say. Her family was concerned.

Had she found a job yet?

What about her painting? Was she making any progress crammed in such a tiny space?

What about food? Was she eating right?

Was she carrying the pepper spray he'd sent over in case she was mugged?

He was worse than an overprotective brother and mother hen rolled into one.

Last night she'd had enough.

When he called, she'd refused to speak to him, leaving Josh to make an excuse. Heart aching, she'd shut herself in her room, sat on her bed in the dark, and cried.

So much for her great plans. They all seemed to be crashing down around her feet, including the one that had seemed the simplest of all—finding a job. She'd never dreamed getting work would be so hard.

Apparently, three years of liberal arts education, with a major in art history, didn't count for much. She'd sent résumés all over town, but so far nada. No one wanted her artistic skills. And to her chagrin, she discovered she was overqualified for the most basic of positions. They wouldn't hire her even as a waitress or a cashier.

"You'll leave, honey," one crusty old manager had told her as he'd handed back her application. "Why should we train you so you can leave?"

"You'll be bored and quit in a week," another one said, ears closed to her pleas to the contrary.

Go back to college.

That was the refrain she'd been hearing a lot lately.

Finish your education.

Well, I'm not going back to college, she thought, one fist squeezed tight at her side. And she wasn't giving up on her dreams, not any of them. She'd vowed to be independent, to make her own way, her own life. To succeed and prosper at her art. And to win the heart of the only man she would ever love, even if she had to get over the hurdle of him refusing that love. Even if he was an infuriating hardhead who made her want to clobber him and kiss him all at the same time.

No, no matter how desperate and dark things seemed, she wasn't quitting. She couldn't afford to quit; she had far too much to lose.

She sighed and came to a halt in front of a boutique window. She sighed again as she gazed at the beautiful designer dress on display, arranged like a slice of sky over an improbably thin mannequin.

Maybe she'd go inside to cheer herself up. She'd just browse, she promised, nothing more.

What could it hurt to look?

A small metal bell on the door tinkled as she let herself inside.

Soft and feminine, the clean, pastel decor wrapped around her like a comfortable breeze, her feet sinking into plush camel carpet as she crossed farther into the space.

Artsy glass shelves and shiny metal racks held an array of merchandise, organized into neat rows, projecting a stylish rainbow of textures and hues. A pair of large cream-colored armoires, painted in the French provincial style with masses of flowers and curling vines and leaves on their fronts, stood in opposite corners, stocked with chemises and scarves, jewelry and other small accessories. A trio of changing rooms were tucked away to one side, a counter and register on the other.

A refreshing hint of beeswax polish lingered in the air, while classical music played at a discreet, soothing volume.

The shop stood empty with the exception of a single female customer who disappeared into one of the fitting rooms. Ivy drifted toward a row of silk blouses and began to peruse the trendy collection, wondering where the shop's clerk was.

She was eyeing a smart little skirt that would be perfect for her sister Brie when the other customer emerged from the fitting room.

"Excuse me," the woman said, approaching. "Could you help me with this dress?"

Politely, Ivy turned to face her.

Pretty, dark-haired, well-groomed. Mid-forties, if Ivy guessed right, with a creeping spread through the middle that ruined what had once likely been a splendid figure. The frown on the woman's forehead spoke to the vulnerability all women experience when trying on clothes, the naked uncertainty and critical self-doubt.

"I'm sorry," Ivy said. "I don't work here."

The woman hesitated for a second. "That's okay. You're a girl. What do you think?"

Reluctant to express an opinion but feeling pressured, Ivy skimmed an assessing look over the garment and the woman wearing it.

Too youthful, was her first thought. *Too short and tight around the hips.* Although the poppy orange color was both vivid and flattering to the woman's complexion.

Gracious, what to say?

"Well," Ivy began, "that shade is fantastic on you, brings out the roses in your cheeks. And the material is lovely, silky and sophisticated, but . . ."

"But? But what?" the woman pounced. "Be honest. I detest fudgers."

Ivy drew a breath. "But the style doesn't suit you. The cut makes the material pull around your hips and puts too much emphasis on your waist."

The woman turned to view her image in a nearby floor-length mirror. "You're right. Makes me look like a sack of meal."

"It's not that bad. Something without much of a waistline, though, might be better, and more tailoring. What's the dress for, by the way? Anything special?"

The woman heaved a sigh. "My daughter's engagement party. I need to look like a mother-of-the-bride, but I don't want to look like a stodgy old crone either."

"You're in no danger of that," Ivy reassured.

She thought about Madelyn and her mother, what they'd wear, and aimed for something in between. She walked over to a rack of dresses, began to flip through. She chose two, both of them sheath dresses, one in a deep rose, the other in violet.

"Oh, I couldn't wear either of those." The woman pointed a finger at the purple dress. "I'd look like a giant eggplant in that."

"Either color should be beautiful with your hair and skin tones. Try them on and see. What can it hurt?"

Obviously reluctant, the woman reached out for the dresses, muttering to herself as she disappeared into one of the fitting rooms.

She emerged a short while later in the rose dress, a bemused expression on her face. "I was certain it would be awful, but it's rather pretty, don't you think?" She did a small turn, moved to the mirror to study herself again.

"Oh, I like it." She smiled.

Ivy smiled back. "It's great. Very stylish. Slimming and elegant." Unlike the last dress, this one hit her just slightly above the knee, showing off a pair of very shapely calves. And without a waistline, her figure problems disappeared, leaving the illusion of a perfect silhouette.

"It is lovely, isn't it?" The woman made another admiring turn and pirouette, checking out her reflection.

"Hmm. Now, let's see you in the violet."

With much more confidence this time, the woman disappeared back into the fitting room.

Ivy strolled over to one of the armoires and studied the selection of printed scarves. She had several draped over one arm when she heard a loud throat clearing.

She turned. "Wow!"

If the rose had been pretty, the violet was fabulous. Rich and vibrant, it was everything she'd imagined and more.

"You look fantastic," Ivy declared.

The woman beamed, then giggled. "I know. I can't believe how great this dress is, and all because of you. I can't remember the last time I felt this special, this sexy." She traced a hand over the material. "I'm going to buy both. Wear the rose one to my daughter's party and save this for my husband. It'll knock his socks off."

They shared a laugh.

Having fun, Ivy held out a gauzy blue and purple silk scarf. "What do you think of this to accessorize?"

"Oh, Mrs. Weinstein, please forgive me for neglecting you." A short, trim woman in black rushed out from a room in the rear of the shop, a harried, apologetic expression on her face. "I hope you've been finding what you need. I'm here alone today and was caught on the phone with one of my suppliers. My usual girl, well, she quit this morning, no notice. And I can't get ahold of my other girl to save my soul."

Mrs. Weinstein paused. "Oh, that's all right." She motioned toward Ivy. "This delightful young woman has been helping me. She's a real gem. If you were smart, you'd find some way to hire her."

Ivy flushed lightly at the compliment.

"I'm going to take this dress and one other," Mrs. Weinstein informed the saleswoman, "and anything else—" She broke off, gazed at Ivy. "What's your name, sweetheart?"

"Ivy."

"And anything else Ivy suggests. Now, let me see those scarves."

The saleswoman stood back while Ivy helped Mrs. Weinstein finish shopping. Once the woman retreated into the dressing room, the saleswoman sidled up to Ivy.

"Twenty-five percent off anything you'd like, Miss . . . ?"

"Grayson. Ivy Grayson."

"Nora Gardner." She held out a hand. "A pleasure to meet you. I'm the manager here."

Ivy shook the older woman's hand.

"I'm greatly in your debt," Nora declared. "Janice Weinstein comes in here at least once a month, tries on half a dozen pieces, and never buys a thing. You've made a real breakthrough today. You aren't looking for a job by any chance, are you?" she added in a joking voice.

Until that moment, Ivy hadn't considered working in a store like this; she didn't have any experience in sales. Then again, she'd actually had fun assisting Mrs. Weinstein—an apparently difficult customer she hadn't found difficult at all. It would be like playing dress-up, only for real.

Should she say something? she wondered. It was now or never, or the opportunity would be gone.

"As a matter of fact," Ivy said, "I am looking for work."

Nora Gardner's dark eyes twinkled. "Really? Excellent. Once I ring up Mrs. Weinstein's purchases, let's have a cup of a tea and we'll discuss your salary and hours."

CHAPTER ELEVEN

"Thanks for agreeing to see me." James rose politely while Madelyn took a seat across the table from him.

She sent him a quick half smile. "No trouble."

The waiter appeared and offered her a menu. He rattled off the daily specials, took her drink order, then moved away.

She placed her menu to one side and looked at James. "I have to admit it was a surprise hearing from you. It's been a long time since we had lunch together."

"Yes, it has," he said. Long enough, he realized, to seem like a lifetime. "So, how are you?"

"Fine. Same as yesterday when you called, though a bit more exhausted. The twins are teething and Hannah was up half the night crying, poor thing. But I'm sure you didn't ask me here to talk about my babies."

"No." Agitated, he picked up his teaspoon and

stirred his coffee. Tapping the spoon twice on the rim, he set it back on the saucer with a clatter. "You have to do something about Ivy."

Madelyn raised an eyebrow. "Why? What's she done now?"

"You know what she's done. She's moved out—"

"Here you go." The waiter placed Madelyn's glass of sparkling water on the table, together with a small green bottle containing a scant inch more. "Have you made any decisions yet?"

"No." James snapped, uncharacteristically irritated by the interruption.

Madelyn sent a small, apologetic smile toward the hapless waiter. "If you could give us a little while longer, thanks."

"Of course." The man shot James a look. "Take your time."

"So, you were saying." She reached into the basket of rolls, chose one covered in sesame seeds.

He took a breath. "I was saying that she's moved out of a comfortable, secure apartment, into a sleazy hovel with those disreputable friends of hers."

"I don't believe Ivy has any disreputable friends, but yes, I'm aware of her move."

"And?"

"And what?" She broke the roll in half and reached for the butter. "The move was her choice, and despite a lot of anxious hand-wringing from our parents, she seems to be doing well."

"*Well*? Do you know she's working in a dress shop?"

"You make it sound like a bong shop, but yes, I

know the place. Reflections is a very fine establishment."

"I don't care how fine it is; it's still a dress shop. Ivy's better than some minimum-wage drudge job. She doesn't need that. She ought to be using her God-given talents, not wasting her time toiling for pennies. She ought to be painting."

Madelyn ate a bite of roll. "From what she tells me, she is painting. As much as her schedule allows. And by the way, she makes twelve fifty an hour, plus commission."

"What?"

"Twelve fifty an hour. A decent step up from minimum wage."

"It's still slave wages," he grumbled, lifting his cup to swallow a hasty mouthful of hot coffee. "But that isn't the point. The point is she didn't need to move. She ought to have stayed where she was. Where your parents wanted her to be. Where she was safe and sound and could have concentrated on her art instead of wasting her time in some ridiculous attempt to prove she can make it on her own."

Madelyn rested an elbow on the table, folded a fist under her chin. "Hmm, and why was it she suddenly felt compelled to do such a thing? She won't tell me— always mumbles something about needing to put a little experience under her belt, gain a bit more maturity. You wouldn't happen to know why, now, would you?"

He fought the urge to squirm under the look she cast him. She always had been too smart for her own good.

Abruptly, he wished he'd never brought her into this. What had seemed like such a good idea yesterday suddenly wasn't. Frustrated beyond measure at the time, he'd wanted to enlist Madelyn's help to see if she could do what he hadn't been able to do himself. Force Ivy to come to her senses.

He'd been stewing, he admitted, furious ever since Ivy'd stopped taking his calls.

How dare she refuse to talk to me?

In her whole life, she'd never refused him anything. Now that's all she seemed to be doing.

Refusing him.

"So," Madelyn continued, "what did happen between the two of you after I left that day? I never heard the details."

He scowled fiercely. "And you won't hear them from me." He turned his head, suddenly eager for an interruption. "Looks like our waiter's hovering again. Perhaps we'd better order before he calls for the manager."

Madelyn gave him another knowing look, then opened her menu.

Once they'd ordered and were alone again, she started in. "So, let's have it. What'd you do to her?"

"What do you mean, what did I do to her?" Before he could prevent it, a guilty flush crept up his neck.

Her eyes zoomed right to the spot. "Other than that," she amended. "I know she wasn't upset about that. I assume you're the one who broke it off."

"Of course I broke it off." He sighed. "That night should never have happened. I should never have let it happen. Hell, I'd think you'd be relieved to know it's over."

The blue of her eyes deepened. "I should be, shouldn't I? So, what did you say to make her run?"

"She didn't *run*; she left. And I told you I wasn't going to discuss details. Those're between Ivy and me."

He tapped his fingers against the tablecloth. "All I'm going to say is, mistakes were made, mistakes that set her off on this foolish course of hers. If it weren't for that, she'd still be living seven floors down from me. She'd still be painting, instead of working at some useless, dead-end job in order to prove something she doesn't need to prove at all."

He reached out, grabbed Madelyn's hand without conscious thought. "Meg, you have to help. You have to convince her to come back. It isn't right, her living like she is. It isn't right, her cohabitating with those men."

He released her hand as a muscle ticked in his jaw. "The two gay ones are all right, I suppose. But it's that dancer, that *ballet* dancer, I don't like. And why the hell is he straight anyway? Who ever heard of a male ballet dancer who isn't gay?"

"How about Baryshnikov or Godunov?"

Ignoring that, he rushed on. "You should see the way he looks at her, like a wolf ready to feast on fresh meat. He hit on her at that Fourth of July party. Did you know that? Got drunk and tried to lure her into his bedroom. And now she's living with him. She thinks he's safe, says he *apologized*. Apologized—ha. He's just biding his time, waiting for the right moment to make his next move. I know men, and they have only one thing on their minds. Sex. He wants to have sex with my Ivy."

He crushed a small cocktail napkin in his fist, too preoccupied to notice the oddly arrested expression on Madelyn's face.

"You have to help me get her out of there," he grated. "She isn't safe. She's trusting, far too trusting for her own good. She just doesn't realize the trouble she's in. I've tried to warn her, but she won't listen to me. You're her sister. Surely you can make her see reason."

A long silence followed before Madelyn spoke, her amazement plain. "You're jealous."

Her words stung him like an electrical shock. "What?"

"Jealous. You're jealous. And what's more, you're in love with her."

He gave a hollow-sounding laugh. "Don't be ridiculous. I'm nothing of the sort. I'm simply concerned for her."

"Hmm-hmm, right. I don't believe I've ever seen you so thoroughly stirred up before, not even over me."

"Stop it, Madelyn. There's nothing between Ivy and me but a longtime sibling affection."

"Oh, so you make a habit of sleeping with women you think of as your sister, do you?"

He shot her a scorching glare.

She ignored him. "Admit it, James. You love her."

"Hey, since when did I become the focus of this conversation?" he said, brushing over her assertion. "This is about Ivy. This is about getting her to move out of that rat-hole apartment she's living in."

"This is about a lot more than an apartment. And when it comes to Ivy, you're always involved. I've recently come to realize that." Her voice lowered, softened. "She loves you, you know."

He scoffed. "She thinks she does, at any rate."

"You mean she's told you?"

"Yes, she's told me."

"And you don't believe her?"

"What I believe is that she's concocted some elaborate romantic fantasy about me over the years, a fantasy that isn't any more real or lasting than a dream. She's infatuated, nothing more, nothing less. It'll wear off soon enough."

"And will it wear off for you too?"

His gut clenched at her question.

Is she right? Do I love Ivy? Even if he did, what difference would it make?

He drained the rest of his coffee in a single gulp, uncaring that it had gone cold.

Their waiter chose that moment to arrive with their meals, food James no longer had any desire to eat. He and Madelyn sat in silence as they were served, his coffee refilled with fresh, her water replenished with a second effervescing bottle.

Madelyn's hand lingered hesitantly over her fork. "I've said too much and you're angry. Perhaps I should leave?"

"I'm not angry." More like shocked. "Eat your meal."

He jabbed a fork into the poached salmon fillet on

his plate and chewed a bite without really tasting it. He drank some coffee, nearly scalding his tongue.

He hissed and put out the burn with a drink of ice water. "So does that husband of yours know we're having lunch together?"

Madelyn swallowed a forkful of pasta, then patted her lips with her napkin. "Yes. He knows. We don't keep things from each other. He trusts me."

"The way I did. Once."

Her face fell. "After your call, after today, I'd hoped you might be ready to put the past behind us. James, I can't ever make up for what I did to you. I can't ever be sorry enough for the pain and humiliation I caused. But what I did was for the best, for us both."

He shot her a look. "You think so?"

"Yes. And you'd see that too if you'd only let yourself. It was never right. *We* were never right together, not as a couple."

"Weren't we?"

She set her utensil aside. "Remember when I first moved to New York?"

He frowned. "Of course. What does that have to do with anything?"

"I didn't live in the best neighborhood, and my roommates always had men over. I even dated a few of them, as I recall. You never went ballistic and told me to move out."

"The situation with Ivy is not the same. She's young and inexperienced."

"So was I, then."

"She's different," he defended.

Madelyn reached out and briefly laid a hand on his sleeve. "Yes, she is. And your feelings for her are different from the ones you had for me. I was your friend first before I was anything else. I was your buddy. But Ivy's not your buddy. She's the girl you protected as she grew up. She's the woman you still feel compelled to shield, the woman you can't let go."

"She was never mine to keep or to let go."

"Wasn't she? You've asked me to help you convince her to come back. But I don't think I'm the right person for the job. You're the only one whose opinion really matters to Ivy."

He sighed. "I told you she won't listen to me."

"Then perhaps you aren't saying the right words. Think about it, James. Do what your heart tells you, not what's in your head."

"Like you did with Douglas?" he said, looking into her eyes again.

"Yes," she said quietly. "Like I did with Zack."

He waited for it, the familiar bitter ache that always tore through him like a knife when Madelyn was near. The memories of what they'd been to each other. The memories of what they'd lost.

What he'd lost.

But even as he waited, the feelings didn't come.

He stared across at her, traced the shape of her lovely face, imagined kissing her soft, red lips, touching her ripe figure and felt . . . nothing, at least nothing remotely akin to desire.

His passion for her was gone.

All that remained was a pleasant warmth and a curious comforting peace along with the lingering remnants of their friendship—a bond that apparently was too strong to die.

Wasn't that why he called her here today, because of that friendship?

She peered at him, a worried expression on her face. *Can it be? Am I really over her?* he asked himself.

Yes, he realized, *it would seem that I am.*

"Thanks, Madelyn."

She looked startled. "For what?"

"For being there. For being a friend."

A wide smile lit her features. "I am. Always. I've missed having you in my life."

"Same here, though you know it won't be like it was before."

"No. Maybe it'll be better."

Ivy had had a lousy day, a hot, sweaty, frustrating day, which got exponentially lousier the moment she walked through the apartment door.

There on the kitchen table, staring at her like an evil eye, lay a sorrowfully familiar package. Its canceled postage and raggedy manila edges a testament to its less-than-tender treatment at the hands of the U.S. Postal Service. The address label she'd attached so hopefully to its front weeks ago smirked back at her.

She didn't need to open the envelope to know what it would say inside.

Thank you for your submission. Unfortunately, your work isn't right for our gallery at this time, blah, blah, blah.

Yeah, right. Why didn't they just write what they really thought?

Get lost, loser.

Deliberately turning her back on the package, Ivy went into her bedroom to change out of her work clothes. In disgust, she tossed her expensive leather shoes—the ones with the broken heel that had caused her so much grief today—into the trash.

Minutes later, clad in faded jeans, a pale peach cotton T-shirt, and socks, she made her way back to the kitchen. She inspected the contents of the refrigerator, settled on a tall glass of grape juice.

She set the untouched drink on the counter next to the sink and gave the envelope another long look. Unable to control the self-defeating impulse, she reached out and tore open the package, needing to know which gallery had sent her submission back.

A CD of her artwork tumbled out along with a piece of white stationery. Turning it over, she read the name embossed at the top and enough of the canned reply below to make her throat squeeze tight. Tears she'd told herself she wouldn't shed welled in her eyes, streamed down her cheeks, warm and wet.

She collapsed onto one of the kitchen chairs and blubbered.

She was sniffing into a crumpled wad of tissues, her face swollen and miserable, when Neil found her twenty minutes later.

He rushed to set aside the sack of groceries in his arms. "Hey, cupcake, what's wrong? What's happened?"

She saw his eyes land on the scattered contents of the envelope on the table, watched his instant recognition.

"Oh, sweetie. I'm sorry," he said.

She buried her nose in the tissues, squeezed out a few more tears.

"Here." He reached out, gathered her in his long arms. "Give me a great big hug."

She did, taking comfort.

"Better?"

"Not much, but thanks anyway." She pulled back, wiped at her reddened eyes.

He took the chair beside her. "Well, they're idiots and you should be glad they didn't want you. Obviously, they can't see talent when it's staring them right in the face. They must be cousins of the casting directors who keep giving my parts to other people. How else can you explain overlooking a pair of artistic geniuses like you and me?"

The remark earned a tiny smile. "Thanks. You know just what to say."

"Hey, I've had loads of practice. Now, let's see that great smile of yours."

She forced her lips to curve upward to mockingly show him her teeth.

He laughed; then she did too, her spirits lifting fractionally.

"Now, that's more like it," he said. "You have a shining gift, Ivy. The whole world will see it for themselves one of these days. Until then, your mission is to keep painting and not give up."

"You either. You're a fabulous actor."

"Damn straight. No way am I going to wait tables the rest of my life."

He stood, crossed to unload groceries from the brown paper bag he'd abandoned when he'd first arrived. "In the meantime, how about one of my famous mile-high hoagies? Hot ham, salami, and provolone cheese with spicy peppers and onions on an Italian roll. Sound good?"

"Sounds great. Want help?"

He shooed her back into her chair. "No, no. The master must work alone." He picked up the glass of grape juice she'd forgotten on the counter and handed it to her. "Yours, I believe."

She sipped her juice while Neil assembled the sandwich.

He rolled the hoagie inside a cocoon of aluminum foil then popped it into the hot oven. After rinsing his hands in the sink, he tossed her a probing look. "All right. Out with it."

"Out with what?"

"Whatever it is that still has you looking so gloomy."

She glanced away. "It's nothing. I'm fine."

"Don't lie to the gay man, dear heart. We're intuitive, you know, like dogs before an impending earthquake. Our senses are finely honed."

"Is that so? Then why don't you work your magic and tell me what's wrong?"

He studied her for a long, hard moment. "I'd say you've got man trouble. *Old* man trouble, if I don't miss my guess."

She scowled at his accuracy. "James is *not* old."

"Well, now, that's a matter of opinion. My oldest brother's younger than him, and I'm the baby in a family of seven kids." He met her expression. "Okay, okay, I'll quit teasing you. What's Mr. Sunshine up to these days?"

"Nothing. And that's the problem. I haven't heard from him in days."

"Maybe that's because you've been refusing to take his phone calls."

"Well, all he ever does is scold me and I—" She paused, taking a deep, shaky breath. "Oh, Neil, I think I've made a terrible mistake. I have a job. I'm proving myself, but it isn't making a bit of difference. James is farther out of my reach than ever. He was supposed to realize by now how much he misses me, needs me. But all he wants is for me to move back to my old apartment and go on the way things were before, before . . ."

"The *night*," he inserted.

Neil knew all about her messed-up romance with James. She'd confided in him only days after the event, needing a sympathetic ear and a sturdy shoulder to cry on.

"Yes, the *night*." She spun her empty juice glass between her thumb and forefinger. "Perhaps I ought to give in, go back. At least I'd see him every once in a while. At least I wouldn't be shut out of his life completely."

"And what good would that do?" Neil folded his arms, leaned back against the counter. "You want him to love you and respect you. He isn't going to do either if you go crawling back on his terms. He treats you like a child. If you do as you're told now, it'll only prove to him he's right, that you are too young, too inexperienced, too immature, especially for him. Call him up. See him if you want to. But don't go back, not like this."

Her shoulders drooped. "If only I didn't love him so much. If only it didn't hurt so much."

"I wish it didn't, sweetie. Personally, I think you could do a whole lot better than Mr. Arrogant Richie-Rich, but there's no explaining the ways of the heart. Give it time. Give him time. If it's meant to be, he'll realize what an asshat he is and come to your door to sweep you off your feet."

"What if he never does? And he isn't an asshat," she defended.

He shrugged as if agreeing to disagree. "Look, worst-case scenario, you'll have your work and your pride and, eventually, you'll find someone else to love. If I were you, though, I wouldn't worry too much about it."

"Oh? Why not?"

"Because from what I've seen of the guy, he's got a real case on you. Jealous, possessive. He practically snarls anytime another man so much as glances your way. Hell, he even tried to scare me off, and we all know I'm no threat in that department. And he *hates* Fred. Do the boy a favor and give him a heads-up if your billionaire boyfriend decides to drop by. Otherwise I fear Fred's dancing days may be numbered."

"If you're implying James would hurt him, you're wrong. James isn't the violent sort."

"Baby cakes, we're all the violent sort given the right provocation."

"Well, he's not. And the whole issue's neither here nor there. I'm not interested in Fred, and James knows that. I've told him Fred and I are friends, nothing more."

He quirked an eyebrow. "I'd love to have heard how that went down. He's got to know Fred would be all over you if you'd just crook your little finger in his direction. A man in lust never entirely gives up hope, my dear. And neither should you."

"No, I suppose not. You're right, and I'm going to try to cheer up, starting now."

"That's the ticket. With that in mind, I suggest you go out and start having some fun."

"I have fun," she protested.

"No, you work. Either you're up at that dress shop selling clothes or here at the apartment locked away in your room, painting."

"I enjoy painting."

"Yeah, but even Michelangelo needed a break every now and again. Josh is playing at a new club tomorrow night. Lulu's in a great off-Broadway musical, and although ballet's never been my favorite, Fred's good for matinee seats at his latest event. You're attending them all."

"When will I have time?"

"We'll make time. Do you want James, the giant poophead, to think you're sitting around moping over him?"

"Neil, behave. James is not a poophead any more than he's an asshat."

He grinned. "Hey, love is blind. So, are you going to fade away in this apartment?"

She straightened her shoulders in sudden decision. "No, I suppose not."

"Then get with it, cupcake. There're some people I want you to meet at a coffeehouse nearby. I think you'd like them. They're artists like us."

"All right."

"Good." The timer dinged for their sandwich. He crossed to pull it out of the oven. "After we eat, we'll head over, see who's around. If we run into a girl named Bianca, don't let her shock you."

"Why would she shock me?"

"Her hair, for starters. Takes some getting used to."

"Why? What's wrong with her hair?"

"She wears it à la the Medusa, as she calls it. Little braids that stick out all over her head like a coil of snakes."

"Sounds different."

"Oh, it's different, all right, especially since she dyed it green."

Ivy laughed.

He divided the sandwich onto plates and passed one to Ivy. "Eat up, cupcake. The night is young, and so are we."

CHAPTER TWELVE

"Do you need me for anything else tonight?"

James glanced up from the stock reports he was reviewing, shifted his attention to his executive assistant. "No. I'm fine, Tory. Go on home. And thanks for sacrificing your Friday evening to finish up those contracts."

"All part of the job." She moved farther into James's expansive office. "It'll be dark soon. Shall I turn on a few lights before I leave?"

The late-summer sun was beginning to lose its brilliance, rays of mellow gold casting a shimmery haze over the horizon, glinting against the broad glass walls that separated the room from the outside world.

"No, I won't be much longer."

She seemed relieved by his statement. "Good. Then I won't need to worry about you falling asleep here again tonight. Imagine my surprise, walking in and finding you on the couch this morning."

He gave her a wry half smile. "Sorry about that. I promise I'll be good and sleep at home this evening."

Instead of saying good night, she lingered, a small frown on her face. "You can tell me to mind my own business, but is everything all right? You've seemed a little on edge lately."

Edgy. Moody. Taciturn. Gruff.

He'd been all those things and more.

Ever since his lunch with Madelyn more than a week ago, he'd been short-tempered and distracted. Just yesterday he'd come down hard on a new employee—a fresh-faced kid barely out of graduate school—for misquoting a series of industry figures in a report.

Easily caught with no lasting damage, the mistake was the sort he should have let pass. Normally he would have, remembering to put a word in the right ears later on to make certain the error got fixed. Instead he'd made an issue of the matter in the middle of a meeting. His few clipped sentences enough to bring mortified color into the young man's cheeks and a sheen of moisture to his overeager eyes.

James thought now of those eyes, a wave of guilt assailing him for taking his personal frustrations out on a young guy just starting out.

He sighed. "It's nothing, Tory. A lot on my mind lately, that's all."

"Maybe you should take a vacation," she suggested. "You haven't had a real break in months."

He picked up his gold fountain pen, turned a page of his report in dismissal. "Yes, but I haven't got the time right now. I'll give it some thought though."

"All right. Let me know if I can clear any of your calendar."

"I will. Have a good weekend."

"You too." She took a few steps toward the door, then turned back. "James."

He looked up. "What?"

"Do something impulsive this weekend, will you? Just for the fun of it."

"Impulsive, huh?"

"Yeah. It's nice to act like a kid every now and again, even if it's not always so easy to feel like one."

"Good night, Tory."

"Good night, James."

He continued working after she'd gone, after the outer office lights had been dimmed and the only sound in the corridors was the distant droning hum of a vacuum cleaner being used by one of the night cleaning crew.

He rubbed a hand over the back of his neck, then laid down his pen. He watched it roll across his desk and come to a stop against his empty coffee cup.

I have to quit thinking about her.

For weeks now Ivy'd filled his mind, his life. First with her vibrant, unpredictable presence, sweeping in like a warm wind to stir up his carefully arranged—albeit mildly tedious—existence. Spreading laughter and sunshine in her wake, beauty and surprise. And passion. She'd brought that to him as well. A pure, un-jaded want that for those few brief hours had made the world go away.

But then it had been over, leaving a void inside him

he didn't understand and hadn't anticipated. He'd known her her whole life, and yet suddenly he no longer seemed to know her at all.

Who was this girl who made him smile? This woman who turned him inside out and upside down?

Was Madelyn right? Did he love Ivy?

Ever since Madelyn had made the suggestion, he'd been unable to get her words out of his head. They'd been there, whizzing around like pinballs, setting off bells and whistles and alarms all over the place.

He still wanted Ivy; he knew that.

Even after all this time, he had dreams. Hot, sweaty, aching dreams that plagued him day and night. It was one of the reasons he'd crashed here on his office sofa last night. He hadn't wanted to face another night alone, lying in his bed where she'd once slept.

Dear God, maybe I really do love her.

The idea shot a tremor straight through him.

And if I do love her, then what?

She claimed to love him.

Maybe he should see where it took them despite all the obstacles in the way.

Do something impulsive this weekend.

Tory's words echoed in his ears.

Impulsive, hmm?

What would Ivy think of Paris?

If they left by eleven, his jet could have the two of them there in time to watch the sunrise crest over the Seine. They'd find a quiet patisserie and breakfast on delicate brioches and fresh, warm croissants with but-

ter and jam and cups of steaming café au lait. Then he'd
show her the city as she'd never seen it before.

He reached out to turn off his computer, then dialed
a phone number before he had enough time to change
his mind.

He rapped his fist on the door to apartment 419. While
he waited for an answer, he eyed the quarter-sized spot
of brown paint that had worn away beneath the pitted
chrome knocker.

"They're all out tonight."

He swiveled his head toward the Queens drawl.

A lanky blonde with a pair of the longest legs he'd
ever seen exited the apartment across the hall. She
yanked her door closed with a hard slam, then jiggled
the key in the lock until the bolt finally slid home with
an audible click.

She turned, rolled her gray eyes, and gave him a wry
smile. "I've complained about this lock a hundred
times. Do they fix it? Of course not." She opened her
purse, dropped the keys inside. "Who're you lookin'
for?" She angled her head toward 419.

"Ivy. Ivy Grayson. Do you know her?"

"Sure, I know her. I know all my neighbors." Eyes
alert, she gave him a quick once-over from head to toe.
"You aren't her brother, are you?"

His jaw firmed. "No. I'm not her brother."

"I just thought . . . both of you being so blond and all."

"Ivy and I, we're . . . old friends," he explained, seeing her curiosity. He held out his hand. "James Jordan."

"Lulu Lancaster. A pleasure." She smiled broadly, taking the hand he offered. "Ivy sure has some nice taste in friends. Attractive, well dressed, and polite. We don't see much of that around here. Though we don't see many classy girls like Ivy around here either. She's a sweetheart."

"Yes, Ivy's one of a kind. You wouldn't happen to know where she's gone this evening, would you? Or when she might be planning to return?"

"Hmm, not sure. She had a date. I know that. No telling where they went. She probably won't be home for hours, if at all, if you know what I mean," she finished on a wink.

"A date?" One hand squeezed into a fist at his side.

"Yeah. Some guy she's been seeing for the past couple weeks. I can never remember his name." She waggled a finger in the air as she thought. "Kirk, Karl, something like that, something with a K. He's an artist."

His gut squeezed, hard and sick. "Is he?"

"Neil introduced them at this coffeehouse where he and Josh hang. Ivy really seems to have hit it off with the guy. They talk art, old masters and all that boring la-la stuff. You should hear them. Very intense—brushstroke this, contrast that. I listen for five minutes and my eyes begin to roll to the back of my head."

She flexed a foot, displaying a long, shapely leg. "I'm more physical. Dancing's my passion."

He stood silently, her words ringing in his ears.

Ivy was on a date.

Ivy was seeing another man.

"Hey, you don't look so good all of a sudden." Lulu stepped closer, tipped her head back for a better angle. "Are you okay?"

He gathered his grim emotions around himself like a heavy coat. "I'm fine. I need to get going." He turned away.

"I'll tell Ivy you stopped by," she called after him.

His footsteps slowed. He tossed her a last look. "No. No need. My visit wasn't important. Nice to have met you, Lulu."

She nodded, a troubled frown on her brow. "Yeah, back at ya."

He took the stairs at breakneck speed; he couldn't wait to get out of there.

Reaching the bottom floor, he pushed outside into the warm, muggy night air. A cat yowled, spooked by his abrupt exit. It darted away on quick, silent paws, disappeared around the corner.

A couple, arms looped around each other's waists, strolled around him where he stood in the middle of the sidewalk. He barely noticed their intimate murmurings as they continued on.

So, he'd been right.

A little more than a month and already she'd found someone new. Kirk or Karl from the coffeehouse, who shared a common interest in art and who knows what else.

Twentysomething, no doubt. Handsome. Charming and penniless as well.

But Ivy wouldn't care about that. She'd never cared about money, never been impressed by it the way so many others were. That's one thing he'd always found so refreshing about her; she didn't like him for his money.

She said she loved me.

Obviously, once she'd moved away, had a chance to rethink her feelings for him, she'd realized her mistake.

A crush, just as he'd figured.

What an idiot he was, believing even for a second that there could have been something real and lasting between them. Thank God she hadn't been there to-night. Thank God he hadn't had a chance to tell her his plans, reveal his newfound feelings, his ridiculous dreams.

Well, those dreams were dead. His feelings, he knew, would take a bit longer to erase.

He walked to his black Mercedes parked at the curb. He turned off the alarm, clicked open the locks, and climbed inside. He sat for a moment, then dialed a number on the car phone.

"Yes, this is Jordan. I ordered the jet for this evening. My plans have changed. I won't be needing it after all."

Ivy tapped discreetly on the dressing room door. "How are you doing? Is the pant combination working out better than the dress?"

"Hmm. I believe it is."

The hinged three-quarter door opened from the in-side, and Ivy took a look at her customer, an energetic, chestnut-haired mother of two. She had small breasts, broad hips, and a no-nonsense attitude that defied any-one to hold her figure flaws against her.

The woman had come into the shop needing something for a party—her party—being hosted in honor of her forty-fifth birthday, which was due to arrive in six days, whether, she'd told Ivy with a mock growl, she liked it or not.

Relaxed yet stylish with just enough kick to make it fun. Dramatic but not outrageous, that's the sort of outfit the client, Rhonda, had told Ivy she was looking for.

So far they'd been through ten outfits.

This was the eleventh.

Rhonda turned in a slow circle, showing off the long-sleeved organza blouse with ruffled collar and cuffs. The material was dyed in feminine swirls of apricot and pink, the wide-legged trousers cut and colored to match in the palest of peach. "What do you think?"

"It's not what I think that's important," Ivy said. "How do *you* feel in the outfit? Does it make you feel pretty?"

"No, no. I'm not saying a word until you give me your unbiased reaction."

She met Rhonda's inquiring brown eyes. "I think it's smashing. Honestly."

"You don't think the ruffles are too much?"

"On anyone else, yes. On you, no way. The cut of the blouse is just right, emphasizing your shoulders and drawing attention to your face. While the pants show off your height and slim your hips. If you didn't have the confidence to carry it off, I would never have suggested it."

Rhonda grinned like a schoolgirl sharing secrets with her BFF. "This is the one. The material's so soft and the color's to die for. When you brought it in, I nearly laughed and sent it back. But you were right. It's exactly what I need for my party. You're a miracle worker, Ivy."

She dismissed the notion with a hand. "Just glad we had what you wanted."

Rhonda pivoted for another look in the set of full-length mirrors. "You have a real eye for design and especially for color. Brilliant."

"Probably a by-product of my art training."

Rhonda cocked her head. "Art training? What sort of art?"

"Oh, painting, drawing. I studied in college. That's my real passion. I'm working here until I can get my art career going."

"Have you tried at any of the galleries?"

"A few. No luck yet."

"Well, it's a tough profession. Even the great ones struggle at first."

Ivy nodded. "Yes. Well, I'll wait for you out front, unless there's something else you'd like to try on?"

Rhonda flipped over the price tag. "No, this will do more than enough damage for one day."

Ivy gathered an armful of rejected clothes from the hooks in the dressing room, then left Rhonda to change.

Her conversation with the other woman had her feeling abruptly disheartened. She was having a hard time lately buoying her spirits even with Neil's determined campaign to keep her busy and active. She had him to thank for a new friend and confidant though, fellow artist Kip Zahn.

He was a sculptor by choice, waiter by necessity. She and Kip had been drawn toward each other by common interests and backgrounds. The youngest son of two distinguished West Coast attorneys, he'd also traded privilege and comfort for a chance to prove himself and succeed at his dream on his own terms.

With less than a semester to go, he'd abandoned college and the career in law his parents had wanted for him. And just like Ivy, he was nursing a bruised and bleeding heart; the girl he loved had been unwilling to leave her old life behind to start a new one with him.

He'd taken Ivy out to dinner and a movie the other night as a kind of thank-you. She was posing for him, her modesty protected by a cleverly draped sheet. Easy as it might seem to find willing models here in the city, the professional ones wanted to be paid, and Kip's job barely covered his rent. Taking pity, she'd agreed to help him out—no charge.

During their sessions, they talked. About art. About life and philosophy. About the miserable state of their love lives.

She hadn't heard from James in nearly a month, despite Neil's hopeful prediction that he'd come to his senses and admit he couldn't live without her.

She was beginning to fear he could live without her just fine.

She'd considered throwing herself at him again, but what was the use? She'd only end up humiliating them both. Then again, what was the point of pride where love was at stake?

"I'm ready," Rhonda sang out, handing her purchase and platinum card to Ivy.

They chatted casually while Ivy rang up the sale. She slipped the garments into a protective plastic bag, turned to hand them over to her client.

Rhonda extended a small white business card. "I have a little place on Thompson Street you might find interesting," she said. "I'm not usually in the habit of doing this sort of thing, but I see possibilities in you, Ivy. No guarantees, but give me a call. We'll see what develops."

Ivy accepted the card, mildly perplexed.

Before she had time to look at it, another customer drew her attention. She tucked the card inside her pocket and promptly forgot all about it.

On break nearly two hours later, she relaxed in a chair in the back room, sipped an iced tea, and rested her weary feet. Only then did she remember the card.

She pulled it from her pocket and read:

West Galleries
Thompson Street, SoHo, NYC
Rhonda West, Proprietor

Rhonda West?

Her mouth dropped open, eyes wide. Everyone in the Western world—or at least in the art world—had heard of Rhonda West and West Galleries. Some of the finest artists working today exhibited their work in her gallery.

She had a little place, she'd said. Some little place!

My God, Pantsuit Rhonda was Rhonda West? She couldn't believe she hadn't put two and two together and recognized her name from her credit card.

And Rhonda had told her to give her a call.

Her heart thundered like a storm inside her chest.

Smoothing out the card with trembling fingers, she stared at it again to make certain it was real.

She had an interview with the owner of one of the top galleries in New York.

Maybe sometimes miracles did come true.

"Good evening, sir. How are you this evening?"

James strode up the sidewalk to his building, brief-case in hand. He gave a friendly nod to the familiar gray-haired gentleman who held open the door with the dignity worthy of royalty.

"I'm well. And you, Barton? Pleasant day?"

"Very pleasant, sir. Particularly so since Miss Gray-son arrived."

"Miss Grayson? You mean Ivy's here?" he blurted before he had time to think.

"Yes. She went up about twenty minutes ago. I pre-sumed you were expecting her."

He wiped the emotion from his face, struggled to conceal the sudden leaping of his nerves. "Of course. She's earlier than I'd planned, that's all."

What was she doing here? he wondered as he con-tinued into the building and onto the elevator.

The delicious murmur of her voice came to him the moment he opened the door. He let it wash over him, sweet as a warm spring rain. He listened for a few moments more before he set down his briefcase and forced himself to move forward into the living room, where she was in conversation with Estella.

". . . and that's exactly what he got," Estella said. "Two cents."

Ivy was chuckling when he entered the room, a gentle smile limning her pink lips.

"Good evening, ladies," he said, striding toward them across an expanse of polished hardwood.

Ivy's head swung his way, her pretty eyes lighting with pleasure. "James."

The sound of his name on her lips slid over him like a caress. The sight of her long feminine form curled on his sofa, a blow to his senses. Through sheer force of will, he kept his features even, in no way revealing the longing that rose within him.

"You didn't mention you'd be stopping by," he remarked, his tone deliberately casual.

"I didn't know I would be," Ivy replied.

"She's got news," Estella said, her excitement palpable.

James switched his attention to the older woman. "I thought you'd be finished for the day by now."

"I am, but I couldn't run off without visiting with Miss Ivy." She flapped a hand and teased. "Don't worry. I won't charge you any overtime."

He snorted softly in reply, crossed to the wet bar on the far side of the room, and reached for the bourbon decanter.

"Go on, child," Estella urged after a pronounced silence. "Tell him your news."

"Yes." He turned, drink in hand. "Tell me your news."

Ivy rose from the couch to face him, dismayed by the hard undertone in his voice.

She'd been so happy this afternoon, so over the moon with excitement, that she hadn't stopped to think. She'd wanted to share her achievement, reveal her triumph to someone who mattered.

Of course, he'd been the first person she'd thought of.

When she'd received the offer, it had been early afternoon. She'd considered surprising him at his office but worried he might be too busy to celebrate properly. So she'd come here to his penthouse to wait.

But now, as she looked at him across the room, she wondered if she'd made a mistake. He looked . . . cold, remote. She'd known him her entire life, yet suddenly he seemed like a stranger. His eyes were so flat and blue.

His look made her want to shiver.

She shuffled her feet. "This woman came into Reflections the other day, you know, the shop where I work."

"I know where you work."

"She wanted an outfit for a party. I helped her."

James rattled the ice cubes in his glass, downed a half inch of the contents as if he were already bored.

She lifted her chin, pressed on. "She was very nice, and as we chatted, my art came up in the conversation. Turns out she's Rhonda West."

He raised an eyebrow. "Of West Galleries?"

That caught your attention, didn't it? she thought.

"The very same," she continued. "She gave me her

card, told me to call her. Well, I did; then I did better. She took a look at my portfolio today, at least what I have finished of it, and she loves it. She said she rarely accepts representational art, but she's giving me a show. It's not solo. I'll be exhibiting with three other artists, but still it's a great opportunity."

He set his drink aside. "You've been asked into the West Gallery?"

"I have."

The chill broke suddenly as he crossed to her, grabbed her up in an exuberant hug.

She relaxed against him with relief, pressing her cheek to his shoulder. She breathed in the musky warmth trapped in his clothes from his long day, savored the delicious, male scent she knew to be his alone.

She closed her eyes, curled her arms around him, and basked in his embrace.

He pulled back but left his hands loose on her arms. "That's wonderful, Ivy. I'm so happy for you, so proud. I knew you'd do it."

"You'll be at the opening?"

"You couldn't keep me away."

"It's scheduled for November first." She stepped back, gesturing with her hands. "I have so much work to do before then. I don't know how I'm going to get it all done in time."

"You have about two months, plenty of time to produce."

"Not really, not with my job. I told Rhonda I'd have at least one more piece, maybe two, done in time for the show."

"Surely you're not planning to keep that ridiculous job?"

"I am. There's no guaranteeing how many of my paintings will sell. Rhonda's very enthusiastic, but even so, it's unusual for an artist to make much profit at first. Chances are I'll still need that *ridiculous job* to make ends meet."

She shouldn't let them, but his words stung.

"You wouldn't need a job at all if you'd let people help you. If you weren't so stubborn," he said, dismissing her statement.

Her shoulders stiffened. "It isn't a matter of being stubborn."

"Well, whatever it is," Estella interrupted with deliberate cheerfulness, "I think Miss Ivy's news is splendid and no reason for anyone to get all disagreeable over."

Scolded like a pair of naughty children, Ivy and James fell silent.

Ivy flushed, realizing she'd completely forgotten Estella was in the room, she'd been so wrapped up in James. Looking at him, she saw he'd only just remembered Estella's presence as well.

She fought to rein in her temper, to regain her earlier high spirits. She gazed at him. "Estella's right. This is a happy day. I thought we might have dinner together tonight to celebrate."

He stared at her for a long moment, a frown marring his even features as if some unpleasant thought had just crossed his mind.

Abruptly, he turned, walked back to the wet bar. He

raised his glass and drank down the last inch of alcohol inside. "Sorry, but I can't. I have plans."

Her smile faded. The chilly stranger was back. "Oh, well, another time, then."

He glanced at his watch. "I don't mean to be rude, Ivy, but you've just reminded me of the time. I need to change or I'll be late."

She stared.

Does he have a date?

A greasy wave of nausea rose in her stomach at the idea. Blindly, she turned away.

She took a long moment to compose herself, then approached the coffee table. Leaning over, she picked up the small, gaily wrapped box sitting there.

She turned back. "Well, then," she said with a brightness she didn't feel, "I'd better give this to you now. It's your birthday present."

For an instant she thought he wasn't going to accept it; then he reached out.

"Promise you won't open it before Sunday," she admonished. "I know how much you hate to wait."

She decided not to ask him how he planned to spend the day. Whether he'd made any special arrangements to celebrate and with whom. It was clear she wouldn't be invited.

"I don't want to keep you." She fumbled for her purse, abandoned in a nearby wing chair. "I'll send you an announcement about the opening. Do . . . do you think Tory would be interested in coming?"

For an instant, his eyes seemed sad. "I'm certain she would."

"Good. Well, then, I'll include her as well."

She crossed to Estella, hugged her quickly. "Take care. Send my best to your family."

Estella hugged her in return. "I'll do that, child. I can't wait to see all that art of yours displayed in a fine gallery, 'specially that picture you did of me. Won't everyone be amazed when they look up and discover this face of mine staring back at them?"

Ivy exchanged another smile with Estella, then swung around toward James. "I'll see you then, I suppose."

He hadn't moved, the present with its shiny black-and-white-checkered paper and curly red ribbon clutched absently in his hands.

"Yes," he said. "Congratulations again, Ivy. I'm happy for you."

She gazed at him, wished he might say more, might explain why he'd turned so distant.

When he didn't, she walked away and let herself out.

The sound of the door closing behind her echoed in the hall like the cry of a lonely little bird.

"Why'd you let her go like that?" Estella demanded, her broad hands sitting squarely on her broad hips. "Why'd you let her think you're meeting another woman tonight?"

"Maybe I am. I don't recall including you in my personal life." He carefully placed the present Ivy'd given him to one side, poured himself another drink.

"Hmmph. If you did, maybe you wouldn't be trying to numb yourself up with what's in that glass. It's plain you love that girl. Why don't you just admit it and put the both of you out of your misery?"

"Leave it alone, Estella."

"She adores you, good-tempered or bad, in a way that's purely uncommon. Don't know what all the trouble's about between the pair of you anyway."

He slammed down his drink, bourbon sloshing over the rim onto his fingers. "I told you to leave it alone, so leave it alone."

Estella fixed him with a hard black-eyed stare, then shrugged. "Fine. It's your grave. Dig it deep as you want, but don't be surprised when it's cold and lonely down there at the bottom."

He turned on the tap, rinsed the alcohol from his hand. "Good night, Estella."

His tone made it clear the subject was closed.

"Good night, Mr. James. I'll be by Tuesday, as usual."

When the penthouse was quiet and he was alone, James topped off his drink. He supposed he should find himself something to eat. He wasn't in the mood to go out. And he certainly didn't want to cook.

Estella'd guessed right. He had lied about the date. There weren't any new women in his life. There hadn't been anyone since Ivy.

He thought of several names—attractive, available females who would no doubt be delighted to hear from him. Perhaps he should look up a number or two, give one of them a call.

He toyed with the idea as he picked up the pretty package Ivy'd brought him. Then he raised his drink and carried both of them into his study.

CHAPTER THIRTEEN

"Want a glass of juice or something?" Kip Zahn inquired from his spot on the wide living room sofa.

Ivy dipped the fine sable bristles of her paintbrush into a blob of the caramel-colored paint. She made a careful mixture of yellow ochre, burnt umber, and titanium white, then stroked the gleaming oil across her newest work, a half-completed canvas she'd set up on an easel shortly after dawn.

The morning light was better here next to the front windows, she'd found, today's crisp, cloudless sunshine a blessing in the early-October sky. She didn't want to dawdle and miss the best moments of the day.

Of course, she could compensate if she had to. Drag the tall pair of photographic lights she used for evening work out of her bedroom, though she'd rather not. The equipment was heavy and hot and she worried she'd blow out a fuse again if she tried plugging them in next to Josh's stereo the way she had a few unfortunate weeks ago.

"No, thanks," she murmured to Kip's question as she concentrated on feathering in a few fine brushstrokes. "I'm good for now."

Kip stood and walked into the kitchen. Opening the refrigerator door, he perused the contents. "Thanks again for letting me crash here last night." He pulled out a pizza box that held the remains of last night's dinner. "Your couch was a godsend."

"No problem. I don't know where your building management expected all of you to go, kicking you out like they did with barely any notice."

"It was fumigate or face court-ordered fines, since the creepy-crawlies were about to carry the place off. After the Lewis kid got bitten by that Chihuahua-sized rat, the pressure was on. Fix it up or else. A couple nights' eviction is worth a critter-free building. Though the place is gonna stink like a toxic waste dump for weeks from the fumes."

"Are you sure it's safe for you to move back in today?"

"So they claim," he said in between bites of pepperoni and cheese. "If I die, ship my body back home to my folks in California."

She pointed her paintbrush at him. "Don't even talk that way. It's not funny. And the sofa's open for as many nights as you need."

He strolled over to her, dropped a kiss on her cheek. "You rock. Almost makes me wish I'd met you first instead of Melissa."

Ivy read the pain in his expression, the longing he couldn't seem to shake for the young woman who'd rejected him.

She knew exactly how he felt.

She didn't want to think about James—hard to do, though, when he happened to be the subject of her painting.

She freshened her brush with a daub of red.

She remembered the day she'd done the pencil study for this painting. A lazy Saturday, she'd coaxed him into his conservatory to keep her company while she sketched some of the plant life housed beneath the high glass skylights above. Surreptitiously, she'd made pencil sketches of him as well, capturing him where he sat bathed in easy arcs of sunlight and afternoon shadow, a faraway look in his eye.

How long ago those days seemed now. How innocent and hopeful and foolish.

Kip stood to one side, studying her progress. "So, that's him, is it? James Edward Jordan the fourth. Rather cool and patrician, isn't he?"

"He only seems that way on the surface. Inside he's warm and generous, kind in a way few people are."

"Still defending him, are you, despite the way he's hurt you?"

"He never asked me to love him. As much as I wish he felt the same, I can't really blame him for doubting my feelings. He's never had much love in his life. His parents are . . . self-absorbed; I suppose that's the best way to describe them. They've spent their lives traveling the world, leaving James behind."

She swished her brush in the turpentine. "Growing up, I remember how my mother always made a point of inviting him to join us for holidays and birthdays. Otherwise he would have been left by himself in that huge rambling house next to ours with no one but the servants for company. I didn't realize until I was older how things were for him. How much he depended on my family, depended on Madelyn, to bring some happiness into his life."

Ivy drew a breath and sighed. "She hurt him. She hurt him badly. I suppose it's no wonder he doesn't trust me."

"You're not her. You shouldn't be blamed for your sister's mistakes."

"No, but some part of him can't forgive her, and therefore, me. Some part of him still doubts anyone will ever truly love him."

James is scared, she realized with sudden clarity. Scared to love, scared to trust again, the way he had once before with a completeness that had been almost blind in its intensity. He wouldn't let himself love again so easily. She'd always known that, but until this moment she hadn't fully understood what it could mean.

Kip voiced the next question. "So how long are you going to wait, hoping he'll change his mind?"

She turned to him, a ripening maturity and a fresh resolve shining in her eyes. "As long as it takes."

Forever, she thought, *if need be*.

If only she could find a way to get close to him again. If only she could make him see she wasn't flighty or fickle. He'd been so remote that day at his penthouse. Almost angry.

Why? she wondered. Was it simply his way of pushing her farther out of his life, or was it something more?

"Please tell me there's coffee," Josh grumbled, interrupting her thoughts.

He shuffled in from the hall, wearing white boxers and a robe dotted with little drums and guitars, baggy red socks on his big feet. His dark, uncombed hair stuck out in crazy rooster clumps all over his head. Bleary-eyed, he all but stumbled into the kitchen.

"There's fresh in the pot," she told him, her mood lightening at the comically pitiful picture he made.

She and Kip watched him retrieve a pair of mugs from the cabinet, bang them on the counter, shovel three teaspoons of sugar into one and coffee into both. He raised the unsweetened one to his mouth, uncaring that he nearly scalded himself on a pair of steaming droplets that sloshed out of the cup.

Eyes closed, he grunted with pleasure.

Frederick, fresh from his morning shower, strolled into the living room. His short hair lay damp and curling, his lean, muscular body clothed in loose gray exercise pants and a long-sleeved blue tank top. "Morning, everyone."

Ivy and Kip returned the greeting.

Josh grunted again.

Fred reached into the refrigerator for a yogurt, then rattled the wobbly silverware drawer open for a spoon. He peeled the foil top off the carton. "You're all still coming tonight, right?" he asked expectantly, taking a bite.

"Coming to what?" Josh asked.

"Tonight's performance. The ballet, remember? I'm dancing the lead."

"Oh, that." Josh picked up the second mug of coffee he'd poured, a cup in each hand. "Sure, we're coming. Why the hell else would I be up so early? I took an a.m. shift today so I'd have the night off." He yawned. "Neil wants his coffee. I want a shower. Later, people."

He disappeared down the hallway. The sound of a door closing rang out moments later.

"Don't mind him," she said, seeing Fred's offended glare. "He doesn't mean to be rude."

"No, he is rude. And it's not your job to apologize for him." Fred chomped down another spoonful of yogurt. "Trouble with Josh is, every time you're on the verge of punching his lights out, he turns around and does something nice. Bastard went and fixed the leaking showerhead yesterday. Did you notice?"

She exchanged a grin with Kip, then wiped her paintbrush on a rag. "Yeah. Rotten of him, wasn't it?"

"At least he could thank me for the complimentary tickets," Fred continued. "I scrounged extra so all of you could come. Should have made him pay for his."

"Well, I'm looking forward to tonight," she soothed. "And I appreciate the free seats."

"Same here, man," Kip seconded. "I've never been to the ballet."

"Then it's about time you went." Finished with what

passed for breakfast, Fred chucked the empty carton into the trash.

"Is that all you're going to eat?" she asked.

Fred laid a hand across his flat stomach. "Can't afford anything more, not today. The less of me there is, the higher I'll fly onstage." He glanced at the time gleaming in red numerals on the microwave. "Which reminds me that I'd better be flying out of here now or I'll be late for practice and rehearsal. Wish me luck."

"Luck," she and Kip chorused.

A knock sounded on the door as Fred approached it to depart, a small vinyl gym bag in hand.

Lulu stood on the other side. "Hey, you leaving?"

He nodded. "Big day. Can't be late."

"How about some company on the subway? We'll ride together if you can hang here for another five minutes."

"All right. I'll wait for you, Lu. But five's your limit."

"You got any Band-Aids? My left foot's one big blister from the new dancing shoes I'm breaking in."

"Sounds like it's your feet that are being broken in, not the shoes." Fred dropped his carryall to the floor. "Hang on and I'll get 'em."

Lulu came farther into the room, raised a hand in greeting.

"Are you okay?" Ivy asked, noticing the other woman's slight limp.

"Oh, sure. Hazard of the trade. I'll be healed up in a couple days. Are you painting?"

Ivy set her brush aside. "Trying to."

"Let's see." Lulu limped closer. "Ooh, that's nice. Will it be in your show?"

"If I can finish it in time."

Lulu pointed at the canvas. "That's weird. I think I know that guy."

Ivy froze. "Who? James?"

"Yeah. That's him. *James*," Lulu said with a snap of her fingers. "Never forget a face, especially when they're as grade-A gorgeous as his. Though you're painting him a tad gloomy, don't you think? Ought to give him a nice bright smile."

Ivy ignored the suggestion. "How do you know James?"

"Oh, he was by here a while back, asking for you. But you were out."

"Here?"

"Yeah. I met him in the hallway. We chatted for a few minutes. Wowza, what a gentleman. Totally *GQ*."

Ivy's stomach gave a peculiar squeeze. "When did he stop by?"

"Oh, one evening four, five weeks ago. Can't remember now. Said he was a friend and not to bother you about it; he'd catch up with you later." Lulu shot her a curious look. "Was it important?"

"No, it's fine."

James had been here? Had driven all the way down one evening to see her? But why? What had he wanted? And more important, why hadn't he said anything to her about it since?

Fred strode back into the room, Band-Aid box in hand. "Here you go, Lu."

Lulu flashed him a grateful smile. "My hero." She dropped down onto the floor, pulled the sneaker and sock off her abused foot, and began tending to her wounds.

"You okay?" Kip asked Ivy after Fred and Lulu had left.

She blinked. "Sure. Why wouldn't I be?"

"Oh, no reason," he said sarcastically. "Just wondered."

She turned a look on him that said she wasn't in the mood to talk, then reached for her paintbrush.

She had work to do.

The houselights came up at intermission.

Ivy stood, together with her friends and the rest of the audience, and joined the slow, meandering procession from auditorium to lobby.

As soon as they were able, Josh and Neil veered off to swap stories with some actor acquaintances they'd spotted on the opposite side of the theater. Kip set off for a quick trip to the men's room, to be followed by a long wait in the beverage line. He'd catch up to Ivy, he told her, once he'd purchased their drinks.

In need of some breathing room and a chance to stretch her legs, she wandered away from the thick crowds toward one of the quieter areas of the building.

Much as she enjoyed events like this, she didn't always enjoy the close atmosphere. Too many warm bodies. Too many designer fragrances swirling in the same confined space. She could use a few minutes of clean air and solitary reflection.

She paused by a poster announcing the ballet company's fall season. Next to the listing for tonight's performance of *Romeo and Juliet* was Fred's name—Oops, she amended, *Frederick's* name—spelled out in small but impressive block letters.

She thought back over the first act. Fred and the entire company had been brilliant, moving with a grace and power that left her breathless. She was so happy for Fred. She knew how hard he worked, how much he wanted this. She understood his passion, the pride he must feel knowing his long years of training and devotion were finally paying off.

She walked on, lured by her artist's sensibilities toward a portion of the theater that contained sculpture and other works of art.

She moved into a large, square room that stood blessedly empty of other people. Recessed lighting cast a mellow glow over the space, an effect enhanced by yards of fawn-colored carpet and warm white walls. Additional lighting was unobtrusively positioned to showcase a pair of huge, postmodernist paintings, as well as a massive marble sculpture that towered skyward in a milky, treelike tangle of arms and legs.

Humanity Grasping at the Heavens was its title.

She stared, absorbed by the visceral impact of the piece, finding it both vile and profound all at the same time.

Unsettling, she decided, definitely unsettling.

Muffled footsteps sounded in the doorway. She tossed a glance to her left, the breath whooshing out of her lungs as her eyes collided with James's.

She didn't know which of them was more surprised.

He took a step backward, then halted. After a moment, he walked toward her, hands tucked into his pockets. "Disturbing, isn't it?"

It took her a moment to realize he was talking about the sculpture.

"Yes," she agreed. "And weird, though I suppose that sounds sacrilegious coming from an artist."

She stifled the urge to reach out, to slip her arm through his or clasp his hand the way she would once have done without thought. Instead, she drew the edges of her pink satin wrap tighter around her shoulders.

"I didn't realize you were in the habit of attending the ballet," he said.

"I'm not, not usually, but it's Fred's big night. He asked us to come see him dance. He's in lead position tonight."

"Well, that solves one nagging mystery. I knew something seemed oddly familiar about Romeo. Apparently, I didn't recognize him sober."

"As I recall, he wasn't the only one who drank too much that evening."

As soon as the words left her mouth, she remembered what else had happened that night. The first and only night they'd made love. She met his eyes, saw that he remembered too.

James looked away, shoved his hands deeper into his pockets. A terrible, awkward silence descended between them. He scoured his mind for something to say. "So how have you been? You look well."

Well didn't do her justice.

She looked beautiful, exquisite. Her cheeks flushed with healthy color, her eyes more brilliant than the sky on a cloudless summer day.

I could drown in those eyes if I let myself.

"I'm fine," she murmured. "You?"

"Oh, fine."

Another silence fell.

He cleared his throat. "And umm, your painting? How are the preparations for the show moving along?"

"Great. I've finished one canvas and am nearly done with another. Rhonda's seen them both and she's pleased. She hopes I'll have time to do one more, but it'll be nothing short of a miracle for that to happen."

"How are things with Rhonda?"

"Wonderful. Exciting. She's very supportive, very down-to-earth. Far more than I would have expected from someone in her position. Being represented by her gallery's the opportunity of a lifetime. I only pray I don't flop."

"You won't flop. The possibility doesn't even exist."

Her eyes warmed with pleasure. "You always say the nicest things."

"Nothing that isn't true." Another quiet moment passed. "I haven't had a chance to thank you."

"Thank me? For what?"

"The present. For my birthday." His voice deepened. "It's beautiful, Ivy."

Her smile widened. "You really like it?"

His thoughts turned to the small oil painting, framed and now hanging in a place of honor in his bedroom. It was a landscape of the woods near their family homes in Connecticut, leaves riotous with color, the ground cool and ready to crunch underfoot. Fall. His favorite time of year.

"Yes," he said. "I love it."

I love you.

"I painted it nearly a year ago," she said, "hoping you might like it." She smiled again, her lips soft and full.

Lord, he wanted to kiss her, snatch her up into his arms and lose himself in the very wonder of her.

"James?" she murmured, her voice puzzled. "I was talking to my neighbor this morning. Lulu. She says you stopped by the apartment a few weeks ago."

"Did she?"

He could see the exact spot on the delicate curve of her neck where her pulse beat, warm and strong; he imagined bending down and pressing his lips just there.

"She says you came to see me. Why?"

Why? Because no matter how many reasons there are why we shouldn't be together, I can't get you out of my mind, my heart.

Because I wanted to carry you away that night and make love to you until you'd forgotten everything and everyone but me.

But maybe it wasn't too late to do those things, he considered. Maybe he should tell her now, take her somewhere they could be alone.

"I knew I'd find you near one of the art displays," a male voice suddenly said. "Hey, neat sculpture."

She turned her head. "Kip."

"Here's your iced tea," he said. "Thought I'd never get through that line at the concession stand."

Absently, Ivy accepted the drink, repressing a frustrated sigh. James had been on the verge of saying something, something important. She'd felt it in her bones.

And the way he'd been looking at her; ooh, she had goose bumps all over her body.

Then Kip had barged in and ruined everything.

Why, oh why, couldn't he have waited just one minute more?

"You must be James Jordan." Kip stuck out his hand. "Ivy mentions you often."

"Does she?" After a brief but noticeable hesitation, James accepted Kip's hand to shake. "And you are?"

"Oh, sorry. Didn't mean to forget my manners. Kip Zahn."

"He's an artist," she interjected, hoping to ease a bit of the tension.

"Yes. I sculpt." Kip jerked a thumb toward the imposing marble statue behind him. "Though nothing as adventurous as the stuff in here."

"Don't be modest," she defended. "Your sculptures are very compelling. Every bit as powerful as these, just different."

Kip grinned. "Not to everyone's taste, she means, but it's sweet of her to say. I'm lucky to have a friend like Ivy."

"Yes," James said, his tone hard. "You are. Do you show your work?"

"Not until recently. I was invited to join an artist's co-op a couple of weeks ago. Several of my pieces are there on consignment. I'm hoping for a sale soon. Particularly now that I've finished the sculpture of Ivy."

"What sculpture of Ivy?"

Reacting to the note of hostility in James's voice, Kip nearly choked on a mouthful of soda. He swallowed with obvious effort. "Hey, relax, man. It's not like she was naked or anything."

James's eyes gleamed dangerously. "I would think not."

A flash of red drew Ivy's attention. She turned her head and saw Parker Manning, sheathed in a long, body-hugging crimson evening gown, glide into the room. She walked over to James and slid a proprietary arm through his.

"So this is where you wandered off to," Parker said. "I've been looking everywhere for you, darling."

James angled his head her way. "You were involved swapping real estate stories with the Domerchis. You know how that bores me. I decided I'd look around."

"Umm, so I see." Parker stroked his sleeve. "Well, I'm finished with that now, so we might as well drift back. The curtain's due to go up on the second act at any moment."

"Yes, you're right," James agreed.

Ivy listened to the exchange. Her fingers clamped around the condensation-slick plastic cup were as cold as the ice inside it. Her throat tightened, an ache spreading through her chest.

She willed James to look at her.

But he didn't.

Instead he moved ahead with the required social niceties. "Parker, allow me to introduce Kip Zahn to you. Zahn, Parker Manning. Zahn, here, is a sculptor."

"Oh, how intriguing." Parker inclined her head and gave him a perfunctory half smile.

"And you remember Ivy Grayson," James continued, still not looking Ivy's way.

"Yes," Parker said, oozing with ill-concealed venom. "Though we've never actually been introduced. Now, dear," she said to James, "we really should be going."

For a moment, Ivy imagined upending her tea on top of Parker's perfectly coiffed head. If only she had the nerve to do it.

"Yes, of course," James said. "Ivy. Zahn. Enjoy the rest of your evening."

Finally, James looked at her. What she saw in his eyes—or rather what she didn't see—made her want to cry.

"James," she whispered, too low to be heard.

Then he and Parker were gone.

She wilted the instant he left.

Kip reached out a supporting arm. "Do you want to leave?"

She did. She wanted to run away, dive underneath the covers of her bed and pretend none of this had ever happened. But she'd promised Fred she would see his ballet, and she couldn't disappoint him by leaving halfway through.

The overhead lights flashed, signaling everyone to return to their seats.

Through sheer force of will, she straightened. "No. I came to support Fred, and that's exactly what I'm going to do."

"Good girl."

But as she sat in the darkened auditorium, she was barely aware of the dancing. Instead, she located a familiar golden head several rows away and watched him while her heart wept.

CHAPTER FOURTEEN

S omeone thrust a glass of champagne into her hand.
Someone else—one of her cousins, she thought—
bussed her on the cheek. Head in a whirl, Ivy stood in
the center of the crowded gallery and marveled at the
minor miracle taking place around her.

Her art was a success. And so, it appeared, was she.

She wondered if she ought to pinch herself to make
sure it was real. She drank a sip of champagne instead,
effervescent bubbles bursting against her tongue, tart
and cool. Silken strains of music floated to her ears; the
lovely, gentle strains were nearly drowned out by the
hum of conversation.

Everyone was here tonight—friends, family, critics,
and curiosity seekers. There were even a handful of serious art lovers sprinkled in among the multitudes, av-
idly perusing the paintings on display. Others nibbled
on cheese cubes and canapés, debating the merits of
this style and that trend.

As the hours ticked by, so did the sales.

Five paintings and three commissions, steady work that would soon have the money rolling in. Oh, not in dream proportions, but comfortable, she reasoned. Enough that she'd be able to quit her job at Reflections if she wanted.

Tonight was only a beginning. As beginnings went, though, it was a damned fine one.

Everything about the evening should have been perfect, *would* have been perfect, except for one rather important detail.

James wasn't there.

She'd masked her disappointment well—at least she thought she had—smiling and laughing, acting as if she were having the time of her life.

Yet even as her heart thrilled to hear the compliments and praise being tossed her way—including an unexpected nod of approval from an influential critic for the *Times*, who'd cooed at length over her brave use of color and bold, neorealist design—part of her remained focused on the door, waiting for the instant when James would arrive.

But he hadn't, and at nine forty-five, a trickle of people were already starting to depart. She would simply have to face facts.

He wasn't coming.

She'd never for a moment imagined he wouldn't be there. In spite of the awkwardness of their last meeting, she'd thought he would come. He, more than anyone, knew how important this night was to her. He'd made a promise, and once James promised, he never went back on his word.

At least he never had before tonight.

Optimistic to the last, she searched the entrance one more time.

Suddenly a long male arm slipped around her shoulders and gave a mighty squeeze.

She jumped, then relaxed just as quickly when she recognized the tall, broad-chested man at her side.

"Hi, Dad." She met his generous smile with one of her own.

"Hey, kiddo. About time I found you alone. The crowd around you has been so thick all night. I was beginning to worry you wouldn't have a moment for your old man."

"Not a chance. You know I always have time for you, and I always will." She flashed him a grin. "No matter how famous I become," she teased.

The idea of that made Philip Grayson's eyebrows soar skyward. Two slashes of coppery red that contrasted strongly with the crown of snowy white hair age had seen fit to deposit on his head.

"Glad to hear it," he declared. "If tonight's any indication, this is only a taste of things to come." His voice deepened. "Your mother and I are very proud of you."

"Thanks, Dad."

"Really, we are, despite any reservations we may have had at first. We never doubted your talent, you know."

"I know. You were just concerned. You're parents and that's what parents do. They worry about their kids."

"Damn right they do." He gave her shoulder another

quick squeeze. "Though I should have known you'd beat the odds and pull it off. Once you put your mind to a thing, there's no stopping you until you get it."

Not always, she thought with an inward sigh as she scanned the entrance one more time. *No, I most certainly do not always get what I want.*

"Come and say good night to your mother," her father said. "We're heading back to the hotel in a few minutes."

"Oh, do you have to leave? I thought we all might grab a late supper together."

"Not tonight, kiddo. Your mom's tired. She'd been running on adrenaline all day, though she doesn't want to admit it."

"She's okay, isn't she? She isn't sick?"

Her father blinked, momentarily taken aback. "No, no, nothing like that." He patted her shoulder. "She's fine, a little worn-out is all. A new florist she hired messed up an entire order for one of her weddings. She was up most of the night doing damage control, arranging centerpieces herself. I offered to help, but she sent me to bed. She was over at the reception hall by seven this morning. Needless to say, she barely slept last night. You'll understand if we beg off tonight."

She swallowed her disappointment as the two of them made their way across the room. "Of course."

"Anyway, your friends must be planning something special for you. You don't need a pair of old fogies tagging along to spoil the fun."

"You wouldn't spoil anything."

Assuming there was anything to spoil. Her friends

had dropped by the opening hours ago, exchanged congratulatory hugs, then deserted her to go their various ways.

They'd all had to work tonight.

All of them.

Neil, Josh, Fred, and Lulu.

Even Kip.

She'd thought at least Kip could have gotten the evening off. But he said his boss was a shrew and had nixed the idea before he'd even opened his mouth to ask for the time.

Maybe Madelyn and Zack would like to do something, she hoped.

And Brie.

She'd been touched that her other sister had flown up from Washington, D.C., just to see the gallery opening. Especially since Brie was serving as lead attorney in an important lawsuit.

Apparently, Brie'd had to twist a few influential arms to get even two days' vacation. But she'd managed, arranging a short postponement before handing over the reins to her cocounsel while she was away.

Ivy knew she was lucky to have such a generous, warmhearted family. Even P.G. and Caroline, who was looking healthier than she had in months, had made the trip into the city. Unbeknownst to her, they'd left a short while ago, their two sleepy children in tow.

"You were tied up," her father explained about P.G. and Caroline departing without saying their good-byes in person. "Oh, and Madelyn and Zack wanted me to pass along their apologies as well."

"What? They've left too?"

"Some scheduling mix-up with their sitter. And Brie received a call from the office. Some problem with one of the legal briefs. She said to tell you she'd phone in the morning before her flight."

Ivy's spirits deflated as fast as a balloon jabbed with a pin. Apparently, everyone was deserting her. Instead of celebrating tonight, it looked like she'd be taking the train home alone and catching up on her sleep.

She worked hard not to let her disappointment show.

"Here she is," her father announced, coming to a halt next to her mother. "Our very own artistic genius."

"Dad, please," Ivy admonished.

"Don't turn modest now. I've got eyes. I know genius when I see it."

"So do I," Laura Grayson declared, leaning over to brush a kiss against her daughter's cheek. "I didn't want to say it before, but these other people who're sharing your show, well, they don't hold a candle to you."

"It's not my show. It's all of our shows. And they're very good too."

"Good perhaps, but not as good as you."

Ivy studied her mother, finding her as lively as usual. For a woman who was supposed to be tired, she didn't look it.

Her father cupped a hand around her mother's elbow. "I told Ivy we were leaving. Since you're so worn-out from last night."

She watched as her parents exchanged some sort of silent communication.

"Yes, yes, I *am* tired." Laura raised a hand to cover a

yawn. "Practically dead on my feet. I hope you'll for-give us, sweetheart, for running out on you on your special night."

"Sure. It's fine." She faked a smile.

But as she looked between them again, she paused, suddenly suspicious. If she didn't know better, she'd think they were lying. But no, why would they lie? Unless—

"Congratulations again on your marvelous show," her mother said, interrupting the thought. She pulled her into her arms. "We'll talk tomorrow before we head home, dear."

Ivy returned the hug, then gave one to her father. "Get some rest."

She watched her parents depart, then stood alone in the rapidly emptying room. A sudden wave of depression hit her. Where had her brilliant evening gone?

Then she saw him, a glimpse of gold wandering among the canvases; James was here after all.

He wore one of his trademark suits, looking debonair in dark charcoal gray—very *GQ*, as Lulu had once called him.

Her feet were moving before she realized she'd taken a step. She followed him as he disappeared around one of the broad, white partitions that split the room into a maze of diagonals. Carefully angled track lights shone from above, illumination pooling like tiny spotlights on each of the artistic offerings displayed.

She found him, his chin tilted upward as he gazed at one of her paintings. She glanced to see which one. His portrait, hanging there like a two-dimensional twin.

He didn't turn his head as she approached, her shoes silent on the gallery's white-on-white tile floor.

"When did you do this?" he asked softly.

"Not long ago. It was the last piece I finished before the show." She stopped a few paces away. "What do you think?"

Nervously, she waited through the long quiet that followed.

"I think you see things in me I barely recognize in myself."

His words surprised her, pleased her. "And the painting? Do you like it?"

He turned. "What's not to like? It's as splendid as all the rest of your work. Not for sale, I see."

"No."

She could never bear to part with a piece so dear to her heart. If she couldn't have him, at least she would have this painting and all the memories that came with it.

She crossed her arms over her breasts. "It's late. I was beginning to think you weren't coming."

"I said I'd be here. You needn't have worried."

"And you didn't stop to say hello when you arrived." Her tone was a gentle reproof.

"You were busy talking to your parents, and I wanted to see the paintings. Where are they? Did they leave?"

She nodded. "Mother's tired, or so she says."

"You don't believe her?"

"I'm not sure. She and Dad were both acting a little peculiar." She narrowed her eyes, her earlier suspicions returning. "You don't know anything about it, do you?"

"Know about what?"

"Whatever it is that's going on."

"Why would you think something's going on?" he said, his face a perfect mask of innocence.

She narrowed her eyes. "Now I'm even more suspicious. What gives?"

James held out for another few moments. "All right, but promise you'll act surprised."

"Surprised by what?"

"The party they're throwing for you at my place. That's why I'm late. I had to stay to let the caterers in."

"A party? For me? I had no idea."

"At least not until I spilled the beans. I told them to draft somebody else to play decoy. I'm no good at this sort of thing."

"It's not you. It's my parents. They're the ones who can barely keep a secret." A thought occurred to her. "So how were you going to lure me up to your penthouse?"

Their eyes met. They both looked away.

"I was supposed to tell you I'd bought one of your paintings and needed help deciding where to hang it," he explained. "Hardly convincing, considering the hour."

"Still, it might have worked." Even a transparent excuse, she reckoned, would have been enough to convince her to go with him. "Were you really prepared to buy one of my paintings?"

"I bought two before the show even opened. It wouldn't have been an issue."

Her mouth dropped open. "You bought two? Why?"

"Why else? Because I like them. It wasn't done out of pity, if that's what you're thinking. You ought to know me well enough by now to realize I don't make frivolous purchases. The ones I bought are worth every penny, and I suspect they'll be a bargain once word gets around about you."

She should be angry with him, she supposed. A sale to James wasn't the same as a sale to a stranger. On one level it smacked of cheating. Then again, she had no desire to be cross with him, especially when she knew he sincerely respected and appreciated her talent.

A spot warmed deep inside her. "Which two did you buy?"

"The *Street Vendor* and the painting of Estella. I couldn't see it going out of the family. It'll be my Christmas present to her and her family."

Her heart swelled with even greater delight. "She'll be so pleased."

Her lips curved.

His curved back.

The connection between them was electric, as magnetic as the pull of the moon and the stars. She watched him watch her and nearly forgot how to breathe, her senses quivering beneath her skin.

He reached out, ran a gentle finger over the strand of creamy pearls encircling her neck. "Is this the necklace I gave you all those years ago?"

"Yes," she whispered.

She remembered the day, the moment, as if it were yesterday. Standing with him beneath the study window in her parents' house, sunlight streaming over them both to chase away the late-winter chill. She'd been only fifteen, the pearls his birthday present to her. They'd been far too indulgent a gift for a girl her age, but she'd treasured them then as she treasured them now.

His fingers moved as if compelled by a will of their own to trace one of the large, luminescent pearl earrings in her ears; he'd given the matching set to her as a sweet sixteen.

She shivered beneath his touch.

Then his hand fell away and he stepped back. "We've probably given everyone enough time to get settled," he said. "Why don't you say good night to Rhonda; then we'll be on our way."

Ivy worked to steady herself, feeling as if she were emerging from a fog. "She's not attending the party?"

"No. Prior engagement. She already offered her regrets, but don't let on that you know. It'll spoil the card and gift she sent along."

"I'll do my best to put on a convincing show."

She wished she were a better actress because getting through the night with James so near was going to take an Oscar-caliber performance.

James didn't know how much more he could take.

Ivy needed to leave.

Soon, very soon.

All evening he'd gritted his teeth, watched her laugh and cavort with her friends. For hours he'd kept a smile pasted on his face, pretending it didn't matter that she sat hip to hip with her new lover on *his* sofa, flaunting their relationship right under his nose.

What on earth had possessed him to invite her crew in the first place? Her friends and that guy, that Kip. What the hell kind of name was Kip anyway? More like something you name a puppy dog than a full-grown man. Then again, the kid in question barely deserved to be called a man. James doubted the boy needed to shave the peach fuzz off his skinny cheeks more than once or twice a week.

He considered pouring himself another glass of champagne, then changed his mind, setting his glass down on a nearby table.

He'd had enough to drink for one evening, he decided. Besides, what was the point? Alcohol solved nothing. Lord knows it didn't deaden the ache or wipe away the want.

When Laura Grayson had called three weeks ago with the idea of having Ivy's party here in his home, he should have given her a flat-out "no." Instead he'd ignored his instincts and gone along with the plan.

Now look what it had gotten him: a miserable evening and a likely hangover in the morning.

But at least Ivy was happy, enjoying herself. No matter what had gone on between them, he wished her nothing but happiness and success.

Unable to stomach another instant of the *Ivy and Kip Show*, he turned away.

Across the room, Ivy snuck another look at James.

Only a little while longer, she told herself, and she'd

be able to leave. Just a little while longer and she could quit pretending she was having the time of her life.

Considering all the trouble her family and friends had gone to to surprise and please her, it wouldn't have been right to let them see how miserable she actually was.

Since the car ride over from the gallery, James had barely spoken to her, spending the entire evening on the opposite side of the room. Desperate, she'd made a show of flirting with Kip, but James hadn't even seemed to notice. Maybe he should have invited that cow Parker Manning to keep him company.

Her stomach burned at the idea.

The night hadn't been all bad, though. The party decorations were lovely—no doubt courtesy of her mother. The food and drink was delectable. The company festive, cracking jokes and telling stories.

She'd sniffed back tears at her parents' prideful toast. Blushed and laughed when her sisters passed around embarrassing baby photos of her, followed by examples of her earliest attempts at art—crayon stick figures and finger-painted smears. No one but she and James were aware the party hadn't come as a delightful surprise.

Only she and James knew a lot of things.

"If you keep looking at him like that," Kip whispered in her ear, "everybody's going to know you're not the least bit interested in me."

She turned her head and met his soulful brown eyes. "Sorry, and thanks for being such a good sport."

"Always glad to help a pal. Sorry Melissa's not here

so you could do the same for me." He slapped his hands on his thighs. "What do you say to some cake? It's chocolate."

When she hesitated, he jumped to his feet and yanked her up off the couch.

She overbalanced and gasped out a laugh. "Well, all right, if you're going to be that way about it."

"So what's the deal with James and Ivy?"

Brie selected a triangle of the pale, creamy cheese that shared her name from a silver tray and set it on her plate next to a clump of juicy purple grapes. She plucked one of the grapes off its stem and popped it into her mouth as she waited for her sister to reply.

Madelyn took her time swallowing a bite of cake, then patted her mouth. "What do you mean?"

Brie pinned her with the look she used to break reluctant witnesses. "Don't pretend with me. You must have noticed the way they look at each other, or rather, don't look at each other. The tension between them's so thick, you really could cut it with a knife." She ate another grape. "So what's up?"

"Privileged information, Counselor."

"Privileged—ha. This concerns family. Nothing's privileged when it comes to family. So give me the 411 already."

Madelyn set down her half-eaten slice of cake. "You always were a nosy pest."

"Hey, lawyer's prerogative. Is he in love with her or what?"

Madelyn looked across the room at James, now deep

in conversation with their father. His jaw was squared in a way that could mean only one thing: They were talking politics.

"Oh, he's in love, though I don't think he's very happy about it."

"What about you? Are you happy about it?"

Madelyn arched an eyebrow and stole one of the grapes off her sister's plate. She let the sweet flavor of the fruit dissolve in her mouth before she answered.

"At first I was shocked, even outraged," she admitted to Brie. "Then I started to think about it and realized they'd be great together. He needs someone like Ivy to put a little pizzazz back in his life. And she's adored him forever, though I suppose until recently, I didn't want to see it. I think, if they'd let themselves, they could make each other very happy."

Madelyn told Brie what she knew of their relationship, how she'd discovered James and Ivy that first time, what James had confessed to her the day she'd met him for lunch.

"Hmm," Brie mused, savoring a forkful of delicate cheese. "Maybe they could use some help."

"Don't interfere."

"I won't. I'm just going to give them a gentle nudge in the right direction."

"*Brie,*" she warned, "stay out of it."

"I could, but since when have I ever stayed out of anything?"

CHAPTER FIFTEEN

The grandfather clock in the hall chimed out the hour. One stroke. Two. Notes played in a stentorian bass that echoed through the empty quiet of the apartment.

Party over, James tugged himself free of his tie and tossed it, together with his suit jacket, over the back of one of the living room chairs. He switched off the overhead lights, leaving a quartet of table lamps to burn throughout the room; then he slumped onto the sofa.

Eyes closed, he leaned his head back and waited for the sense of relief to come.

But it wasn't relief he felt, only sadness sweeping through him as raw and unforgiving as a bitter winter wind. He pinched a pair of fingers over the bridge of his nose and fought the ache.

It will pass, he told himself. *It has to pass.*

He sat for another long minute, then decided he might as well go to bed.

"Where is everyone?"

He jerked, spun around. "*Ivy?* Where'd you come from?"

"The powder room. Where's Brie? She and Malynn were supposed to wait for me while Zack went to get the car."

He climbed to his feet. "Are you sure? They all left minutes ago."

She crossed her arms over her chest. "Of course I'm sure. They were supposed to wait."

"I assumed you'd gone home with your—" He broke off, unable to say the word "boyfriend." He swallowed and began again. "Why didn't you leave with your friends?"

"They wanted to go late-night clubbing. I wasn't in the mood. Brie said I could tag along with her and Zack and Malynn. They said they'd drive me out to my place and drop me off."

He tucked his hands in his pants pockets, tried to ignore how fresh and pretty she looked despite the late hour. "Maybe you misunderstood."

"One of us obviously did." Her arms dropped to her sides. "I guess I can take the train."

He frowned. "Not at this hour. I'll drive you home."

"There's no need for both of us to be up all night. Look, I'll take a cab, if it will make you feel better. Okay?"

He straightened. "I said I'll take you home."

A small war of emotions raced over her features; then she shrugged. "Suit yourself."

She looked away. "By the way, if I didn't say so before, the party was lovely. Thank you."

"You're welcome. But the person you ought to be thanking is your mother. She did the majority of the work."

Ivy nodded. "Still, it was very generous of you to put up with all of us, particularly my friends. I don't imagine you were jumping up and down with excitement being asked to invite them into your home."

"I don't have anything against your friends."

She arched a skeptical brow.

"I've never objected to them personally. Well, not all of them," he corrected, thinking of Fred and Kip. "It's your living arrangements I've taken exception to. You're entitled to be friends with whomever you like."

Silence fell—the awkward kind that came so often between them these days.

His sadness returned. "I suppose we ought to go."

"Yes." Her gaze fell on the trays of food, the used plates and cups and glasses scattered around the room. "Why don't I help you clean up a little first?"

"That's not necessary."

"I'd feel guilty if I left you with this." She crossed to the coffee table, began gathering dirty dishes.

"Estella will take care of it tomorrow."

"Why don't we give her a break for once? If we work together, it won't take us long to clear things away."

Dishes in hand, she headed down the hallway to the kitchen.

Knowing when he was beaten, James picked up a pair of hors d'oeuvre trays and followed her.

He could count on one hand the number of times he'd done dishes. But with Ivy at his side, he found the

274   Tracy Anne Warren

process strangely enjoyable. He washed while she dried. Neither of them hurried, savoring the simple chore and the brief time together.

They were nearly finished, counters wiped clean, dishwasher loaded, when James reached for one remaining glass.

The goblet slipped in his wet hand, then tumbled to the floor. The delicate crystal shattered, jagged pieces flying everywhere.

Instinctively, Ivy jumped out of the way to avoid the sharp fragments.

"Are you all right?" he demanded, his voice harsh with concern.

"Yeah. What about you?"

"Fine." He waved off her worry, then crouched down to pick up the pieces.

"Hey, don't do that," she cautioned. "Let me get the vacuum."

Ignoring her, he began to stack a few of the larger shards off to one side. He hissed as he misjudged a piece, a ruby-colored line of blood beading across his palm.

"Oh God, look what you've done." She rushed forward, glass crunching under her shoes. "How badly have you cut yourself?" She grabbed a dish towel from the countertop and gently pressed it to the wound. She pulled the cloth away moments later to check the cut.

"It doesn't look too deep," she murmured. "Still, you might need stitches." Fresh blood welled into the gash. She wrapped the cloth around his palm again, vivid splotches blossoming on the material. "Maybe we should take you to the emergency room."

"I don't need the emergency room. It's nothing."

"It's not nothing. You're hurt."

"A little cut. I'll recover. All I need is a Band-Aid."
He laid his other hand over hers. "Ivy, I'll be fine."

Her lips tightened, clearly irritated by his male obstinacy. "Are there any bandages here in the kitchen?"

"I don't think so. I have a box in my medicine cabinet upstairs."

"Then let's go find one before you bleed to death."

"In a minute. Let me finish cleaning up this broken
glass first."

"The glass can wait," she said, glaring at him. "That
cut on your hand can't."

She took hold of his uninjured hand and pulled him
along behind her. She paused on the kitchen threshold
to step out of her shoes, indicated to James that he
should do the same.

"We'll leave our shoes here so we won't track any
glass," she explained.

He tossed her a look, wondering when she'd gotten
so bossy. Deciding it wasn't worth fighting over, he did
as he was told. She led him upstairs into the cool tiled
expanse of his spacious bathroom.

"Sit," she ordered, motioning him toward a chair
near the bath's one window, blinds closed against the
night.

Obediently, he sat.

She rummaged in the medicine cabinet, found the
bandages, then opened a pair of drawers on either side
of the sink to gather cotton balls, ointment, and a bottle
of hydrogen peroxide.

"Put that stuff away," he complained, gesturing toward the peroxide. "It stings."

"Don't turn crybaby on me now." She set her supplies on the counter next to him. "You're the one who vetoed any real medical attention, and this'll keep out an infection. Now, let me see your hand."

"Won't soap and water do?"

"No." She pinned him with a stern eyebrow.

Reluctantly, he offered his hand. Her touch gentle, she unwound the bloodstained cloth and inspected the cut.

"The bleeding's stopped at least. I still think you could use a stitch or two, but if you want to risk a scar, that's your choice."

She reached for the antiseptic, soaked a trio of cotton balls, then pressed them to the cut.

He sucked in his breath. "Jesus Christ, that stings."

"It'll feel better in a minute," she soothed, continuing to clean the wound.

"Easy for you to say."

"Hey, I've had my share of cuts and scrapes over the years. I know how it feels." She tossed the last bloodied cotton ball into the trash, then bent closer to inspect the gash on his hand.

He jolted in surprise when she stroked a fingertip across his palm just beneath the cut. Mesmerized, he sat statue still as she raised his hand and blew a cooling line of air across the wound.

His belly muscles tightened, desire flaring to life. His hand trembled in hers.

"Better?" she murmured.

Hardly, he thought, though he had to admit the cut didn't hurt anymore. He'd practically forgotten it was there.

Long moments ticked past. Slowly, she glanced up and met his eyes.

The power of her gaze struck him like a fierce wave crashing to shore, sweeping him in and under. All the longing, all the pent-up need inside him rushed to the surface, demanding to break free.

Suddenly he could be silent no more. "Do you love him?" he asked, his voice rough.

Her eyebrows rose in obvious surprise. "Love who?"

"That guy, that Kip," he spat. "The one you've been seeing."

"Is that what you think?" she murmured.

"What else am I supposed to think?" He swallowed past the lump in his throat, lowered his eyes to their still-joined hands. "Well, do you?"

She sank to her knees before him. "No. He's my friend, nothing more."

"Not your lover?" he asked, the question all but wrenched from him.

She shook her head. "You're my only lover."

Reaching up, she stroked her palm, soft and smooth, over his cheek. His eyelids lowered to half-mast, her touch radiating all the way to his toes. "I want no one else," she said.

He whispered her name, murmuring it like a prayer. He bent to kiss her, but she stopped him with a hand.

"What about her?" she asked.

"Who?"

"Parker."

He curled a finger beneath her chin. "There's nothing between Parker and me, not anymore." He brushed a thumb across her cheekbone and confessed. "There's been no one since you. How could there be when you're the only woman I want?"

"Oh, James." She wrapped her slender arms around his neck. "I thought . . ."

"What did you think?"

"That you were back with her. That you realized you were completely, totally over me."

His mouth twisted in irony. "Then it would seem we're both damned good at fooling each other these days. It's been hell without you, Ivy, pure hell."

She pressed her mouth to his, her yearning caress one of wonder, relief, and delight. The contact sent sparks whirling between them.

He tugged her up into his lap, took the kiss deeper. He breathed her in, losing himself in the scent and texture of her skin, the honeyed flavor of her lips on his.

"I love you," she whispered on a shivery sigh.

His heart caught inside his chest. Until that moment, he hadn't realized how much he wanted, even needed, to hear those words, sentiments he'd once distrusted and dismissed. Could he trust them now? Did she truly love him? Would she, now and forever?

He leaned his forehead against hers. "Tell me again."

"I love you."

He kissed her gently, tenderly. "Oh, Ivy, what is it that you do to me?"

"The same thing you do to me." She skimmed her mouth along his jawline.

"I've tried to fight these feelings for you, but it's just no use. I can't get you out of my head. Or my heart. I love you, Ivy. So much sometimes it frightens me."

She smiled, joy spreading inside her eyes like a brilliant sunrise. "You don't know how long I've waited to hear you say that. Sometimes I despaired you ever would. But don't be afraid. Not of this, not of me, not ever of love."

He kissed her again, unwilling to wait even a second longer to claim what he'd been so long without. He tangled his fingers in her hair as she tightened her arms around him, returned his kiss with a fervor that sent hot blood rushing through him.

He reached for the zipper on her dress. "*Ouch*," he said, fresh pain from the cut stabbing through his palm.

"Oh no, your hand . . ." Ivy pulled away. "Is it bleeding again?"

"I don't know." He didn't much care, either. All he cared about was getting her out of her clothes. He settled his mouth on her neck, trailing a line of kisses over her satiny skin.

"Let me see." She reached around, caught hold of his arm. She cradled his palm to her breast. "Oh, it is bleeding." She snatched a few tissues from a nearby box, pressed them against the cut.

He leaned over to steal another kiss.

She pulled away after a quick peck. "Stop it, James. Let me take care of your hand."

"You can take care of it later. Right now we have more important things to do." He located her zipper tab, grasped it with his good hand, and slid it home, straight to the base of her spine. The dress sagged around her shoulders, exposing her breasts, clad in sheer, lacy white cups. He buried his face against them, breathed in her scent.

He groaned in frustration when she pulled away, climbed off his lap.

"There's no need to rush," she said, letting the dress slide into a pool at her feet. "We have all night." She leaned forward, feathered a kiss over his lips, against his cheek. "I'm not going anywhere, I promise. Now, why don't you relax and let me take care of everything?"

"Everything, hmm?"

She reached for the box of bandages, an irrepressible gleam in her eyes. "That's right. Everything."

Considering the possibilities, he extended his palm. "When you put it that way, how can I refuse?"

In bra and panties, she bandaged his cut, unaware of the incredibly sexy picture she made.

When she finished, she tidied the countertop, rinsed and dried her hands, then turned to him. "Come along."

She led him into the bedroom, over to his wide, king-sized bed. She pushed him down on the mattress, where he landed with a slight bounce.

"No using your injured hand," she warned. "Let me take care of you."

Ivy stepped between his legs, then reached out to

undo the buttons on his shirt. She watched his eyes darken.

A shiver of anticipation slid through her, turning her molten inside.

He loved her. He wanted her.

Tonight was everything she'd waited for and more. And whatever difficulties might lie ahead, she knew they would weather them together.

She pushed his shirt off his shoulders, unfastened his cuffs, and eased the garment free, careful of the cut on his hand. His eyes closed as she glided her hands over his exposed flesh, his body acquiescent beneath her touch. Powerful, masculine, he could have taken over their lovemaking in an instant, controlled every nuance and sensation. Instead he gave himself to her, and she reveled in the gift of his trust.

She leaned down and kissed his neck, using her lips and tongue to learn its shape. Pressing her mouth to the hollow of his throat, she swirled her tongue over the spot in a way that made him quiver.

Taking her time, she worked her way downward, scattering licks and kisses across his firm chest. She gazed up at him to take in his strong, beautiful face, taut with arousal.

Her long hair slid over his knees as she bent to remove his socks. He reached down with his good hand and threaded it into her tresses to massage her scalp. She shivered, loving the way he touched her.

Her eyes lowered, landed between his legs. Suddenly some of her bold nerve deserted her as she stared back up at his belt buckle. Her fingers trembled as she began to reach for the metal clasp.

He reached down and with one hand pulled her to her feet.

"Enough, Ivy," he murmured, clasping her around the waist.

Falling onto his back, he tumbled her across him, then crushed her mouth to his. She yielded with a heady sigh, all thoughts and inhibitions floating away on a wave of delight.

They helped each other finish undressing. Her bra and panties found their way to the floor, his trousers and boxers tossed after.

They twined together, sharing ravenous, open-mouthed kisses, touches that scalded skin and singed nerves.

Using only his mouth and his one good hand, he soon had her writhing beneath him. She clutched the sheets as he brought her to the edge. Panting, heat pouring through her like a furnace, she was lost as he sent her over with a kiss to her core that was as shocking as it was profound. She cried out, eyelids fluttering as the earth rose up, then crashed down around her.

She reached for him, half delirious as she pulled him up and over her. Unlike their first time together, when he thrust inside, there was no pain. Only a raw, exquisite need.

Matching him, move for move, she gave as he gave, took as he took, reveling in their shared closeness, knowing this time he felt each moment with not only his body but his heart.

He brought her to climax twice more, leaving her sobbing from the power of her final release.

When he took his own satisfaction, he shouted out her name, shouted out his love for her.

Afterward, he buried his face in her neck, warm and replete as he murmured sweet endearments in her ear.

Happy, so happy, she cradled him to her and murmured back.

James woke at dawn with Ivy touching him like a siren bent on enslaving his soul. Fully aroused, his body was hard and hot, aching for release, as her mouth and hands ranged over him. Silken, savage, seemingly everywhere at once. He moaned and shifted against the sheets as he reached for her.

She eluded him, bending low to do something thoroughly wicked with her teeth and tongue. He moaned again and willed his body not to explode, not just yet anyway. He stretched his arms up over his head, linked his fingers together on the pillow, and fought for control.

She rose, straddling his hips. Her long hair brushed his chest, his face, as she leaned over and locked her mouth on his to share a deep, wet, penetrating kiss.

"Good morning," she purred. "Are you awake?"

"God, yes," he groaned.

She laughed, then kissed him again until his brain heated to the consistency of mush. He began to lower his arms, eager to touch her, but she stopped him, her soft fingers encircling his wrists.

"Don't move," she whispered, pressing his arms

into the pillow. "You're injured, remember? Stay where you are."

"Like this?"

"Hmm. Exactly like that. Stay there and let me." She rocked up, rocked down, sheathing him inside her warmth. "Just let me, let me, let me," she chanted.

He heard her breath catch, sigh, sing out, as she moved upon him. As he had only hours earlier, he willed himself to relax and allow her to do as she pleased. Allow her to take him in a way he'd never been taken before.

Branded. He felt branded in those moments. Bonded to her, a girl who was more woman than any woman he'd ever known, more feminine that any female in existence.

She sent him skyward—high, high, higher, until he shattered, until both of them shattered, drifting as one back to reality.

Gradually, his senses became his own once more, his thoughts clearing, his breath growing even once more.

In those moments, he knew one thing. He would never be free of Ivy again. He would never want to be free of her.

In the lightening day, holding her to his heart as she slept, he wondered exactly what he was going to do about it.

"We should get married," he stated hours later over brunch in the sunny breakfast room off the kitchen.

Ivy paused, a slice of bacon halfway to her mouth. "What?"

"Seems like the logical thing to do," he hurried on. "And it's what you want, isn't it?"

She set down the bacon and wiped her fingers on a linen napkin. "It always has been," she murmured softly.

"Good. Then that's what we'll do." He stabbed a fork into the last of the eggs on his plate.

He proposed, she thought, mildly stunned.

Though, as proposals went, that one lacked a certain essential something. In fact, on the face of it, it had kind of sucked.

Somehow, when she'd imagined this moment—and believe you me, she'd imagined it plenty of times—his proposal had been special. With sweet music floating on the air, a little champagne bubbling in a pair of long-stemmed glasses, James down on one knee telling her he couldn't imagine another instant without her as his wife.

But there'd been nothing the least bit special or romantic about his blunt declaration said over a plate of cooling eggs.

And he hadn't actually asked, had he?

Hadn't spoken the words "Will you marry me?"

He'd said "should."

They "should" get married, not "I want to marry you. Please say yes."

Then again, a proposal was still a proposal, she supposed, no matter the circumstances or the words.

She listened in silence as he rattled on.

"I'll take you by your apartment when we're finished eating," he said. "You can change clothes; then we'll go pick out an engagement ring."

"What about your great-grandmother's ring?"

His great-grandmother's ring was a huge, old-fashioned emerald-cut canary yellow diamond roughly the size of a shooter aggie. He'd given it to Madelyn years ago when they'd been engaged. As she remembered, her sister hadn't much cared for the style, though Madelyn had worn it graciously because of the sentiment involved.

Why wasn't he offering it to her?

"You don't want that old monstrosity, do you? Surely you'd rather have a ring of your own."

"I don't think it's a monstrosity. I've always loved that ring."

And she meant it. She'd always thought the stone was exquisite, the old-fashioned setting graceful and charming.

"Really?" He looked skeptical.

"Yes, really. It's beautiful, and it's an heirloom handed down through four generations of your family. I think that's lovely."

He paused for a long moment. "Well, all right, if that's what you want. The ring's up at the house in Connecticut."

"I can wait."

Briefly, he drummed his fingers on the table. "Maybe we shouldn't wait at all. Maybe we should elope."

"*Elope!* You know my mother would turn three shades of puce if we eloped." She caught the troubled look on his face and laid her hand over his. "James, what is it? What's wrong?"

"Nothing."

"Don't start fibbing to me now." She hesitated, then asked the question uppermost in her mind. "Are you sure you want to get married?"

"Of course I do. Haven't I said so?"

He stood, paced across the kitchen, the floor swept clean of the glass he'd broken the night before. He refilled his cup of coffee, then left it untouched on the counter.

"Actually, you didn't," she pointed out. "What you said is that we *should* get married, not that you want to get married." She pushed aside the remains of her breakfast, her appetite gone. "You don't have to marry me, you know."

He met her eyes. "Of course I do. What other options are there? Living together's completely out of the question. Your family and mine . . . Well, I don't even want to think about their reaction if you just moved in. So that leaves marriage."

"It also leaves simply dating for a while. I'll come here. You can come to my apartment. I've been thinking of moving closer anyway. There's a girl I work with at Reflections who's looking for a roommate. With my art income, I should be able to afford the extra rent."

He scowled, crossed his arms. "So what are you saying? That you won't marry me?"

"Yes," she said, her answer as much of a shock to her as it was to him. "I guess I am."

What have I just done? she wondered. *How could I turn down the proposal I've been waiting my entire life to accept?*

Once, she would have been ecstatic, willing to take him on any terms. Even six months ago she would have jumped at the chance, however begrudgingly offered, to call herself his wife.

But she wasn't the same naive girl she'd been then, when she'd set out on her quest to make him love her. Now she wanted him to come to her with a willing heart. No games, no guilt, only a confident assurance that a lifetime commitment to her was exactly what he desired most.

She left her chair and crossed to him. "Ask me again when you're sure marriage is really what you want. When you know you're ready."

"How do you know I'm not ready now?"

"Because if you were, we wouldn't be having this conversation."

His face paled, his eyes intensely blue. "I don't want to lose you, Ivy."

"You won't lose me." She slid her arms around his neck. "I love you, and that's never going to change. And despite your fears, I'm not going to leave you either. But until you believe those things with your whole heart, none of the rest of it matters."

He huffed out a breath. "When did you get to be so smart?"

She shrugged. "I've always been smart. You've just never noticed before."

He rested his forehead against hers. "I do love you, you know."

"I know. And I know you need more time. I'm

young, as you never get tired of reminding me. I can wait."

He gave her a penetrating look. "Can you?"

"I've waited twenty years. What's a couple more?"

He clutched her to him, burying his face in her hair. "I'm sorry, sweetheart. I don't deserve you."

She blinked against the sudden moisture in her eyes. "Probably not," she teased, "but you've got me anyway." She pulled away, forced a bright smile. "Now, where are you taking me for dinner?"

"Anywhere you want, anywhere at all. How about Rome?"

"Rome! As in Italy?"

"Yeah." He grinned. "I know just the place on Via Zanardelli. They serve spaghetti carbonara that truly is to die for. And over there I can ply you with wine, no age limit."

She laughed. "I don't think I need much plying, but if you say it's wonderful, then okay."

He tugged her against him and kissed her until stars burst behind her eyes. Finally, he released her. "Go call your family and tell them you've decided to spend the weekend with a—"

"Friend," she inserted.

"Right. A friend. I don't want them worrying about you."

"I'll have to call Rhonda too."

"Fine, call Rhonda; then we'll be off."

"I need to stop by the apartment to pack a few things."

"Just grab your passport. Don't bother with the rest. We can pick up whatever you need in Rome. Otherwise, we'll never get out of here."

She smiled. "All right. Ooh, this is exciting."

"You haven't seen exciting yet. There's a bedroom on the plane. I'm looking forward to seeing how you like making love at thirty thousand feet."

Chapter Sixteen

The weekend in Rome was divine and left Ivy floating on a cloud for days after.

While in the city, she and James dined on fine Italian food, shopped for new outfits and accessories for her at the best designer stores, and slept in a palatial seventeenth-century suite in a bed with a tall, blue and gold satin canopy and real silk sheets.

During the day the two of them played tourist, walking the streets hand-in-hand as they took in the sights: the Colosseum, the dome at St. Peter's Basilica, the Spanish Steps.

At night they would share an intimate dinner, then dance for hours at some popular nightspot. Later they made love, losing themselves in each other until dawn spread in pale pink ribbons across the sky.

Far too soon, the weekend ended and she and James returned to New York.

They settled into a new routine: days spent at work,

nights spent wrapped in each other's arms—usually in his big bed at his penthouse. It wasn't an ideal arrangement, but for now it suited both of them fine.

For convenience' sake, she began leaving some of her things at his place. First she hung a couple of outfits in his closet. The next week she slipped a stack of clean panties in the drawer next to his underwear. Later she purchased a duplicate set of cosmetics, feminine sundries, and doodads so she could get dressed in the morning before work without having to race to her apartment.

If James minded finding her belongings all over his apartment, he never once complained, silently making room for her things on his countertops and in his drawers.

And if a niggling tension remained, an unspoken worry that he might decide to pull away from her again, she kept her fears well hidden. She'd promised him time, and no matter how it killed her, she was going to give it to him. At least while she was waiting for him this go-round, she wouldn't have to wait alone.

Busy in ways she'd never conceived, she cut way back on her hours at Reflections, much to her boss's disappointment. Still, her boss, Nora, couldn't contain her pride at Ivy's talent and blossoming success, urging everyone she met to go see Ivy's paintings at West Galleries on Thompson Street.

Perhaps in part because of Nora's glowing word of mouth, she sold two more paintings over the next month and earned a commission for another.

She also moved uptown, leaving the guys behind

amid tears and promises to visit often. Her new room-mate, Amy, was as sweet as she was sassy, with a tongue in her head that sometimes made Ivy gasp in shock and then roar with laughter.

She used her new apartment mostly as an art studio and a place to check the business phone messages that stacked up like cordwood on her answering machine. Except for Madelyn and Zack, her family knew nothing about her increasingly intimate relationship with James. A part of her hated keeping them in the dark, especially her mother, but another part of her wanted this time with James.

Just the two of them. Alone.

Recently, though, he'd surprised her, and pleased her, by taking her to the opening of a Broadway play. At intermission, he'd introduced her to a few of his friends and acquaintances, who'd studied her with fas-cinated speculation. She'd done her best to be charm-ing and polite and to look as if she belonged on James's arm. Despite the scrutiny, she'd enjoyed the evening very much, and as far as she could tell, so had James.

He'd surprised her again last week by asking her to accompany him to a black-tie holiday charity event. She'd held her own at the dinner table despite an obvi-ous age gap between her and rest of the diners. She discussed the latest fashions with the women and the upcoming football play-offs with the men.

James had smiled softly at her, an enigmatic glint in his eye, as he'd helped her on with her coat at the end of the evening. She'd asked him what he was thinking, but he'd kissed her instead, then taken her back to his penthouse, where she'd promptly forgotten everything else but him.

Now Christmas was upon them, only a few days left before the big day, the crisp smell of snow hanging in the chilly air.

"I wish you'd come with me," she said to him as they relaxed on his sofa sipping cups of hot coffee. She set her drink down on the end table, turned to trail her fingers through his hair. "My folks would love to have you."

He shook his head. "You know I don't usually spend Christmas at your parents' house anymore, especially when Madelyn and Zack are going to be there. I think your parents would wonder why I suddenly decided to put in an appearance this year."

"Tell them you and Madelyn have finally buried the hatchet and everything's cool between the two of you again. Mom and Dad would be thrilled to know all the hard feelings are in the past."

He gave her a look. "They'd also want to know exactly how Madelyn and I came to make up after all these years. Your mom would be twisting my arm to get the full story, and I'm not sure how I'd explain without your coming into the picture."

"Oh." Ivy thought for a moment. "Just say you've met someone and you're over Malynn. You don't have to tell them the someone is me."

"And when my mystery girlfriend doesn't show up with me, then what?"

Ivy shrugged. "She's spending the holiday with her own family. It wouldn't be a lie."

He gave a half laugh and rolled his eyes.

She jumped up onto her knees beside him. "Please come. At least come for Christmas Eve. There're always so many relatives packed in the house, you'll hardly be noticed in the crowd."

"Well, gee, thanks."

She made a face at him. "You know what I mean. Everyone always asks about you anyway. This year they won't have to. Besides, you live next door. All you have to do is say you decided to spend the holiday in Connecticut this year and dropped by like a good neighbor to wish everyone a Merry Christmas."

"A Merry Christmas, huh? Maybe I should slip on a red suit and bring a sack full of gifts?"

"Quit avoiding the subject." She leaned back, folded her arms over her chest. "If you're not going, then I'm not going. I'll tell everybody I'm staying here in the city this year."

He frowned. "You can't do that. The moment you don't show, your mother'll be on the phone to both of us demanding to know what's wrong and why you're not coming home."

She shrugged. "It's up to you. I'll only go home if you come with me. I refuse to be parted from you for the holidays."

"That's blackmail, you know."

She grinned. "Is it working?"

He glared at her for a long moment, then let out a huff. "All right, I'll come for Christmas Eve—"

"And Christmas dinner the next day."

He rolled his eyes again. "And Christmas dinner the next day."

"Yes." She lunged forward, wrapped her arms around him, and planted a big, smacking kiss on his mouth.

"But—," he continued in a stern tone.

"But?" she repeated, smiling but trying not to gloat.

"We'll arrive separately, and we can't spend the evening hanging all over each other."

"You mean I can't sit in your lap and feed you eggnog and cookies?"

"No." He barked out a begrudging laugh. "You're incorrigible, do you know that?"

"But you love me anyway."

His gaze grew serious. "Yes. I love you anyway."

"As long as you do, that's all I need to be happy."

But is it enough? he wondered a few days later when he arrived at her parents' house, buried under an armload of gifts. Was she truly happy with things the way they stood? Was he?

He'd opted to leave the red suit at home, dressed instead in a black crewneck sweater and a pair of dark wool pants.

He searched for Ivy the moment he came inside but couldn't locate her in the crowd. She'd taken the train up three days before to help her mother with the preparations, and he'd missed her each and every moment since.

Christmas Eve was in full swing at the Grayson home, the large, gracious rooms jammed elbow to ear with as many family members as would fit. Bejeweled for the season, the house boasted holly berry wreathes and twisted strands of gaily striped ribbons in reds and greens.

Fragrant pine garlands adorned fireplace mantels, newel posts, and staircases. Ruby-hued poinsettias were set high and low to display their pretty foliage. Beeswax candles melted in slow drips beneath lighted flames while Nat King Cole crooned about chestnuts and children who wanted to know if reindeer really did know how to fly.

In the center of it all, inside the massive great room, stood the Christmas tree. Rising upward like a majestic queen, it reigned as though garbed for a coronation in glittering glass balls, twinkling lights, and bunches of silvery tinsel. Twelve feet high, the tree's massive limbs sheltered a mountain of presents, gifts of all shapes and sizes ready to be unwrapped.

He walked forward to add more to its bounty.

Laura Grayson found him moments later, gave him an enthusiastic hug and a kiss on the cheek, then led him to the refreshment table for a cup of hundred-proof eggnog and a plate of goodies. Philip Grayson stopped by next, grabbed his hand for one of his famous crushing handshakes, then launched into a discussion of horse racing—he'd recently developed an interest.

James soon found himself passed from relative to relative, Ivy's aunts, uncles, and cousins—all of whom he'd known for years, ever since that first Christmas at sixteen when he'd spent the holiday as a kind of adopted member of the family.

The atmosphere was infectious, and he couldn't help but be touched by the spirit of the season. Suddenly he was fiercely glad he'd let Ivy talk him into coming. He hadn't realized until now just how much he missed being with them all.

Where was she? he wondered again. He'd seen or talked to nearly every member of her extended family, Grayson and Bradford alike, but he still hadn't seen her.

Suddenly someone nudged him from behind and slipped an arm around his waist.

He didn't even need to turn to know it was Ivy. Her sweet, clean scent drifted to him, the lithe, lean shape of her that he'd come to know so well pressed to his hip.

He swung around, barely restraining the urge to clutch her to him and smother her lips with a heated kiss. He settled instead for a peck on her soft cheek and a rather sexless hug that was as unsatisfying as it was short.

Her eyes twinkled as she smiled at him. "Hi," she said, her voice husky with suppressed excitement.

"Hi back," he murmured quietly. "Where have you been? I got here half an hour ago, at least."

"Locked in the kitchen, frying up oysters for the starving masses. Mom took pity and said she'd finish them up."

"Oysters, hmm? I'll be sure to eat several since you made them."

Though what he'd rather take a bite out of was her. With her cheeks dusted a pretty pink, she definitely looked good enough to eat.

But enough of that sort of thinking, he warned himself. After all, he was the one who'd decided to keep their relationship under wraps.

They talked for a few minutes more; then Ivy moved away to circulate. Needing something to occupy him, he retreated to the buffet table.

He loaded a plate with finger-sized ham sandwiches, an array of relish choices, and a circle of saltines mounded with Ivy's golden, crispy fried oysters. He topped them with several dashes of fiery Tabasco sauce and began to eat.

As he did, he couldn't keep his gaze from drifting toward Ivy. She stood on the opposite side of the Christmas tree in conversation with Caroline.

Caroline's recovery was clear to see, her cheeks blooming anew with healthy color, the once-gaunt lines of her cheekbones filled out with much-needed weight. The new doctors and latest treatments appeared to be working. Everyone, family and friends alike, had heaved giant sighs of relief, joyful to hear the news that her cancer was in remission.

Ivy gestured to emphasize some point she was making, her expressive hands punctuating the air. A glimpse of straight white teeth flashed as she smiled, lighting an answering smile within him.

How lovely she is, he thought, *beautiful both inside and out in a way few people are. How lucky I am that she loves me.*

He frowned, then ate a forkful of cranberry conserves.

Zack Douglas stepped up to the linen-draped table and dug a handful of spicy nuts out of a decorative candy dish. He tossed a couple into his mouth and chewed. "Jordan," he said, nodding brusquely.

"Douglas."

They stood, awkward in each other's company. A full minute passed in silence.

"Good nuts," Zack commented, scooping up another handful.

"Everything's excellent."

Several children chose that moment to race up to the buffet table. Skidding to a noisy halt, they grabbed handfuls of cookies, then dashed away again amid shouts and laughter to resume whatever game it was they'd been playing.

"I predict somebody's going to have an aching belly tonight," Zack said.

"What's Christmas for if you can't overindulge?"

"True, but you don't have to listen to 'em cry. Wait till you have a couple of your own; then we'll talk."

Without fully realizing it, James scanned the room for Ivy, discovered her talking to one of her aunts. His gaze lingered, warmed.

"So how long are you going to wait before you make an honest woman of her?"

His gaze veered to Zack. "Who?"

"*Who?*" Zack snorted. "What other woman have you spent the night staring at? My little sister-in-law Ivy of course."

"I haven't been staring," he said coolly. "And I don't believe my relationship with Ivy is any of your business."

"Maybe not, but it's my wife's business and her family's. Considering you guys are practically shacked up together, you really ought to break down and marry her. What are you waiting for anyway? It's plain as pitch you're crazy about her."

James set his plate down with a snap. "If you must know, I've already asked her to marry me."

Zack's dark eyebrows lifted. "And what? She turned you down?"

"No. Yes. Not exactly. She wants to wait."

"*She* wants to wait?" The skepticism in Zack's voice rang clear.

"For a while. She's young yet." James's eyes settled on her again, unaware of the stark need reflected on his features. "There's still a chance she might decide marriage to me isn't the best choice for her."

"She could," Zack said. "Then again, she's had a lot of time to think about it. Known you her whole life, hasn't she?"

James crossed his arms. "Yes. What of it?"

"Just proves she must know what makes you tick. If she hasn't seen through your flaws by now, I doubt she ever will."

"She sees through my flaws."

"Then it's odd she still loves you. Just goes to show there's no accounting for taste."

As if she sensed their interest, Ivy turned her head, her eyes immediately alighting upon James. Her lips curved, a look on her face that couldn't be mistaken for anything but what it was—an expression of deep, abiding love.

"Yep," Zack remarked softly. "I can see how much she wants to wait." He scooped up another handful of nuts. "I'd better go find my wife."

James barely heard him, his senses, his entire body and mind attuned to Ivy.

What am I waiting for? he wondered, Zack's earlier question repeating in his head.

Was Zack right? Was he being a stupid, stubborn fool, refusing to make a lasting commitment to Ivy?

She'd refused his offer of marriage because she said he needed time. But was time really going to change anything between them? Would a few more months, a few more years, give him any more reassurance than he already had?

He'd challenged her to prove her worth out in the real world and she had, astonishing him with her resourcefulness, her resilience, her undeniable talent and determination.

He'd accused her of not knowing her own mind, her own heart. Told her what she felt for him was nothing more than an immature fantasy, an infatuation that would run its course, burn hot and then sputter out as fast as a match striking tinder. Yet despite living in a city teaming with thousands of available men and having friendships with two who would have leaped into her bed at the slightest come-on, she wanted no other but him.

He'd told her she was too young and he too old, that the years between them left too many gaps in tastes and experience. Yet in her company he was never bored, never weary of life the way he'd sometimes been before she'd burst into his world and turned everything upside down.

And she got along well with his friends despite a

few raised eyebrows. Even his older business acquaintances liked her, finding themselves enchanted by evening's end with her poised manner and effortless, friendly grace.

In all the ways that counted, she was his perfect match. When he was with her, he was happy. She satisfied him physically, intellectually, emotionally. What more did he want?

What it all boiled down to was trust.

Did he trust her enough to believe her promises? Did he love her enough to risk everything and take a real chance on her love?

One day she might outgrow him, grow bored with him, want something else, someone else. But wasn't that a risk every person took when they married, when they committed themselves to another, whatever their age? Either he was willing to take that risk or he wasn't. Love, not time, was the only force that could make the right choice for him.

He gazed across the room again, found her, and felt his heart constrict at the sheer, sweet radiance that made Ivy the woman she was.

Knowing suddenly what he had to do, he made his way to the front hall, slipped into his coat, and left the house.

Ivy sipped at her mug of eggnog and wondered where James had disappeared to. The last time she'd seen him he'd been talking to Zack. Unusual since the two men generally steered well clear of each other on the rare occasion they found themselves in the same room.

It was nearly time to open presents. Per family tradition, everyone was allowed to choose a single gift tonight. The rest of the presents would remain beneath the tree to be opened in the morning.

People were beginning to gravitate toward the tree, the scents of pine and anticipation strong in the air. The older ones secured themselves a seat near the action, while the children scampered here and there, barely able to contain their excitement.

She searched again for James without luck, then went to stand on the fringes of the group, behind one of the sofas.

Her young cousin, Clara, a bashful twelve-year-old with an overbite and braces, had been chosen to be this year's Santa's helper. According to tradition, she had the honor of passing out gifts.

Seated in front of Ivy, Granny Bradford received her present. With agonizing slowness, the old, gnarled fingers set to work, picking at the Scotch Tape oh so carefully so the paper wouldn't be damaged.

Ivy forced herself not to lean over the sofa back from where she stood and help the process along with a hearty rip. She was still watching the tortuous process when James slipped up next to her.

She turned to him, her voice quiet. "Where have you been?"

"Had a little errand I needed to run," he murmured in reply.

He smelled of cold, fresh air. An outdoorsy chill radiated off his hair and skin, a tinge of winter pink staining his cheeks.

"What sort of errand?" she asked.

"Come with me and I'll tell you."

She followed him but made it only a few steps before a voice stopped them.

"Where are you two sneaking off to?" Brie questioned. "You haven't opened your presents yet."

Ivy and James paused.

"We're just stepping out for a minute," Ivy said. "We'll be right back."

An odd sparkle glittered in her sister's gaze. "Stepping out to do what?"

Listening in, several curious relatives waited for her answer.

"James wants to tell me something."

"What could be so important it can't wait?" Brie insisted. "Come and open your gift."

Ivy opened her mouth to refuse, but James stopped her with a gentle touch.

He cleared his throat. "Actually, what I have to say is important, and not only to Ivy. Perhaps it would be best if I simply said it here and now."

Resting his hand against the nape of her neck beneath her hair, he stroked his thumb against her skin with an intimate and proprietary touch. She stiffened and made a halfhearted attempt to step away. He prevented her with a light squeeze.

Her eyes flew to his. "What's gotten in to you?" she whispered. "What are you doing?"

"What I should have done ages ago," he told her in a voice meant for her ears only. "I'm not afraid of what's between us, Ivy, not anymore. Having you with me makes me happy. *You* make me happy. Isn't it time we shared our love with the people we love?"

Stunned surprise and joy melted her heart. He wanted to tell her family about their relationship? He wanted to openly announce they were a couple? She hadn't thought it possible, but she loved him more in that moment than she already had her entire life. Her throat swelled tight with emotion as she nodded her agreement.

The few desultory conversations still taking place in the room ceased, all attention focused on her and James as he led her toward the tree in the center of the room.

He stopped, straightened his shoulders, and turned to the assembled company. "Sorry to interrupt the festivities, but Ivy and I have something we'd like to say. As you all know, she moved to New York this past summer. What you don't know is that the two of us have been seeing each other for a while, romantically." He slipped an arm over her shoulders, hugged her to his side. "Ivy and I are in love."

Across the room, Philip Grayson's bright red eyebrows shot upward like a pair of flames. Beside him, Laura merely smiled as an assortment of indrawn breaths sounded from all directions.

James turned to face her parents, directed his next words specifically to them. "We didn't mean for it to happen." He cast a quick glance down at Ivy. "Lord knows, *I* didn't mean for it to happen. What started as friendship changed, became more, became deeper, stronger. I tried to deny my feelings, argued with myself a thousand times over about all the reasons why we shouldn't be together. Ivy's too young. She's just starting out and doesn't need to be tied down in one place, to one person. She can't know what she's getting into, and she'll have regrets."

He looked at Madelyn, standing with her husband and little girls. On her face was an expression of understanding, reconciliation, and happiness—for him, for her, for them all.

"But Ivy says she loves me," James continued. "Says she will no matter how hard I try to convince her she shouldn't. She says she'll keep loving me, always, no matter what. And I believe her." He turned, took her hand, his heart shining in his eyes, open for all to see.

"I've been afraid to believe you, but I do," he said, speaking now to her alone. "And whatever comes, comes. Love's about taking a chance, and I want to take that chance with you."

"Oh, James."

She could tell he wanted to kiss her, and Lord, if she didn't want him to. Then he remembered they had an audience.

He looked again toward her parents. "I hope you'll give us your blessing. I'll understand if you can't, but it won't change my intentions or how I feel about Ivy."

Her father glared, obviously trying to come to terms with the news he'd been dealt.

Her mother had no such trouble. "Of course you have our blessing," Laura said. "How could you think otherwise?" When her husband didn't say anything, she gave him a gentle poke in the ribs.

Briefly, he met his wife's gaze; then his features relaxed. "You'll have to give me some time to get used the idea of you and Ivy"—he broke off, waving a hand—"being together as a couple. My God, James, you've known her since she was in diapers. I've got to tell you that the idea is really messing with my head."

He gave it a mild shake, causing laughter. "But if you love my girl as much as I can see that you do, and if Ivy feels the same, then how can I stand in your way?"

James smiled and sent Philip a grateful nod. "Then there's only one thing left for me to do."

Taking a step back, he turned to face Ivy and dropped down onto one knee. A velvet-covered jeweler's box appeared in his palm.

Her lips parted on a silent inhalation, her hands flying up to cover them as he opened the box. Inside lay his grandmother's ring, the one she adored. The huge canary diamond winked, brilliant and beautiful as a star.

He reached up, gathered her trembling hand into his. "Ivy Jasmine Grayson, I love you as I've never loved anyone before or will ever love anyone again. You're like pure, sweet sunshine, and the light you cast fills all the dark, empty spaces in my soul. I can't do without you. Say you'll be mine. Please say you'll marry me."

"Are you sure?" She bent down, a tear trailing over her cheek. "You don't have to do this, you know. I said I'll wait."

"We've waited long enough, don't you think? I know my own heart," he said, repeating the words she'd once said to him, "and it's yours, completely yours. I don't need any more time. Just say yes, sweetheart."

"If you're sure, then yes. Oh, heavens, yes!"

Laughing, crying, she flung her arms around him and crushed her lips to his in a joyous merging—a union they knew would withstand all the tests of time.

CHAPTER SEVENTEEN

"Maybe we should elope after all," James said two days later.

He and Ivy sat snuggled comfortably together on the sofa in the family room of her parents' house. A cheery fire burned in the stone fireplace, their empty cocoa cups forgotten on the wide cherrywood coffee table.

Ivy lifted her head from his shoulder and met his eyes. "Shh. Don't even joke about such a thing. Mom might overhear."

"Who says I'm joking? Okay, okay, don't look so worried. Here," he said, "let me take your mind off things." Smiling, he leaned in for a kiss.

Her pulse kicked into a faster rhythm, her eyes closing as a familiar rush of desire swept through her. She wished they could go over to his house next door and put the king-sized organic mattress and four-hundred-thread-count Egyptian cotton sheets on James's bed to good use.

But her father was still adjusting to the idea of her and James being intimate, so to spare his feelings, Ivy had decided to stay in her old room here at her parents' house for the rest of the holiday.

Of course, that didn't mean she couldn't sneak over to James's place for some alone time, which she'd done just that morning as a deliciously fun predawn, day-after-Christmas present to them both.

She moaned softly against his lips as he reluctantly eased away. "We'd better quit," he murmured. "Otherwise we're going to get caught on this couch like a pair of teenagers."

"I'm willing to risk it if you are," she said, pulling his head down for another kiss.

He kissed her back for several long, intense moments, then broke away. "This is why we should elope. Your mother's already talking about us waiting a year or two so there's plenty of time to plan a big wedding. That's too long for me. Way too long."

"For me too, but you know everyone will be so disappointed if we don't have a big blowout." She ran a palm over his thigh, feeling an answering quiver. "But I'm going to move into your penthouse as soon as we get back to the city, so it isn't like we won't be together. The time will go fast."

A small pair of lines creased his brows. "So you genuinely want a big wedding?"

"Yeah, I kind of do. The gown. The flowers. The cake. I'm only going to get married once, so I'd like to do it right." She laid a hand against his cheek. "I'm not going to ditch you at the altar. You know that, right?"

He met her eyes, gazing deep. Then he relaxed. "I do. We'll have whatever kind of wedding you want. Just set the date and I'll be there."

She smiled and pressed her lips to his again—soft and slow and infinitely sweet.

"It's too bad, though," he said after they came up for air. "I was looking forward to flying to Vegas and having Elvis do the honors."

She laughed.

"What's this about Elvis and Vegas?" Brie walked up and dropped down into an overstuffed chair. "Holy crap. You guys aren't thinking about eloping, are you?" She tossed a glance over her shoulder. "Mom will have ten cows, all in different shades of purple, if you run off. Then again, having the King marry you . . . hey, sounds fun."

"We aren't going to Vegas—at least not to get married." James leaned back against the cushions, his arm draped over Ivy's shoulders. "Ivy says she wants traditional, so traditional it shall be."

Brie looked between them. "Well, whatever you choose, I think it's great you two are getting hitched. Like I told Madelyn weeks ago, it's about time."

"What did you tell me?" Madelyn asked as she strolled up to join the group. Zack followed, taking a seat next to his wife on the opposite sofa.

"We were just talking wedding plans," Brie answered.

"Mom's in heaven," Madelyn said. "She's already started calling all her favorite vendors to put them on alert for the big day. If you want any peace, I'd advise picking a date soon."

"I know." Ivy nodded. "She hints at me at least once an hour."

"Personally, I think an autumn wedding would be lovely," Brie volunteered.

"I do too, but I'm not sure we could get everything arranged in time for this fall," Ivy said.

"Then how about spring?" Madelyn suggested.

James sat in silence and played with a strand of Ivy's long hair.

Zack slapped a hand on his thigh. "Hey, a bunch of your relatives are playing video games in the media room. I think I'll go gun down a few of whatever it is they're killing."

"No, you won't." Madelyn gave him a gentle tap. "Now, behave."

Zack grinned, his eyes only for her. "That's not gonna happen. You know you'd get tired of me if I did."

She smiled back. "Impossible. I could never get tired of you."

"Ditto, baby." He leaned in for a kiss.

"Now I'm the one who should leave." Brie looked at the happy couples. "Way too many happily-ever-after pheromones flying around."

"What you need is to find a great guy of your own," Ivy told Brie. "What happened to Caleb?"

"Same thing that happened to Will and Xavier. They turned out to be jerks." Brie shrugged. "Anyway, I'm busy with my career and don't have time to worry about finding my soul mate. Frankly, I've kissed so many frogs that I don't think my prince is out there."

"Oh, I wouldn't be so sure," Zack said. "When I met Madelyn, love and marriage were the last things on my mind, but she changed all that for me. I never dreamed I'd have what I do with her now."

Madelyn nodded and clasped Zack's hand, smiling.

"He's right," James said, "though I'll deny I ever said I agreed with him about anything if you ask me later." He tugged Ivy closer and kissed her temple. "Don't ever give up on love, Brie. You never know when it might be waiting just around the corner. It found me when I least expected it, and I'm so glad."

"Exactly," Ivy agreed. "Who knows? Maybe the next man you meet will turn out to be 'the one.'"

"Right, and I'm going to win a huge lottery jackpot while flying pigs whiz around my head." Brie laughed. "Come on. Enough of this talk. Let's all go play Xbox and blow something up. I'm definitely in the mood for some mayhem."

They all laughed and got up from their seats.

But rather than follow, Ivy and James hung back.

"Do you really want to play video games?" James asked, his arms looped around her waist.

Ivy met his eyes and saw a desire in them that mirrored her own. "I'd rather play games alone with you. Do you think we can sneak over to your house without being seen?"

"Frankly, I don't care if we are seen." He pressed his lips to hers for a slow, seductive kiss. "You're mine now, and the whole wide world can know."

Read on for an excerpt from
Tracy Anne Warren's next novel,

MAN OH MAN

Coming in 2015 from Signet Select

"Now, remember, we're here in the Hamptons for a weekend of fun, sports, and relaxation," Barrett S. Collingsworth IV said in a tone that was as smugly patronizing as his name.

Fun, huh? Brie Grayson wasn't so sure about that. She tapped the edge of her tennis racket against one trim calf and gazed out over the manicured grounds of the exclusive private club.

True, the May air was a perfect seventy-two degrees, the sky a cloudless blue. From the courts around them came the quiet *thwack* of rackets hitting fuzzy yellow tennis balls and the low murmur of multiple conversations interspersed with an occasional grunt of frustration or shout of success.

Yet in spite of the undeniable bennie of spending the weekend in the Hamptons, this was still a working weekend, whatever Barrett S. might otherwise say. He wasn't called ol' BS at the office for nothing.

It had taken her less than a day when she'd started at Marshall, McNeal, and Prescott eight months ago to figure out that Barrett was mostly full of crap—a sentiment almost universally shared by not only the associates but most of the partners too. Still, for all his shortcomings, he wasn't as stupid as he looked or acted—he had earned his Juris Doctor from Harvard, after all, just as she had.

The most important thing to know about Barrett, though, was the fact that he was the nephew of one of the senior partners and that he never hesitated to whine to his uncle about anyone or anything he didn't like. So, as irritating as he could be, she'd made a point of staying on his good side.

She supposed that's why she'd been chosen to accompany him this weekend—or maybe punished was a more accurate description. Still, she had plans—upwardly mobile plans—and she wasn't about to screw up her fast track toward making junior partner. So, if it meant putting up with ol' BS for a couple of days, then she'd put up with him. As for the shutting up, well, she'd see how much of that she could stand.

At least the weather was truly beautiful, she reminded herself again, same as her surroundings. She turned her fair-skinned, SPF 45–protected face up to the sunshine and drank in the rays, relishing a slight breeze that ruffled her stylishly cut, chin-length blond hair. Maybe if all went well this afternoon, she would have time for a quick dip in the pool when they got back to the hotel.

"Just play tennis and let me decide when it's time to

talk business," Barrett said, interrupting her thoughts in order to continue the lecture he'd started hours ago on the drive down from Manhattan. "We've been trying to land Monroe for years, and we can't afford to let him slip away again."

She kept walking, deciding silence was the best response.

"He's a huge get." Barrett jabbed a finger in the air for emphasis. "In the past decade, he's built a line of luxury hotels here in the States and in Canada that are second to none. Rumor has it he's about to go international. If we can convince him to come on board with us before he takes the business global, it'll be a massive coup. Might even earn me a promotion."

Since I'm part of this deal, it had better earn me a promotion too.

"And you really think playing a round of doubles with Monroe is going to change his mind?" she asked.

"The game is only a warm-up. The deal will happen afterward. Clients love attention and flattery. The trick is to get them good and relaxed; then, when their guard's down, pounce like a tiger with a powerful business angle. *Wa-la*, deal done."

Brie kept her face as expressionless as possible, trying not to smirk at the idea of Barrett as a tiger. More like a house cat—some really annoying, overly pampered Persian maybe? Although the comparison was unkind to cats everywhere and Persians in particular.

No, Barrett might think he was James-Bond smooth, but somehow she didn't believe a self-made entrepreneur like M. J. Monroe was going to be swayed by flattery and attention. If getting him to sign on the dotted line was that easy, he'd have put his Montblanc to paper a long time ago.

She tapped her racket against her leg again, the attorney in her demanding that she argue her point, however unwise. "But you said yourself that no one has been able to convince him to switch firms before, so why should he now? Surely he's already been buttered up lots of times before this?"

He came to an abrupt halt and stared at her, a look of supreme arrogance on his knobby-chinned face. "Not by *me*, he hasn't. That's why Uncle Wendell sent in his big gun this time. Monroe just needs the right man to explain to him what the firm can do. Our billables alone are enough to impress even the most hardened businessmen. To say nothing of our client roster and winning track record when it comes to settlements and litigations."

Big gun, huh?

Brie just barely held back a snort. Not that Barrett was mistaken about the power and prestige of Marshall, McNeal, and Prescott and what it could offer. Indisputably, MM&P was one of New York City's top law firms—if not *the* top. But somehow she still didn't think that fact would sway Monroe. If he hadn't already been lured by the mystique of their one-percenter-heavy client list or their admittedly excellent reputation for winning lawsuits and making sure their clients didn't pay out a dime more than necessary for their legal transactions—except to the firm itself, of course—then he was looking for something else. Something more. Exactly what that something more might be was the key to acquiring his business.

"Besides," Barrett said, pausing only long enough to take a breath, "I went to a lot of trouble to arrange this match—"

"You mean *I* went to a lot of trouble, considering it's my sister's fiancé who has a membership here. And the fact that James is the one who very graciously accompanied us here today so we could use the amenities."

"Yes, but *I'm* the one who wrangled the court time with Monroe. I won't tell you how much it cost me to bump the couple who was originally scheduled to play."

Brie managed not to roll her eyes. "I still don't see why we couldn't have just met Monroe in an office like normal people rather than resorting to all these schemes."

"Because we're not normal people. We're lawyers."

She paused, realizing that for once ol' BS had a really good point.

Then they were courtside, the court number painted in a neat white on the carefully maintained grass.

Showtime!

She put on her best professional smile and followed after Barrett, only to stop dead seconds later. An odd shiver went through her as she stared at the man standing on the other side of the court, his head bent to one side as he listened to whatever his attractive brunette partner was saying.

He was tall and athletically built without being overly muscled, solid without an extra ounce of fat anywhere on him. She guessed he was close to her own thirty-three years and in his prime. His dark brown hair was short and neatly trimmed but not in a big-city, five-hundred-dollar-a-cut kind of way. His tennis clothes were the same—good quality but not obscenely expensive.

Brie scowled, her heart rate suddenly picking up beneath her crisp white Burberry Brit sports shirt. She gave herself a quick shake and looked away. Eyes on her white sneakers, she trailed Barrett over to the bench that lined one side of the court and set down her bag.

What is wrong with me? I've never met M. J. Monroe before in my life. So why the freaky reaction?

The man was a complete stranger. She'd even taken a quick look at an Internet photo of him when she'd done her prep work for the weekend and it hadn't sparked any unusual reactions. He'd seemed pleasant-looking enough in a business-hardened, square-jawed kind of way, but he hadn't made her senses go on full alert like a breach in security at the Pentagon.

Yet now her instincts were flashing like red sirens, warning her that there was something about him— something oddly familiar.

Maybe she was dehydrated and delusional. She just needed to drink some water and rebalance her electrolytes, although they had seemed fine two minutes ago.

Looking for a distraction, she pulled a bottle of water out of her gear bag, unscrewed the top, and took a long drink. From the corner of her eye, she saw Barrett lope his way over to Monroe and his companion and introduce himself with far too much enthusiasm. She stayed where she was, careful not to turn. Extra careful not to look again.

Another minute and I will be calm, cool, and collected, she assured herself, *all hints of weirdness gone.*

She smiled inwardly, well aware that being "weird" was the last thing anyone would ever accuse her of. Serious and intense with workaholic tendencies that her mother worried would drive her into an early grave—those were qualities that most people would use to describe her. Not flaky and certainly never weird.

She took one last pull from the bottle, then sealed it and stowed it away. Picking up her racket, she turned, sure she had herself under control once more. She pasted her professional smile back on her face and strode confidently forward.

"Here she comes now," Barrett said with a toothy, well-oiled grin. "M.J.—I hope I can call you M.J.?—and Lila, his most exquisite doubles partner——"

Lila, the exquisite, gave a throaty laugh.

"Let me introduce my partner of the courts—tennis courts, that is." Barrett waved a hand toward her with a flourish. "Ms. Brie Grayson."

Monroe's head turned and he looked straight at her. But instead of a handshake and a hello, he stared, running his eyes slowly over her, head to toe.

Her inner alarm went off again like a banshee, the weirdness crawling back over her skin. She was too good a litigator, though—and Texas Hold'em player— to let any hint of reaction show on her face.

But inside . . .

She shivered.

His eyes were dark, the brown of rich teak. Under other circumstances, she might have thought them beautiful. Instead, all she could see was their shrewdness, their keen understanding. It was as if he were privy to some joke she hadn't heard the punch line to. And if there was one thing she really hated, it was knowing that someone else knew something she didn't.

Suddenly he grinned. And not just any grin but one that was wide and shit-eating.

She was still considering his peculiar reaction when he spoke, his voice deep and smooth. "Why, if it isn't the creamy little cheese herself. How many years has it been, Brie-Brie?"

Her mouth fell open, her mind racing backward to her childhood.

No, it isn't possible! It cannot be him.

She looked closer, comparing her memory of the hateful boy she'd known in junior high school to the sophisticated man who now stood before her.

Christ Almighty, it is him!

How could she not have known? How could she not have realized that M. J. Monroe and Maddox Monroe were one and the same? No wonder her body had been sending out warning signals. It's a wonder she hadn't broken out in hives—or convulsions.

Yet here he was, live and in person, her worst nightmare come back to life—the bully who'd turned seventh grade into one great big slice of pure hell!

*   *   *

Maddox stared at Brie Grayson, unable to look away.

Of all the people he'd expected to run into here at the club, it wasn't the girl who'd starred in every one of his immature, twelve-year-old male fantasies for an entire school year—and a long while after that, if he was being strictly honest.

Back in those days, he'd thought she was the cutest girl he'd ever seen.

She'd thought he was a pig.

And he probably had been; adolescent boys weren't much known for their tact or thoughtfulness.

Of course he'd noticed her the moment she'd walked onto the tennis court a few minutes ago—how could he not, with her head of sun-bright blond hair, gorgeous long legs, and a tight little ass that practically begged to be squeezed through her short white tennis skirt?

When she'd been a girl, he'd thought that she was adorable.

But as a woman full-grown, she was a real knockout!

Still, one thing that apparently hadn't changed over the years was her reaction to him. Judging by her narrow-eyed glare, she hated him every bit as much now as she had in the seventh grade. Although he supposed he was partly to blame, aware he shouldn't have renewed their acquaintance by baiting her the way he had.

Then again, that had always been the problem—she brought out the very devil in him. He hadn't been able to control his reaction to her when he was twelve, and it would appear he couldn't control it any better as a grown man.

He hid a smile, certain the afternoon was going to be a whole lot more entertaining than he'd imagined.

Brie's blowhard tennis partner looked back and forth between him and Brie, a frown of confusion on his face.

Boyfriend? Maddox wondered. He eyed Brie again, speculating. Surely she had better taste than to hook up with Barrett whatever-his-name-was. But you never knew with women. Taste could definitely be a subjective thing when it came to relationships.

Barrett, the blowhard, frowned harder. "Do you two know each other?" he asked.

"No!" Brie shot back.

"Yes," Maddox said at the same moment, meeting her eyes with amused contradiction.

She stared back, her body bristling with tension and challenge.

Barrett's head swiveled back and forth between them. "Well, which is it?"

"Yes?" said Lila. "Do you know each other or not?"

His date, who until that moment he'd forgotten was even there, crossed her arms over her chest and waited.

Maddox met Brie's gaze again and arched a single eyebrow.

"Yes," Brie admitted reluctantly, "but it was a *long* time ago. I didn't even recognize him."

"I recognized *you*," Maddox said, not breaking eye contact. "Even in junior high you were the kind who was impossible to forget."

Brie scowled, her fist tightening around the handle of her racket almost as if she was considering using it—on him.

He nearly laughed.

His date picked up her own racket. "So, are we going to play or not?" Lila said in a peeved tone. "We're wasting court time."

"You're right," Maddox agreed without looking away from Brie. "We should play. Would you like to serve first?" he asked Brie.

She tapped her racket edge against the palm of her hand and looked back with a barely hidden sneer. "You betcha, Monroe. Game on!"

Grinning, he moved to his side of the court.